I0731263

J.D. GRUBB

There was Music

Copyright © 2020 by J.D. Grubb

All rights reserved. No part of this publication may be reproduced, stored or transmitted in any form or by any means, electronic, mechanical, photocopying, recording, scanning, or otherwise without written permission from the publisher. It is illegal to copy this book, post it to a website, or distribute it by any other means without permission.

Requests for permission to make copies of any part of the work should be submitted online at www.jdgrubb.com/contact.

This novel is entirely a work of fiction. The names, characters and incidents portrayed in it are the work of the author's imagination. Any resemblance to actual persons, living or dead, events or localities is entirely coincidental.

First published by LOD Press 2020

The Library of Congress Cataloging in Publication Data:
Grubb, J.D.
There was Music/J.D. Grubb--1st ed.
ISBN: 978-1-953028-00-6
1. Cost of Survival—Fiction. 2. Journey of Identity—Fiction. 3. Healing from Trauma—Fiction. 4. Power of Music—Fiction.

To the survivors, the healers, the pioneers.

Contents

Warning

This story contains some scenes with torture, sexual assault, rape, and suicidal thoughts.

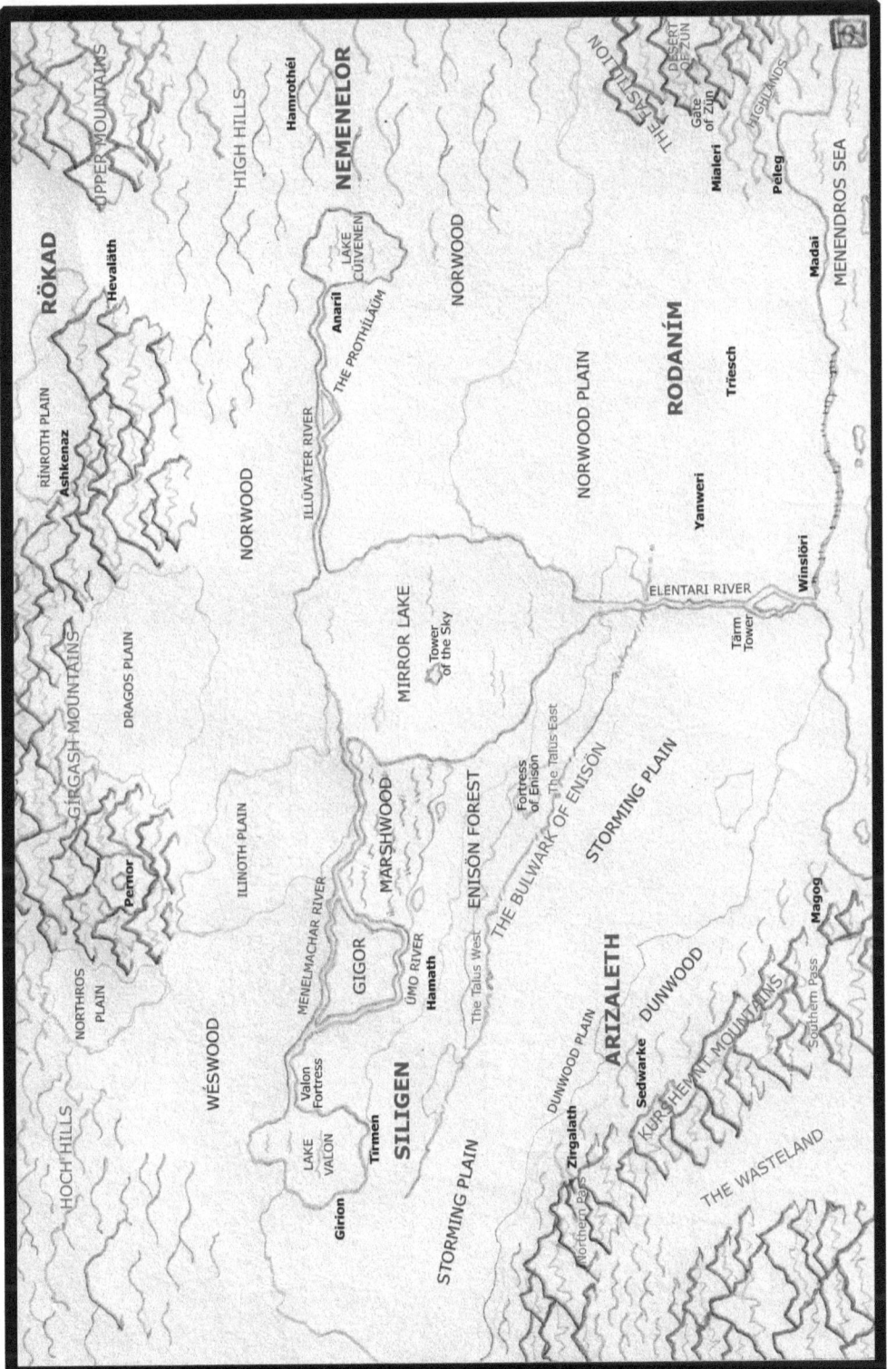

Prelude & Fugue

I wander in abstraction—this place between my past and future, where even the present is hard to grasp. I am conscious, aware of my surroundings and responsive to them; I can touch and feel, so I am not entirely a phantom. Yet what does it mean when the external and internal do not agree? The summer sun shines, but I am cold; there are people, but I feel alone.

Does time add meaning? Can it connect everything: body, people, history? Stitched together, do they reveal the whole of me?

Who am I?

This stranger says that my past contains hints of the answer. He asks about my life; but what does he really want to know, and why does he care? Is he trying to categorize and judge me, to imprison and control me like so many others?

I am more than one idea—more than daughter, sister, criminal, survivor; I am all of these and none of them. I am past, present, and future: memory, pain, and hope. I am complete in my incompleteness. I am contradiction: power and frailty. Is that not true for everyone?

I could tell him about resolve, but to what end? My resolve has faded. Where once there was flowing water, now there is only sand. I ache with thirst. For so long I have sought to be strong, to do more than cope. What I really want now, I think, is not more resolve, but acceptance. With all that has happened to me, with all that I have done, I struggle to accept who I am—what I have become. I seek something that will last through the difficulty of healing—patience, grace, love? I used to reject such needs as weakness, but now I am not sure.

I am weary of doubt, longing, hate.

"Do not give up," Father would say. "Fight on," Mother might add. "Triumph comes to those who endure." All my life, these ideas nurtured my hope. Yet the truth is that hope does not always last. It can turn the heart into a wasteland, barren of the belief in goodness.

If good is still out there somewhere, I am tired of looking for it.

I am weary of words, of thoughts spinning round and round in my head. My will has grown as calloused as my flesh. I do not think that is bad, however. After all, I have lasted this long. I am still here, in this land between waking and sleeping that we call life.

This stranger says that healing begins with sharing my story; that by claiming it, the fragments of my life can be reassembled to form a whole. Some are visible—the scars lining my skin—while others are invisible, maybe lost.

I do want to feel again.

I want to try.

Part 1: Prison

Children singing, laughing, playing, dancing; over a field of yellow flowers, cloud-dappled skies of liveliest blue. An echo, it is all only an echo.

Was it ever true?

Why are you here?

Her eyes flickered open.

Cords held her wrists to the arms of the chair. She clenched her fists to ward off the swelling of her hands, against the pain. Her feet were also bound, and gloved hands held her head in place. For a moment, she struggled to think as her vision remained blurred and her temples hurt.

The air smelled musty, with a sting of urine. It did not disgust her anymore, as it first did; she had grown accustomed to the stench.

Slowly, details of the chamber came into focus, shadowed but for a lamp glowing dimly above her. Decay colored the stone walls: smoke stains and bloody pigments framed in black mold. A long table stood against the left wall. Chains dangled from the far right corner. Near her, a smaller table displayed tools for painting the room with human suffering.

"I will repeat my question, Prisoner 43-1-12," a mellow voice said. "Why are you here?"

Her head throbbed at the sound.

A guard slowly poured water onto her head. The water slid down her face and neck, drenched the coarse threads of her tunic, and dripped down from her fingertips. A pool formed around her bare feet. The cold of the room clung to her with renewed fervor. She shivered.

"Answer my question," the voice said, still calm.

The speaker materialized from the shadows: Nabilak, the prison warden. As he crouched before her, she stared at the thick scar running from the corner of his lip down his chin, drawing that side of his face into a grimace. She still could not decide if it was an expression of disgust or amusement.

"Well?" Nabilak pressed.

"You know why," she replied, her throat burning, barely managing a whisper. "What do you want from me?"

A part of her sought to move, to fight back or flee; but another part of her ached. She felt exhausted. Faltering, she realized with a pang of despair that the strand connecting her body to her will was beginning to fray.

* * *

My unraveling began during the Illirium War. It did not happen at once, or obviously, but with a gradual isolation. So many women were widowed. Fatherless children and orphans ran wild in the streets, many found dying of disease or hunger in corridors and alleyways. Most of the good men had been killed in the fighting. Those who returned, even in victory, were not the same.

The truth is that none of us were the same. Desperation and loss pervaded our town of Hamath. Life entered a new age, bidding us to bury the past; yet death is not easily forgotten, no matter how hard we try.

The previous age, that of the Alöwean Empire, stirs confused sentiments: awe and contempt, a sense of security and fear. Opinions vary, but for better or worse that empire has fallen. Another has risen in its place.

I am no historian. Until more recently, what happened outside Hamath meant little to me. There is a lot I still do not understand. Growing up, I mostly did not care. I was young and my world did not extend beyond the borders of our clan. I had met a few Alöweans, and knew none personally. Youth has a way of shielding one from the differences of others, and prejudices are generally taught. Unlike many of my fellow Illiri, I never felt any bitterness toward the Alöwean people. I suppose I learned that from my parents, especially my father.

The few Alöweans I had met acted courteously, but also seemed so distant, serene, ageless—quiet but attentive, as if they perceived a world beyond our own. Is that what makes our two races so different? Except for their pointed ears and the crimson in their complexion, they look the same as us. Some of them refer to us as "Mankind." What led to such distinctions, to the antagonism between our two races? I do not understand politics and war; they seem little more than games where the stakes are power and peoples' lives.

When I think of the Alöwean Empire, I mainly remember one man. He was not even an Alöwean, but a fellow Illiri who served their empire. At least that is what my brothers, Ürstus and Sindor, would say. Father, on the other hand, considered the man's appointment an opportunity for our people to gain influence. My brothers contended that Father's views were rare. Most others, Alöwean and Illiri alike, considered the man a threat or even a traitor to our people.

That was before the war. I was five years old when I met the man, too young to grasp such opinions. I mainly remember his eyes: two bronze suns of welcome. They looked at me with such warmth.

He would kneel to meet my eye level and talk to me like an equal. Sometimes he would lift me off the ground, hold me high above him as if I was gliding like a hawk, and then sit me on the fence of our main corral. As he held me securely in place, we would watch Father lunge one of our horses.

I wish I could remember the man's name. Mother would probably know, for she had a good memory.

The first time the man with bronze-colored eyes came to our ranch was to purchase one of our horses. He was accompanied by an older, grim-looking Alöwean who held some important rank in the Empire. I think they referred to themselves as Guardians. The Alöwean knew of our ranch, which was encouraging, for Father worked hard to maintain his family's legacy of being the best horse breeders and trainers west of Mirror Lake.

After a second visit, the man with bronze-colored eyes settled on my favorite courser, Swiftsoul. Swiftsoul had speed, stamina, and agility. I had named the hazelnut-colored steed myself, helping Father raise him. Swiftsoul was a true stallion, full of spirit and power; he suited his new master well. Though I was sad to part with Swiftsoul, I was glad his new master sought to foster peace between us Illiri and the Alöweans. The man passed through our town often during those early years, which I appreciated, for it allowed me to see how Swiftsoul was faring. Seeing him happier and stronger made me glad.

I share this because it was when I was the happiest. Those were moments soaked in sunset, the most vibrant colors I have ever known. Time was simple. I was enamored by everything. The memories comfort me, just as the presence of the man with bronze-colored eyes once comforted me. I am not sure why he made me feel that way. Nonetheless, the memories also fill me with sadness, for they remind me of what has been lost.

So much has been lost.

* * *

"Take her out of here." The prison warden's calm voice sounded disappointed. Or was it calculating?

Prisoner 43-1-12 felt the cords loosened from her wrists and ankles. Rough, gloved hands reached under her armpits like hooks and pulled her from the chair, which stuck to her legs a moment then fell to the floor with stark wooden echoes.

She gritted her teeth against the burning pain of her bare knees and the top of her feet dragging along a stone hallway. A door creaked open ahead, but she could not lift her head to see it. Inside, the cell was dark. As the gloved hands released her, her head struck the floor, leaving her vision blurred and spinning. The door clanged shut, and a gust of stale air passed over her body.

She shivered and coughed. The damp material of her tunic itched, yet it was the only clothing she had—the only layer against the cold. She crawled toward the back of the cell, but quickly tired from the effort. Lying still offered some relief. She tried to pull her tunic down, but the cloth was not long enough to cover her knees. So she clutched her legs against her chest while her hands grasped her arms. The movement provided little improvement, though her body eventually calmed in numb submission. If only she had more hay to insulate her from the stone floor. If only her head would stop throbbing.

How often had this routine occurred, and for how long?

Everything from before seemed little more than a dream.

A soothing voice: Mother humming a lullaby. Her tender fingers stroke my hair, their touch whispering like the leaves of trees outside my window. A child's voice joins the melody—my voice.

Mother, where have you gone? Who stole you from my side, leaving me alone in the night? Who will sing to me now, or sing with me?

I miss you.

I have tried to be strong like you. Have I made you proud?

For a moment, she thought she heard a melody. Had she been humming to herself, or had it been in her mind? She was not sure.

Her throat hurt.

Conscious of a trickling sound, she recalled how moisture gathered at the corner ceiling of the cell and fell in steady drops to a puddle below. Her thirst overcame her exhaustion. She crawled on her hands and knees to the puddle. The water quenched her parched throat, and eased some of the tension in her body. She accepted the dirty stone taste, for the water revived her a little, and the choice to drink from it was something she could control.

The darkness of the cell no longer seemed so pervasive. It must be morning, she thought. The day brought relief; for only at night did her tormentors come. Only at night did they really try to break her. She had lasted this long, however long it had been—days, weeks, months. She resolved to defy them still. They would not break her; not her spirit, anyway.

Touching her head, she remembered that her hair was a few inches long. It had been shaved upon her arrival to the prison. She tried to calculate how much time had passed by the length of her hair, but could only guess. It did not really matter. Knowing would not improve her situation. Knowing might actually make it worse.

She felt her face and winced. The fresh bumps were tender. She wondered what they looked like, what she looked like—filthy, unkempt, hollow, she imagined. Would they tire of looking at her in such a state, and leave her alone? Growing up, people had commented on her beauty. It used to fill her with confidence, but now she considered it a curse, a beacon to predators.

* * *

"You are a lovely young woman," Mother commented.

Having finished brushing my long hair, she braided it back to look like hers. Only, while her hair was blonde, mine was auburn—dark like Father's. I was thirteen years old, and could tend to my own hair, but I think she sometimes liked to do it just to be with me. It provided one of the few opportunities we could be alone together. I never protested, for those times were when I felt closest to her. She otherwise acted so withdrawn, as if behind an invisible shield. It sounds strange, but those small moments of letting her brush my hair reminded me that she was a woman like me. That we shared something unique between us, something my father and brothers would never understand—something deeper. I am not sure what to call it.

"Men will take increasing notice of you," Mother continued, her hands working my hair methodically. She stood behind me as I sat. "Some may be quick to say they love you."

"Is that wrong?" I asked.

"You need to be careful," she replied. "Look beyond their words; observe the patterns of their behavior before opening your heart to them. A man's so-called love may have no regard for who you actually are as a person. Such a man may only care about using your image or presence for himself. Therefore, do not embrace a profession of love too readily, for it could be a lure."

I had an idea of what she might mean. A year or so earlier we had discussed my body, examining and considering its distinct features. I understood what sex involved, at least the concept of it. "A lure to what exactly?" I asked, wanting to make sure I understood.

"It is not only about preventing a man from claiming your body," Mother replied, avoiding my gaze in the mirror. "No matter how hard we work to protect ourselves, we do not always have control over our circumstances. So it is more about protecting our hearts, such as from becoming unwittingly bound to another's rule. Be wary of physical attraction, charming words, and enticing gestures alone; they can be used to manipulate our trust and remove safeguards. Do not take your current freedom for granted."

"But are all men as you suggest?"

"No."

I wondered if something had happened to her when she was young, but I did not know how to ask—or whether I should. Instead, I asked, "Do you love Father?"

After a moment of silence: "Yes."

"How did he gain your trust?"

"You know how we met." Finished with my hair, she handed me the brush to put away.

"I know that you met here in Hamath," I said, putting the brush into a drawer, "and that you were sick."

"It was more fatigue than sickness," she corrected.

"Well, I do not remember why you were fatigued," I pressed. "How did you get here, or what happened exactly?"

"Why do you want to know?"

I wanted to know her better, but saying that seemed strange to me. So I tried to engage her practical sensibility. "How else am I to learn to distinguish between real and false love?"

Mother appeared to consider this.

"Very well," she said after a while. "Your father and brothers will soon return from their morning chores. We can talk further while preparing breakfast. Come along."

I followed her out of my room to our kitchen, which smelled of herbs and wood smoke. With the cooking fire crackling in the large kitchen hearth, the space felt warm and inviting. Outside the window, the landscape radiated with the soft light of an amber dawn.

As we worked together, Mother spoke. "I did not grow up in a peaceful household, in Yanweri." With the knuckle of her thumb, she carefully rubbed her temple near the bridge of her nose and then sighed. "I became fed up with it and left when I was twenty-one." She passed me a jar of flour, for I usually made our bread. "I was unmarried and uninterested in the men of our clan," she continued, "and anyway I wanted to explore more of Rodaním."

"You traveled alone?" I asked, while mixing ingredients into a bowl.

"Yes," she replied. "That did not bother me in the least. I was well equipped to navigate the wild and defend myself. Remember, I come from a family of warriors."

I remembered, though Mother rarely spoke about her family in any detail. I only knew that my grandparents had met while serving together in an armed contingent at the Gate of Zün in eastern Rodaním, and that eventually my grandfather lost the ability to walk, which became a matter of contention between him and my grandmother.

"I mainly followed backcountry paths," Mother continued, "and befriended a few other explorers and hunters. For the next five years or so, I made many trips, eventually going beyond the borders of Rodaním. Once, I joined a caravan of traders who let me earn my way as we journeyed north into Nemenelor, to Anaríl."

"You went to the eastern capital of the Alöweans?" I exclaimed. Why had she not mentioned this before?

"Yes," she replied. "But that is another story."

My questions were mounting, but I stored them away for another time. Mother did not like too many questions at once, so I tried to control myself.

"From Anaríl," mother continued, "I bartered passage on a boat, which went west down the Illüväter River to Mirror Lake."

I glanced at Mother's small framed map of Illirium, which hung on the wall overlooking our dining area. Father had given it to her as an anniversary gift years earlier. I liked to study the map sometimes. Yet aside from the few landmarks labeled around Hamath, the rest of Illirium was little more than a collection of names to me. A significant space separated Hamath from Anaríl, with Mirror Lake in between, or even Hamath from Mother's hometown of Yanweri. To me, they were intangible spaces; yet for Mother much must have been tangible and linked to memory. I envied her. I wanted to know everything she knew. I was determined to be more assertive in asking her questions about her travels, to learn all I could.

"Focus," Mother said, pointing to the dough I had stopped kneading. "That should have been in the oven already."

"Sorry," I replied, resuming my work.

"This is not a good time to tell you all this."

"Please," I said, more abruptly than intended. "I will be better focused. I want to hear more."

Mother tended to strips of sizzling meat on a frying pan.

"Very well," she conceded. "After Mirror Lake, I returned home for a while because I missed my sister."

"Aunt Corine?"

"Yes." Mother removed the frying pan from over the fire. "I asked her to join me, but she would not leave Yanweri. So I set out on my own once again, this time westward across the Elentari River. Travel was liberating to me. I had heard tales of a thirteenth Illiri clan dwelling somewhere in Marshwood, so I made my way north along the western shore of Mirror Lake. I did not get far into Marshwood, foolishly thinking I could find my way alone through that swampland. I was lucky I only got sick. I could have gotten myself trapped in a bog or worse. While I managed to recover somewhat from the sickness, it left me weary. The summer was very wet that year. I needed to find a dry place to rest, and the closest town was Hamath."

The kitchen door swung open. Father wiped his boots outside and then stepped in. "It smells good in here," he commented with a smile. Having replaced his work boots for his indoor shoes, he came over and kissed me on the check. "How are you, my flower?"

"Mother is telling me about how you both met," I replied.

"Oh, is she?" He looked at his wife with affection. "Well, do not let me interrupt then."

"You could tell it better than me," Mother said, focusing on her task, looking at neither of us.

"What did you first like about her?" I asked him.

"Her spirit," he replied. After sitting down at the dining table, he gazed at his wife. "Even in her tired state, she held herself up with dignity. There are few stronger than her in all Hamath."

"Is that the fresh milk?" Mother turned to look at the container Father was holding. He nodded and offered it to her.

Silence followed, interrupted by the light clatter of Mother's kitchen work. Her back was to us. I did not understand her suddenly reserved attitude. Having placed the ready dough in our stone oven, I glanced at Father. He caught my eyes.

"You know," he said, as if reading my thoughts, "I forgot to wash up. I will be back shortly." He winked at me, slipped back into his work boots, and stepped outside.

"Set the table," Mother said softly.

"You have not answered my question," I commented, doing as she asked.

"Which question?"

"How Father gained your trust."

"Oh . . . that." Mother sliced some apples. "Very well. I met your father at the eastern border of this ranch. He greeted me amiably, we talked about my predicament, and he offered me a place to stay—in what is now your room, actually. His grandmother, your great grandmother, was still alive then. She tended to me, made me feel safe and cared for. All the while she spoke highly of your father; how since his father died, he had worked hard to keep the ranch going to support his family.

"Once I felt recovered, I spent most of my time with him. He taught me about managing a ranch, and some tricks to horse training I did not know. In short, I came to admire his work ethic. I also felt a harmony in his home, which was unlike anything I had ever known." She put the knife down. Her posture relaxed somewhat, and her expression was pensive. "While your father and I shared a passion for horses and working with our hands, what drew me most to him was his calm, kind manner. No matter what the circumstance, that did not change. It still does not."

Slowly, she inhaled then exhaled. With the back of her hand, she moved a lose strand of blonde hair from her face before resuming her work with the knife. "Eventually, we professed our love for one another and were married—after I first returned to Yanweri for a time."

"Are you still attracted to him?" I asked.

"Of course."

"Are you happy?"

"I do not think about my life in terms of happiness," she replied. "I am as happy as I could hope to be. That is as much as anyone could want."

I recalled some of Mother's earlier warnings to me. "Did Father profess his love first, or was it you?"

"He did." Mother looked at me for a while, but then her eyes wandered down. "I thought it before he said it. He is unlike any man I have known. Though he is no warrior, he makes me feel safe, or more so at peace. I have never known such peace." Her eyes returned to mine. "Does that answer your question?"

Before I could respond, my brothers burst through the kitchen door, arguing noisily. Father followed close behind them, quiet but attentive to their conversation. An amused expression lined his eyes.

It was not my mother who made me most conscious of my appearance, but my friend, Jed. He and I grew up together in Hamath. Outside my family, he was my best friend. Jed was closer to Sindor's age, but got along with me better. Our romance did not begin with appearances, but the happy adventures of childhood. I trusted him, more than my brothers in a way.

Jed was fourteen years old when he visited Hamath after his first year of training in the north—in Pernor, the so-called pinnacle of the Alöwean Empire. Though the Alöwean Empire was ruled by a king in the east, Jed said the twelve Alöweans comprising the Council of Pernor had the true power. His opportunity to serve there was possible because the man with bronze-colored eyes was opening doors between the Illiri and Alöweans.

From my perspective as a thirteen-year-old girl, Jed no longer looked like a boy. He acted more aware and in control of his body, less awkward and hasty. His gaze was more focused on his surroundings. The lines of his profile were firmer. He still could not grow a beard, which I was glad for. For without it, he retained a glimpse of the boy I knew—though that boy now dressed like a man. He wore a maroon tunic over leather armor. The color complemented his brown eyes.

I remember walking together to our favorite stream, which ran along the foot of the forest hills north of Hamath. It was a sunny day, one of the last that year. Jed told me about his experiences in Pernor, how he had finished a preliminary phase of training with the Pernor Guard and would be placed in a scouting contingent under the command of some captain.

Jed was excited about his new post. "It means I will not be confined within the walls of the fortress," he explained. "I will be trained as a Pernor Hunter, protecting Pernor's borderlands. The mountains encircling Pernor are taller and wilder than anything here. I want to explore every corner. Someday I will show you."

Jed was always fond of nature.

"That would be wonderful," I replied, finding myself interested less in the where than the who. "I am proud of you," I added, hoping to focus our attention on us.

"It is settled then," he replied with a grin.

I pictured myself like Mother. Except that, instead of being the wife of a rancher, I would be the wife of a soldier. Would we be allowed to live together in Pernor? The idea appealed to my imagination, for my parents did not raise me or my two brothers for leisure. In our own way, we were close to the land, to dirtying our hands—to disciplined work. I loved horses, but my eldest brother, Ürstus, would inherit the ranch. I did not mind. I wanted to see more of the world, and I envisioned myself doing so with Jed.

I was too shy to share any of this with him, of course.

Instead, I rambled about Father and the ranch, about how a noble from the Illiri city of Girion had purchased most of our trained destriers. I mentioned how Father had brooded the rest of that day, and how that was unusual. Jed listened attentively, asking some questions about the noble, but ultimately said nothing more.

Later, I came to understand that Dwairian, Lord of Girion, was preparing to challenge Alöwean rule through a military uprising. The five western Illiri clans were not unified under one ruler. Each clan, of which Hamath was one and Girion another, was ruled by its own lord who was ultimately subservient to Alöwean authority. Dwairian saw himself as the king our people needed. Apparently, many Illiri agreed.

As I have mentioned, I did not think about what was happening outside my life at that time. I was content. Jed and I only had a few days together before he needed to return to Pernor, so I did not want to waste any more of our time with such seemingly irrelevant talk. My world was small, and Jed was a warm light in it.

He kissed me for the first time that day, while we stood next to that woodland stream. I was not ready when it happened; my lips were caught limp, unresponsive. Excited and embarrassed, I felt myself blush. It was then that I was sure our relationship had changed; that we could never go back to the way it used to be.

"I love you," he said, timidly. "I think I have always loved you."

My heart leapt within me. I blushed again.

"I love you too," I mumbled. I said it because it seemed like the right response. But I did not really know what love meant.

I still do not.

We kissed again, better this time, and longer—we were learning—and then walked back home hand-in-hand. My heart beat so ferociously in my chest the whole time, I was sure Jed could feel me trembling. Still, it was a sacred moment.

If there ever was a seed of love planted within my heart—if that was supposed to be its first blossom—then it has long since withered and died. The memory to me is a youthful cliché. How naïve we were. The sound of Jed's young voice is like a distant murmur. Though I can recall what I felt, I struggle to remember the actual sensation of being kissed by him, the joy of it; or the gentle strength of his hand, and how I relaxed into its security.

There is no more warm sunlight, only burning heat. There is no more quiet winter, only piercing chills. I yearn to remember the tangible touch of affection, to be gathered into a caring embrace—the vulnerable hope in all of it. But those sensations are now ghosts. The light has dimmed. The past no longer seems real. Reality has become shadows: darkness, cruelty, and more darkness—an endless revolution I cannot escape.

For years, I have fought to protect my spirit from being overrun while my body is assaulted. Again and again, I tell myself that my mind is still my own, my bastion of freedom, and that my memory preserves one last bridge to good. I have defended it with every measure of power I can muster. But now I wonder if I was deceiving myself. Perhaps that part of my mind has also been overrun.

* * *

Footsteps echoed outside. Keys rattled.

The cell had darkened again: nightfall.

The lock clicked, and the door swung open. Tall silhouettes came forward and picked Prisoner 43-1-12 up off the ground.

She did not resist them. She had tried that many times before, but it was useless to resist what happened next. She had to focus all her strength on fortifying her mind: to shut down her thoughts and sensations so that her body could become a shell, her spirit protected behind barriers of resolve.

Yet it was never easy.

They dragged her to the room. Inside, the prison warden waited. Dressed in gray, he studied her as the guards placed her before him. She collapsed to her knees, too weak to stand. Hands seized her arms to bring her back up.

Was that a shade of compassion across Nabilak's face? Why did he look at her like that?

"I admire your stamina, 43-1-12," he said.

Why did his voice remain so gentle?

Nabilak nodded to the guards. They brought her to the long wooden table, pulled off her tunic, and stretched her face-down on the dank surface. Her limbs were bound and stretched to tension. She cringed, but could not move as frigid water was splashed over her flesh. Her arms began to ache. She gasped for breath.

"Remember that you have a choice," Nabilak urged calmly. "This lasts as long as you wish."

Damn you and your voice, she thought.

"It can end right now," he continued. "Say the word, and I will help you."

Damn your word.

Nabilak crouched down to look at her face, which was half-buried by her extended left arm. He ran his fingers lightly down her back. "Just one word," he said. "It is it not difficult, 43-1-12. It does not require much. Just say the word. Why subject yourself to more of this needless abuse?"

Her body trembled. She clenched her teeth and closed her eyes. She had defied oppressors before, and would do so again. If only she could stop shaking.

Nabilak sighed and stepped away.

There came a whooshing sound. Pain stung the nerves on her back. She let out a soft cry, and cursed herself for doing so.

Nabilak continued to speak, louder, as if proclaiming a verdict. "I will not allow you to persistently defy the authority of this prison."

The whooshing sound of the cane returned, its sting more painful this time.

"Striking a guard will not be tolerated." Nabilak suddenly came closer, his voice softening again. "But I can protect you, 43-1-12."

Again, the cane struck.

"Let me save you," Nabilak continued.

Again.

"Just say the word and it will be over."

Again.

Each time the pain escalated. She wished she could contain her cries, but her body was not strong enough. She tried to dissociate her mind from it, yet each time the pain escaped her throat.

"How long will you pretend you can endure such needless suffering?"

Again, the cane struck.

17

"Continuing this would be long and meaningless."

The flogging continued. Soon it would begin on the back of her legs. She prayed for strength, for detachment. She prayed for the pain to end. She prayed . . . to what? Her will, the air, some unseen presence? She did not know. The people of Hamath worshipped no deity. For most, there was only the Dryden, Keeper of the Dead, and the effort to evade it as long as possible.

Would dying free her of pain? She thought she caught the glimmer of the Dryden's flaming blue body at the corner of her eye. Was it there watching her, waiting?

No, she could not think about death. She would defy it like all the rest. Instead, she would focus on enduring; for therein might be the power to overcome her adversaries.

But it was never easy.

Horses running, the sound of their coming like the wind when it pounds against the outside walls of our home during a storm. Down the slope the horses gallop, a fiery sun rising behind them.

Two young men, each riding his own stallion, drive the herd skillfully toward the corral. Ürstus and Sindor, my brothers.

Father scolds them for hitting the mounts too hard with their riding crops. They were slow to learn.

* * *

"Get up," Mother said.

I looked pleadingly at her, but her expression offered only appraisal as she waited to see what I would do.

"Get up," she repeated more firmly.

With her arms crossed, she stood under the shade of the trees, which bordered the small field where three times a week she instructed my brothers and me on techniques of self defense. Today, we were focused on hand-to-hand combat.

My knees stung. I looked at their dusty, scraped flesh. Both elbows were no better. Blood swelled from a deep gash at the base of my right palm. I gritted my teeth against the pain, knowing that tears would invite more harsh words from my mother.

"You pushed her too hard," my eldest brother, Ürstus, scolded Sindor. They were two years apart. I was the youngest by three years, only nine at the time.

"I did not," Sindor exclaimed. "She exaggerates everything."

"Quiet," Mother said. "No one is to blame." She focused back on me. "Are you going to keep lying there?"

I glanced at my brothers.

"Why do you look to them?" Mother asked. "It is not for them to determine what you do. You must decide. Hesitate, and you will be at their mercy. Act, and they may be at yours. So get up."

"Why?" Annoyed, I sat up. "I do not want to be a warrior."

"You think people will show you compassion simply because you are a girl?" Mother took a step toward me. "That is not the world we live in. You have to be strong, assertive, protect yourself and adapt as needed."

"But they are older than me." I indicated my brothers. "They are boys, and boys are stronger."

"No," Mother countered. "Do not use your age or sex as an excuse. Men may generally be stronger, but we are often more resilient. Anyway, there are ways to turn a stronger adversary's power against him."

"Mother?" Sindor interjected.

"Yes?" she replied, her tone softening. She shifted her head toward her second son, but her eyes remained on me.

"Why do you teach us how to fight, but not Father?"

She glanced at Sindor.

"She is a Daughter of Rodaním," Ürstus commented. He looked at Mother for affirmation. She nodded. "She is from the Yanweri Clan, and they are all fierce warriors—even Grandmother Kathryn. The Hamath Clan is agrarian. You know that Father comes from a family of ranchers."

"Does that mean Father is weak?" Sindor asked.

Mother sighed, addressing us all in a calm voice. "I love your father deeply.

19

He is good, and strong in the best of ways. But I will not rely on him for my protection. Each of us has a responsibility to take care of ourselves. Your father and I will do everything we can to protect you, but we cannot do all. Your protection begins with your minds, your attentiveness and choices. From there, it continues through the actions of your bodies."

She stared at the seasonally dry creek that cut through a portion of the meadow. Her head lowered slightly, her demeanor softening further. "Carelessness," she said, glancing at my brothers, "or complacency," she focused on me, "will lead to heartache or worse. None of us are safe from mistakes. Therefore, we must remain vigilant . . . of our strengths and weaknesses; first for ourselves as individuals, but then also for each other as a family."

* * *

43-1-12 awoke still lying on the table in the prison room, her arms and legs no longer bound. She tried to flex her limbs, but stopped as a wave of nausea passed over her. Turning to her side felt slightly better, as did lying still.

Reopening her eyes, she noticed her discolored wrists. Would she die in this room? Something within her still resisted, fought for life, yet she questioned it. What was there to live for?

She wanted to cry.

Slowly, she sat up. She felt too weary to maintain an upright posture, but her back hurt too much to remain slouched over. Gritting her teeth, she slid off the table to the floor, but her legs immediately buckled under her. Her arms scarcely managed to shield her head before she struck the ground. Her shoulders cramped upon impact, and the skin on her back screamed. She closed her eyes and rolled over, moaning, waiting for the pain to pass.

Noticing her ragged tunic on the ground a few paces away, she clambered over to it. The coarse threadwork burned against her raw back and upper legs, but offered some protection against the chill of the floor.

She looked over at the stone hearth, at the dust and ash.

* * *

Light flashed through the kitchen window. The ground shook. Apprehensively, my parents and I went outside our home. I was fourteen years old. My brothers had already left home.

What followed was a vague progression of moments.

Eerie cries reverberated across the night sky. We stared in disbelief as hands of flame grasped the walls of Hamath across the valley to the south. A strong wind was blowing from that direction, the fire already crawling from the town toward the border of our land.

Why had there been no warning?

"We cannot stay here, Siméon," Mother urged Father. She grabbed my hand and walked briskly toward the stables.

Ahead, I spotted one of our colts collapsed near the arena. Passing by, I was horrified to see that a short spear had punctured its ribs and that its head had been partially severed. Sprawled out and groaning miserably, it was somehow still alive.

"Look away," Mother said, not stopping. Her face looked stoic, focused. I saw the glint of steel. The long knife she always kept strapped to her waist was held ready in her other hand.

Across our property, the horses were in a frenzied state. Some had managed to break loose and were running about in confusion. When we reached the stable, Father was already there. I am not sure how he arrived ahead of us.

"Hurry." Mother pressed me toward Father, who quickly saddled my gelding, Yüllen.

Father was sweating, his brow and gaze tense, but the movements of his body remained controlled and methodical as he prepared each horse—the practiced rhythm of a horse master. I took Yüllen's reins from him as Mother mounted her mare, Yenna, bareback.

While Father finished saddling his stallion, Charger, Mother directed me to follow her back through the stable's main entrance.

The horses became more restless.

Mother halted. "Back," she whispered severely, pulling her reins. "Back."

Slender creatures appeared around the side of our home a few hundred strides away. They moved like us, their bodies the same shape, yet stood about half the height of an average man. Their faces were pale. Large round eyes glowed yellow, while the pupils were white. The creatures' ears were wide and pointed, like bats. Later, I learned that the creatures are called Ülak; to me at that moment, however, they were demons.

Many bore torches. They divided into two groups. One entered our house while the other moved toward us.

"Mercy," Mother whispered. Having sheathed her knife, she leaned out from her horse to seize an arm-length wooden shovel hanging from one of the stable's support pillars. She held the shovel like a sword, rested the shaft against her right shoulder. She inhaled slowly, her posture straightening while at the same time remaining limber.

The image of her sword mounted on the wall inside our home struck my mind. I wished she had it instead of the shovel. The history of her sword remained unknown to me. I had only glimpsed her skill while she gave us sparring lessons, yet at those times we used crude wooden swords. I had never seen her use her actual sword, and had not given it serious thought until that moment.

"Hedda, turn around," Father implored, trying to keep quiet. Still on foot, he had managed to back Charger up and turn him. "We can escape out the back."

Even as Father came and guided my horse around to face the rear door of the stable, my attention remained fixed on Mother. What was she doing?

The Ülak reached the stable entrance. Each wore some assortment of rusting black armor. Most wielded short swords and spears. They threw torches into the stalls, some of which still had horses in them. Our horses' screams filled my ears. When the Ülak spotted us, a gleeful, high-pitched cry resounded from their wide mouths.

Mother waited calmly on her horse with the shovel in hand. "Go," she said to Father and me, shifting her head slightly in our direction without looking back. "I will find you."

A few Ülak notched their bows and raised them.

"Hedda," Father cried.

A gust of wind surged through the stable door, lifting Mother's slender blonde braids. She kicked her heels into Yenna's flanks and drove into the line of Ülak. Yenna knocked aside the two Ülak archers and trampled a third. Meanwhile, using the shovel, Mother deflected the spear thrust of another Ülak and then swung the shovel down hard onto the creature's head.

More Ülak appeared in the yard outside the stable. They hesitated at the sight of Mother's composed ferocity and the bloodied shovel. A horn blared through the night.

"Go," Mother shouted back at us. She directed Yenna forward, increasing speed, as she charged into the rightmost wing of the gathering Ülak line.

I did not have a chance to see what happened afterward, for two Ülak were still in the stable with us, having somehow evaded Mother's attack. They looked at me hungrily, drooling and licking their lips, which were curved into smiles with sharp teeth. Father pulled a hatchet from his belt and threw it. The hatchet cleaved into one creature's skull before it had time to respond. I winced. I had seen an animal butchered before, but this felt different.

The second Ülak hesitated long enough for Father to grab a metal pitchfork. The Ülak lunged at him with its curved scimitar, but Father parried the attack and thrust the pitchfork into its belly. As it collapsed, more Ülak arrived at the main entrance, which was now ablaze.

My stomach tensed.

Father leapt onto Charger, facing the rear door. "Ride."

With my heart pounding, I overcame the queasiness in my gut, followed Father out the back of the stable, and veered left around the arena. The decapitated bodies of two of our ranch hands lay nearby. Our house and stable burned brightly, lighting our initial escape.

The moon also shone from above, but little more than a face staring down passively at the chaos. Its pallid light reflected on the spires of black smoke now rising from our home and across the countryside. In the distance to our left, all of Hamath was wreathed in red flames.

In the wide valley separating our ranch from the town, I thought I saw the glint of swords. Later we learned that a battle occurred between the Ülak's main force and an army of mounted Alöwean soldiers from the Bulwark. Alas, they had come too late to save Hamath.

The Ülak were everywhere. Spotting us, they gave chase on foot. I glimpsed Mother's horse ride past us in the opposite direction with two arrows protruding from its left hip.

Where was Mother?

Father drove his heels firmly into Charger's side. I did the same with Yüllen.

Ülak materialized from the darkness ahead of us, barring our path. Those following behind were closing in fast. Father urged Charger to run faster. The horse was a courser trained for war. I hoped my mount would keep close to Charger without hesitating. Yüllen was a good horse, but also older and more timid.

The Ülak raised their spears as we reached their line.

Yüllen screamed and reared. Jerked forward, I crashed into his neck, which made my feet slip from the reins. I tensed, trying to press my thighs into Yüllen's side to keep me upright, but I lost contact. Empty space surrounded me until I slammed onto the ground. Gasping for breath, I forced myself to sit up. Ülak were standing over Yüllen's body, stabbing it repeatedly. One grabbed my neck from behind, but I twisted free and ran.

Where was Father?

Disoriented and struggling to breathe, I tripped and fell onto another Ülak whose back was to me. On my hands and knees, I found a fist-sized rock, straightened, and thrust it into the fallen Ülak's face. The impact stung my wrist, but I ignored the pain. I seized the dead Ülak's short spear and extended the tip outward, pivoting left, blindly hoping to create a space between me and my assailants. Instincts drove me, engrained through Mother's training.

Ülak gathered around me.

I heard Father calling, and spotted him still mounted not far beyond the Ülak encirclement. I called to him. He saw me, redirected Charger, and galloped in my direction. Some of the Ülak turned to face him.

24

As he was about to reach the Ülak, their line collapsed. Many fell with arrows jutting from their necks or torsos. Three winged shapes swooped low over our position. I spotted the Alöwean Sky Riders atop their eagle-like mounts as they circled, released another volley of arrows into the Ülak ranks, and then flew on toward the billowing darkness that encompassed Hamath.

Father reached me. I seized his outstretched hand and was lifted atop Charger. I then clung to Father's waist from behind as we rode across the plain to the protection of the forest. My heart pounded. Father's breaths were tense and irregular.

I cried.

I have tried to drive the image of Mother lying dead like the two ranch hands out of my head, yet it lingers stubbornly. Though I never saw what happened, though we never found Mother's body, the idea is part of my consciousness.

It never ceases to haunt me.

Mercy.

* * *

One day, the prison guards brought 43-1-12 outside.

She sat against a sun-saturated wall in a small secluded courtyard, reminding herself how it felt to be warm. Judging by the temperature and the cheerful sound of birdsong, she guessed it was spring in the outside world. The thought evoked images of flowers and tall grass swaying with the breeze outside Hamath. Though she could visualize colors, she could not recall the fragrance of flowers. She remembered sitting among the blossoms when she was a little girl, dreaming the daylight hours away. She missed the cheerfulness of their presence, the soft flesh of their bright petals.

Her reverie crumbled with the clang of hammers and pick-axes on stone. Once a great Alöwean city, Tïrmen was now being rebuilt as an Illiri prison fortress. She wondered how long it would take before there was nothing left of the old world.

**

I witnessed the city of Tïrmen twice before it was a prison. The first was when I accompanied Father on business. I remember little from that trip, except how Tïrmen's large stone ramparts conveyed such strength and security. They still exude power, but now it is one of bondage. It is hard to comprehend how such a grand city was conquered.

Tïrmen was the second largest city of the Alöwean Empire, a symbol, my father said, of their hegemony in western Illirium. Concern lined his voice whenever he discussed the tension mounting between the city's Alöwean and Illiri inhabitants. That was before the war.

"Things are changing too quickly," he said one night. Our family sat at the dinner table in our home.

"It's time for change," my brother, Ürstus, replied.

I half-listened to their conversation, distracted by the memory of kissing Jed a few weeks earlier.

"Most Illiri are fed up with foreign control," Sindor added. He brushed strands of blonde hair away from his forehead. "We want to be free."

"But what does that mean?" Father replied calmly. Finished with his food, he set his utensils down, crossed his arms, and leaned back in his chair. "You make it sound so simple."

Father rarely agreed with such dissentious talk. Most of the Alöweans he had met were honorable people.

"Freedom will begin when we drive the Alöweans out of the west," Ürstus said, "out of Siligen. These are our lands. We were here first."

"While it is true that our forefathers settled here long before the Alöweans," Father countered, "Siligen exists because of the Alöweans. You are mistaken if you think the clans of Hamath and Girion would coexist peacefully without Tïrmen, let alone be secure without the protection of the Alöwean garrisons."

"The clans of Arizaleth thrive well enough," Sindor said. "The Alöweans only have a small presence there."

"Don't bring Arizaleth into this," Ürstus chided his brother. "Let's try to focus on Siligen right now."

Sindor's confident tone retreated slightly against his older brother. "I still think Hamath and Girion could work together without Alöwean interference."

"I agree," Ürstus said.

"Yet that would be at the cost of Hamath's autonomy," Father commented. "Girion is larger and better armed."

"I see nothing wrong with that," Ürstus replied. "Lord Dwairian is a smart leader. He recognizes Hamath's value, that we provide a majority of Siligen's produce and livestock. He knows that Girion needs us."

"What of Tírmen?" Father asked. "In this imagined scenario of driving the Alöweans out of the west, out of Siligen, what will become of their western capital?"

"It could remain a center of trade," Ürstus replied. "At least a third of the city is populated by Illiri anyway. With the Alöweans gone, or most of them anyway, it would not be that different."

"You forget that most of the city's wealth comes from the east," Father countered, "from Nemenelor. Moreover, it is a complicated and costly task to maintain armed defenses like the Alöweans do in the Fortress of Enisön or the Bulwark, let alone Tírmen."

"But what are they protecting us against?" Ürstus urged. "Their armed presence merely serves their own interests: preserving the Empire."

"He has point, Siméon," Mother said, meeting Father's gaze. "The clans of Rodaním have long been united against foreign dominion. The Alöweans respect Rodaním's strength, and do not dare challenge it. Perhaps they fear the same could be true in the west."

"Exactly," Sindor exclaimed. "Siligen could be as strong, especially if united with the clans of Arizaleth. We outnumber the Alöweans at least four to one."

"The peace in Arizaleth has never been more than fragile," Father retorted, "and the clans of Rodaním share a deep kinship unlike the five western clans. Unification is challenging. Once again, we risk oversimplifying the matter. Besides, I doubt that Lord Dwairian is equipped to maintain the sovereignty let alone unity of so much territory, especially considering the cost of an uprising—in lives, resources, time. Even if the Illiri somehow managed to win, assuming that enough people would muster behind Lord Dwairian, I do not see what there is to gain that we cannot acquire more peacefully."

"We want the freedom to define our own future," Ürstus said.

"Maybe you have lived too comfortable a life, Father," Sindor replied. "Alöwean support has made you soft."

"Careful," Mother said. The sternness of her voice startled me to full attention. She stared at Sindor and then at Ürstus. "Your father's life has never been easy. Neither of our lives has. Rodaním is far from perfect. Anyway, you talk about freedom, but you would do well to remember the power of duty. We have wanted for nothing as a result of your father's dedication to this family and our people. His work has provided you a means to contemplate your dissatisfaction, to consider life beyond your present—beyond surviving. Never take that for granted."

"Forgive us," Ürstus said. He glanced at Mother, but settled his attention on Father. "We do not mean to sound ungrateful."

"I know," Father replied. "It is all right. I am glad that you boys feel free to speak your minds; that you can give voice to and explore your frustrations. Do not stop contemplating what is happening beyond our borders. Ask the difficult questions. But do not let them grow into anger alone. Seek practical answers and outcomes beneficial to all."

"I agree with Father," I said.

"You would," Sindor commented.

"Be respectful," Father scolded. Sindor looked away, frowning. Father focused on me. "What else do you think?"

With everyone now looking at me, I hesitated. "I wonder if violence is the only way to determine change."

"Sometimes it is," Mother replied.

"But most of the time there are peaceful solutions." Father offered a smile, but it was edged with sadness. "There are many ways to adapt." He looked at my brothers. "That can begin with adjusting your own point of view."

Ürstus and Sindor were two years apart, but they did everything together. They played together, learned together, ran away together. When news came a month later about Dwairian mustering an army in Girion, they did not seek Father's approval to join. My parents and I simply awoke one morning to find that Ürstus and Sindor were gone.

A brief note was all they left, written in Ürstus' firm, controlled hand. "We are done talking about change," he wrote, "Now is the time for action."

"They will be all right, Siméon," Mother said to Father, though her tone lacked conviction. She seemed both proud and saddened by her sons' choice.

Father remained silent for days. He just somberly focused on his work.

I was just angry that my brothers had not said goodbye.

The second time I saw Tïrmen was after the attack on our ranch. Father and I rode through the night, our progress slow as we navigated dense woodlands in order to avoid the main roads. At dawn we stumbled upon a group of Hamath survivors gathered in a damp meadow. Everyone smelled of smoke. We were greeted by Nelle, a stout woman with graying brown hair. She wore a dirty sheepskin coat, and appeared to be in charge.

"We're making for Tïrmen," she explained upon Father's questioning.

"That is, unless you have a better idea, Siméon," Ozath, Nelle's brother, added. Ozath was a farmer whose land bordered our own. His two children, a boy and a girl, hid behind him, each clutching one of his large hands.

"There's nowhere else to go," Nelle stated impatiently.

"Let Siméon speak," another woman said. Others murmured agreement.

"We should keep moving," Nelle muttered.

No one moved. Everyone looked at Father, waiting.

"Nelle is right," Father said at last. "Tïrmen is our best hope. We can continue west through the forest, taking advantage of its protection."

Everyone agreed. During the next seven days, Father became the unspoken leader of our company. On the seventh day, we reached Tïrmen. The only trouble we experienced along the way was foraging for food and tolerating rainstorms.

Reaching the plain, which ascends to Tïrmen's eastern gate, we discovered a large camp of Illiri.

"We're no longer permitted within the city walls," a woman said, noticing our confusion as we entered the camp.

"What has happened?" Father asked. But the woman had already walked away. She appeared to be looking for someone.

An older man, observing us from where he sat on a barrel, called out to Father. "It's the damn Alöweans."

Father turned to him. "Excuse me?"

"The Alöweans think we're rising against them."

"Why do they think that?" Father asked.

"Who's to know?" the old man replied. "We've heard rumors of skirmishes in the south, and news of an army being mustered in Girion."

I thought of my brothers.

There was bitter irony in the man's tone. "Thus the Lord of Tïrmen, in all his Alöwean foresight, asserts that precautions have to be made—for the security of the city, you see. Thus we've been banished from within its walls—from our own homes."

"It is true," said a familiar voice.

Father and I turned to see Hamath's lord, Ïdathor, standing next to us. He was covered in mud and specks of dried blood. Behind him was a grim, battered contingent of Hamath soldiers tending to their horses.

Ïdathor's movements were slow with fatigue. He placed a hand on Father's shoulder. "I am glad to see you alive, Siméon." He acknowledged me with a nod then glanced around. "Where is Hedda?"

Father's eyes wandered down. He shook his head.

Ïdathor's shoulders sank. He rubbed his eyes then pulled Father into a hug. "I am sorry."

My heart ached. Tears formed, but I could no longer release them. I had cried a lot lately. After a moment of silence, I asked, "Any news?"

"I am learning what I can," Ïdathor replied, stepping back from my father. He ran his fingers back through his short white hair. "Aside from my own warriors, you are the first Hamath survivors I have seen. Everyone else has been scattered or slain . . . an entire city lost." He motioned around him. "As to what is happening here, it is proving difficult to find reliable information. We will have to find refuge elsewhere, it seems.

"Where should we go?" Father asked.

"I have been thinking about that," Ïdathor replied. "To start with, we need to get organized—find the leaders of our Illiri brethren here."

Ïdathor eventually rallied the entire Illiri camp, though I remember little of what was said. I recall a great deal of confusion at first, both angry and fearful. In the end, Ïdathor called for us to return to the ruins of Hamath; claimed he had received word that aid would be given to all who sided with Dwairian, the newly proclaimed Illiri king. That Hamath could be rebuilt greater than before—something about a glorious future free from the Alöwean Empire. I do not know where he got such information. I was tired and consumed with grief.

"Dwairian's message is spreading quickly," Father commented to me as Ïdathor roused the crowd. Father seemed neither pleased nor disturbed, just worn out. "What is important now is survival." He held me close, exhaling slowly. "We will find a way to survive, you and I."

Survival.

Change.

At the time, I did not really understand what was happening. Father looked uncertain about Ïdathor's plan, but perhaps could not think beyond his own sorrow. Mother was gone. My brothers were probably in Girion. Our horses had been slain or driven off, and our ranch was no more than a smoldering skeleton of a home. What was there to return to?

We returned, nevertheless.

Mother, why did you go?

Was there no other way to protect us?

Have you found the Fields of Gedáron, that eternal paradise about which you sometimes spoke? Or were you claimed by the Dryden, Keeper of the Dead, who seeks to claim us all?

I miss you.

Can I find you in the world beyond this one, if such a world exists?

* * *

The nightly beatings subsided. Three guards regularly brought 43-1-12 out to the small courtyard for fresh air and light. They began to feed her better. One day, a female healer named Ida tended to her wounds—her bruised face and scarred flesh. The decrepit tunic was replaced with a newer one, along with worn breeches and boots.

43-1-12 felt her health gradually return, yet it also made her wary. What were they doing? She could not let herself become too comfortable, she decided. She had to keep vigilant, ready for anything.

One morning, Nabilak came to her cell. Two guards stood behind him.

43-1-12 remained seated, her back against the far wall of the cell, watching him.

"I am returning you to Ward 12," Nabilak commented, avoiding her eyes. His posture was somewhat slouched. "I trust you have learned to be more submissive."

She clenched her jaw. He could think whatever he liked.

"Remember why you are here," he continued with a firmer voice, still avoiding her gaze. "Your sentence has not yet been finalized, and your actions so far have endeared you to no one. The Arbiter of Siligen does not look kindly on defiance. There will be no more fighting with anyone, especially not with prison guards. Is that understood?"

Continuing to stare at him, she said nothing.

Stiffening, Nabilak took a step forward. "Is that understood?" he shouted.

As she stayed silent, the two guards stepped in and lifted her roughly to her feet. "Answer the warden, bitch," one barked into her ear.

She nodded to Nabliak, beginnnig to sense a power over him. For one, her mind was still her own. He had not breached it. "I understand," she said calmly.

Nabilak's posture relaxed. His voice softened as he looked at her. "This prison is your home, 43-1-12. So think carefully about what kind of home you would like it to be. Think about my offer."

He nodded to the guards and then turned away.

She hoped to never see him again.

Summer came.

Working outside invigorated her spirit. The women of Ward 12 did not have to excavate rock from the ruined city like the men of the other wards. Under King Dwairian's decree, the women were not to perform heavy labor at all. Furthermore, they were to be kept separate from the male inmates, and their health looked after, which was marginally done. The rationale was that if the women could be redeemed, they were to be returned to society to help replenish the dwindled numbers of Illiri lost during the war—to help build Dwairian's new empire. No one took that seriously, however.

Each day, the women of Ward 12 mixed ground stone into a compound that served as a new kind of mortar. No one knew much about it except that Dwairian already used it to bolster his castle west in Girion. The mortar was supposed to be stronger than its predecessors. Some said that Rök chemists had been contracted to create the compound. 43-1-12 knew little about the Rök, or Dwarves as some called them, whose kingdom was somewhere far away in northeastern Illirium. She did not care.

At night, before lying down to sleep in the musty barracks of Unit 1, which was positioned at the eastern end of the ruined city, or during the day when the women were allowed periods of rest, she would steal away to a quiet spot to condition her body and mind: exercises with a stone, lunges, jumps—anything. Her limbs became stronger, her flexibility increased. She was grateful that no one stopped her. She wanted to sustain an edge of physical and mental discipline. That is what her mother would do, she thought. It was difficult with such low rations, but she resolved not to be weak. She would keep her ferocity alive as best as she could.

She did not speak much with the other women. Some were insane. Those that had tried to bully her at first had learned from broken noses to keep their distance. Most were in prison for murder or insurrection, but some for lesser crimes. 43-1-12 thought of herself as a rebel, though being labeled as mad could have its advantages.

One day, in the labor yard adjacent to Ward 12, she bent over a large vat half-buried in the earth. The dusty yard was lined with them. Two women worked at each vat. Her partner that day was a middle-aged woman named

33

Yetta who stirred the contents of the new mortar compound slowly, keeping them mixed and soft. Each time one of the prison's free workers came to take some of the mixture away in a pail, 43-1-12 would add more of the ground substance and water into the vat.

Yetta's right jaw line bore the mark, *27-2-12*. Everyone in Tïrmen Prison had been given a number: a small tattoo that followed the jaw line. On 43-1-12's family's ranch, their horses had been marked with small ink numbers. The number conveyed ownership, though the horses had received far better treatment than the inmates of Tïrmen Prison.

The last set of numbers, the "12", was the same for all the women in Ward 12, which was the only female ward in the prison. The first set of numbers referred to the progressing count of inmates in that particular ward. She had recently seen a woman with *62-2-12* marked on her jaw, the "62" showing her to be the sixty-second prisoner brought into Ward 12. The population of the ward was small, but steadily growing. A few new prisoners arrived every week. An equal number either died or were taken elsewhere; she did not know where.

The second number referred to one of two units. Unit 2 was for thieves or those who had committed petty crimes, and included the mentally deranged. Unit 1 was for the dangerous ones, generally kept separate from those in Unit 2. Nearly all of the women in Ward 12 awaited a final sentence for their alleged crimes. Guilty or innocent, each had been marked. Therefore, even if they were ultimately released back into society, their image would be permanently tarnished by suspicion.

Still, the number provided a degree of anonymity. To 43-1-12, it elicited an identity displaced from and at war with society. It meant resistance, a form of assertion. For now, she would accept the label as a mask, a defense—an attempt to turn the prison's weapon against itself.

She poured more water into the vat and then addressed the middle-aged woman. "Do you know what year it is?"

Yetta looked up from her work with a blank expression. "Eh?"

She repeated the question.

Yetta considered it for a while. "Why, I think it has been a few months since you arrived, my dear." Her voice had a musical gaiety to it, as if she was reasoning with a child. "I remember that day." The woman returned her attention to mixing the mortar. "You were a feisty one." But then she gazed at the sky, squinting for a moment. "As to the year, it's 630 EP, I think, or 4 AEP—or whatever you choose. I don't care for this new dating system. It's made things awfully confusing. Granted, the name 'Elíbom Prímom', EP, means nothing to me. Who decided to qualify years like that anyway? It's all nonsense, so who cares if years are now deemed 'After' him, AEP, or not."

"I do not know either," 43-1-12 commented.

"You were absent from us for a while there." Yetta looked up at her with a puzzled expression. "I thought they'd might have let you go."

"No," she replied, looking away.

"That would have been a shame," Yetta added.

43-1-12 focused back on their work, trying to ignore Yetta as she spoke about the odd things her husband used to do before he was killed in the war. She blocked the woman's face from view with the rim of her straw hat while the fingers of despair brushed against her focus. The truth weighed heavily upon her heart. Had it only been four months since she arrived to the prison?

It had felt longer.

A swift sun: morning and evening; days pass with little utterance.

    Faces: some sad, some angry—all weary.

    How to cope with the aftermath of war? How to handle anonymity? What to hold on to? Where to look?

    All so weary.

"Did you hear me, Prisoner 43-1-12?" the man said.

She sat in the shade of the Unit 1 barracks, resting her left leg out in front of her while her right leg was held up by both her hands clasped at her knee. It was her midday break. Her eyes closed, she had been trying to focus on the sounds of birds and trees outside the prison walls, but the effort was proving futile.

35

The Captain of Ward 12 kicked her left boot. "43-1-12?"

She opened her eyes and glanced up at the captain, squinting to adjust her eyes to the light that reflected off the conical helmets of the two guards behind him. The captain looked to be a little older than her, maybe in his early twenties. The brown tunic covering his chain mail shirt looked new. She guessed that he had not been in Tïrmen for long.

"Someone is here to see you," he said.

She rose to her feet, ignoring the captain's extended hand. His gesture surprised her. Why did he not have the guards force her to stand?

With the two guards following behind them, the captain led her to the edge of Ward 12 and through the crude gatehouse. She spotted a few guards watching her from behind the wood palisade. Quickly looking again, she wondered if she had seen Nabilak among the guards. He was not there, however. Maybe she had imagined it.

When she arrived at the gate, she was frisked. She glared at the guard in front of her as the second guard's hands lingered longer than necessary while sliding across parts of her body. She frowned at the captain, but he diverted his eyes.

Passive, she noted. Perhaps that could be used against him.

The routine completed, the captain nodded to one of the gatekeepers. "Open the gate."

She followed the captain outside, noticing a group of tall figures with brown bark-like skin to her left. They were a race she had never seen before. She wanted to look closer, but was promptly directed to the right. The guards pressed her into a small square courtyard, which was part of the Ward 12 palisade, and shut the door shut promptly behind her.

Ambling to the other side of the courtyard, she studied Tïrmen's central keep, which looked down on her from the left. Having seen it from that angle years before during her first visit with her father, though not so close, she thought how gloomy it now looked. It had felt so alive before. The war had emptied it of life, and the scars still showed. Various merlons had been broken away. Black stains like bruises marked the castle's stonework, especially at the tops of its towers or along the battlements where the hoardings had been devoured by fire. The numerous yellow and green Alöwean flags, which had once waved briskly, illuminated by the sun, had been replaced by one solitary blue flag: the pennant of Siligen, the symbol of King Dwairian's new empire. It hung limply from a pole protruding from the tallest tower. Lined with white and bearing a gold lion at its center, its life had been absorbed by the more brilliant afternoon sky. In such light, one barely noticed the flag at all.

Empires rise and fall and rise, she mused.

The door creaked opened behind her, and someone stepped in. Without turning around, she listened to his footsteps, noting how they hesitated then stopped. The door closed again. She listened to the newcomer exhale slowly, as if trying to check himself.

Turning around, she saw that the young man was slightly taller than her. Beneath a black cloak, he wore leather plate armor, the lion of Girion branded at the center of the portion protecting his chest. He bore no other armor aside from leather greaves, gauntlets, and knee-high riding boots. Here was a soldier equipped to travel swiftly.

She glanced at his sheath, but the sword had been removed, presumably by the guards outside as a precaution. Looking up at the man's face, he seemed familiar. The tanned, bearded expression was firm, but the eyes were unsure, almost sad. He reminded her of someone, but she could not think who. A thick discolored scar ran from his left cheek across his nose to his right brow. His hair was brown and drawn back from his shoulders with a small cord.

Where had she seen him before?

He looked at her expectantly.

"Rhoda?" He whispered the name, as if hardly believing what he saw.

The voice was familiar. The name was familiar. Recognition poured through her consciousness. She took a step back.

*　*　*

My father's father and grandfather were horse masters. He inherited the business when he was a young man, the only surviving child of his family.

Despite the grief of his youth—a mother who suffered three miscarriages, dying with the third, and a father whose heart stopped ten years later—Father managed to maintain the family's legacy in western Illirium. Better than that, he increased its reputation. Our family was one of the wealthiest in Hamath.

After the Ülak raid and flight to Tïrmen, we returned to Hamath with nothing. Father did not know what else to do. The town offered scorched memories; the work and amount of resources needed to rebuild felt overwhelming. Hamath was incredibly vulnerable, yet no one bothered us. I am not sure why.

For days, I only wanted to sleep.

"Get up," Father said one morning, having stuck his head through the entrance of our small tent.

I pretended not to hear him, and continued sleeping. My thoughts wandered in a fog of weariness and heartache. I heard him exhale slowly and step inside the tent, closer to the edge of my cot.

"We cannot keep doing this," he said more firmly. "This is not the way."

"Not the way to what?" I replied curtly, my voice muffled by the blanket across my face.

He pulled the blanket back. "Look at me."

It took a moment for my eyes to adjust to the brightness. Sunlight saturated the faded white of the tent cover. Father knelt beside me.

"What?" I asked.

"We have all suffered." He sank to a sitting position on the grassy ground, leaned back against the edge of his cot opposite mine. "Yet we cannot withdraw into ourselves. We cannot hide from the present. There are more productive ways to cope."

I pressed my face into my pillow.

"I know it is not easy." He brushed a strand of my hair back behind my ear. "But we must adapt. That is part of what it means to survive. We help each other. We force ourselves to stand up and claim opportunities."

I shifted my face against my pillow so that one eye could glance at him. He tried to offer a smile, but it lacked confidence. I reminded myself that he was also grieving, probably deeper than I understood. He needed for us to be strong together.

I felt so tired.

"Come," he urged, rising to his feet. "Get dressed, wash your face, and have something to eat with me. We can start there for today."

Though the war did not last a year, it felt longer.

Aside from the warriors under Ïdathor's command, and a handful of other survivors like my father and me, nearly everyone who returned to Hamath came from Tïrmen. The Illiri of Tïrmen were a different kind of people. They had different expectations, and were more ambitious. But the old town of Hamath was dead. A new city would be built, and Father and I had to find our place in it.

The war ended when King Dwairian's authority was recognized by what remained of the defeated Alöwean Empire. Dwairian commanded the Illiri clan lords who had remained loyal to him, such as Ïdathor, to then direct most resources toward agriculture. The people of Siligen, our so-called new Illiri Empire, needed to be fed. As Father and Ïdathor had been good friends since childhood, the Lord of Hamath allowed us to keep our old lands, much of which had yet to be cultivated, under the condition that for five years its main produce be distributed to the community.

"We have to work on behalf of each another," Ïdathor said, "for the common good." Apparently these were Dwairian's words.

Father agreed.

I wish Mother had been there with us, and my brothers—and Jed. But Mother was gone, and no one knew if my brothers had survived the war. Jed was probably also dead. Rumor of Pernor's destruction had reached us in the first weeks of the war. Nothing was certain except that Pernor's fate had been similar to that of Hamath: consumed by flames. I was not surprised that the Pinnacle of the Alöwean Empire, the stronghold of its high council, had been targeted. Still, I wept upon hearing the news. I imagined Jed as a blackened shape amidst blackened ruins—like our burned home. I cursed the war. I curse it still—and Dwairian for inciting it. I longed for my old family. Working together, so much might have been different.

Three years passed. I reached my sixteenth birthday. Our family land prospered. Many of Hamath's residents wanted to partner with Father. His honest, hard-working character was well respected. After two more years, we could begin converting our land back into a horse ranch. Father and Ïdathor discussed ways to acquire some well-bred horses. To rebuild the family business would be in the interest of the new empire.

I will never forget the day Ürstus and Sindor rode into Hamath among a contingent of Siligen soldiers. It was in that third year after the war, the autumn of 628 EP. They were only passing through; apparently their commander had correspondence for Ïdathor from Dwairian. Happening to be present when the contingent arrived to the new city square, Father and I tended to their horses while they waited. A large fountain was at the center of the square. The streets were paved with stones. Once more, traders had begun to come from throughout Illirium, including Dwarves from as far as Rökad, selling their wares, exchanging news. Prosperity was returning to Hamath.

I wish the reunion with my brothers felt the same.

Seeing Ürstus and Sindor after four years away reminded me of a past that could not be regained. I did not know what to say to them. They did not recognize me at first, actually. They said little to Father, though he stood beside me the whole time. He mainly focused on the horses.

"I am glad you are alive," I offered, not knowing what else to say. I meant it.

"Where is Mother?" Ürstus asked.

I felt my thoughts tensing with indignation. "Dead."

"What?" Sindor said, clearly surprised. "How? When?"

"You should have been here," I said, grief mixing with anger. "She might still be alive if you had not abandoned us."

"It was an Ülak raid," Father said softly. "When Hamath was attacked."

Sindor glanced at Father then back at me, his expression still exposing disbelief. I nodded. As the weight of the truth settled, his eyes lowered.

Ürstus clenched his jaw.

"I'm sorry," Sindor said.

"She died a fighter," Father added. "It is what she wanted."

"Still," I said, looking at my brothers, daring them to meet my gaze. "You should have been here."

"Many have lost those precious to them," Ürstus stated, finally looking at me. "But they did not die for nothing. Our freedom has been won. A new age has begun."

My brothers explained that they were part of a new force in Siligen, a small mounted army of distinguished warriors called the Riders of Valon. They spoke briefly of the war, of being part of the final battle—how it had been a massacre, how it had been glorious. They mentioned enemies with names like Küllka and Boldei, who remained scattered and resisted the new empire.

"We are going to hunt them down," Sindor said. "Most have fled to the Kurshemnt Mountains."

We had to say farewell too soon. As my brothers rode off and the dust settled, I did not know what to feel. In a way, I did not feel anything. I looked at Father beside me, observed his frown slowly weaken to what I thought was sorrow strained by regret. My heart ached for him more than for my brothers' departure. I reached my arm around Father's waist, and he placed his arm around my shoulder. Though my brothers lived, Father and I would face the future alone.

I have struggled to forgive Ürstus and Sindor. Sometimes I have hated them. More often, I feel indifferent. After all, that is how they treated us. But it is a mournful indifference.

So much might have been prevented had they stayed that day.

A body floats down through the water. The head is smashed. A small cloud of blood surrounds it like a halo.

More bodies follow. All dead.

The stream winds on, joined by others as the mountains empty themselves of violence. Yet the violence remains.

There is an ache, a hunger: winter's haunting.

* * *

"What are you doing here?" 43-1-12 asked her brother in disbelief.

Ürstus watched her with heavy eyes, as if burdened by shame. "Forgive me."

"Why did you come?"

"It took me a while to find you." He took a step forward, but she stepped away, the firmness of her expression warning him not to come closer. He pulled back and raised his hands in submission. "I'm not going to hurt you."

"You have done enough," she retorted.

"Rhoda."

"Do not call me that."

It had been so long since she had heard the name spoken. Amidst the sorrow and struggle of the last few years, she had buried it—to preserve it, maybe even to forget it. She had become a survivor, on her own without anyone to help her. It was easier to defy everything without the thought of her old identity.

"Leave me." She turned away. "I have nothing to say to you."

Gritting her teeth, she tried to sort through confused emotions. Anger at her brothers' abandonment lingered within her, as did a defiant indifference, but so also did a desire to be reconciled. She realized that she missed them. A pang of hope struck her heart. Could their remaining family be made whole again?

She turned around and leaned against the wall, slowly sliding down to a sitting position, all the while staring at her brother's boots. They could have been anyone's boots. "Where is Sindor?"

Ürstus had not moved. "He's dead, killed in a skirmish with the Boldei . . . in the Kurshemnt Mountains." His voice was quiet, his eyes fixed on the ground in front of her. "It was a few months ago, during our summer raids. Sindor fell from a great height, and we could not retrieve his body. . . . Many fell that day."

Her heart shuddered. The three of them would never be together again. "Why are you here?" Her eyes settled on the black contours of the lion on

Ürstus' breastplate.

"You're my sister," he began. "I had to find you."

"But why now?"

"I heard what happened." He hesitated. "Is it true?"

She stared at him. "Are you here to condemn me like everyone else?"

"No," he said, but then seemed to think about it more. "No. You did what any of us would have done in your place. You did what Mother taught us." He shook his head to himself. "I'm sorry I wasn't there." He knelt down, brushed his finger across the dusty ground. "I'm going to get you out of here. Somehow."

He glanced at her apologetically, but she looked away.

"There is nothing you can do," she said, standing, brushing the dust off of her trousers. She turned to look up at Tïrmen's towers. "It is too late. If Ïdathor could not help me, you certainly cannot."

"I'm not giving up," Ürstus said behind her.

She heard his footsteps approaching, felt his hand on her shoulder. He had never touched her so tenderly. Her heart beat faster. Eyes resisted a desire for tears.

He sighed. "I wish I could stay."

She stiffened, brushed his hand from her shoulder while still keeping her back to him.

He explained, "I have to return south to the mountain campaign, but I'll try to call in some favors. In a few months, I should have enough money to pay for your release."

If only it were a matter of money. "Do not worry about me," she said. "Go, take care of yourself. Survive. That is all any of us can do now."

"Rhoda, I'm so sorry."

He placed both his hands on her shoulders, but she shook them off. "Stop." She turned to face him. "I am not that girl anymore."

He appeared about to protest, but she would hear none of it.

"I am Prisoner 43-1-12." She pointed to the tattoo on her jaw. "Nothing else."

Her heart pounded. Her eyes were fixed on his, but he could not sustain such a firm gaze. She embraced the anger, felt its power over her brother. Yet at the same time she also hated that she was unleashing it upon him. A part of her wanted his love while a part cautioned that it would soften her defenses. She wanted him to hug her, to take her with him. Yet she also wanted him to leave.

"You're my sister," he said, meeting her eyes once more. "Nothing will ever change that. Don't give up."

After another moment's hesitation, he turned, strode to the door, and knocked. As it was opened for him, he looked back at her one last time. "Fight on, little sister."

There was a tone of respect in his voice that she had never heard from him before. It made her feel emboldened. It made her feel regret. She wanted him to come back so that she could hold him close, to remember what goodness felt like.

But the door closed behind him.

Rhoda: a flower, evergreen.

What color remains? The petals have faded and fallen. What is left that survives? What is left to cultivate?

Passive time. Hungry eyes.

In a world measured by steps, life framed in glances and breaths, all goodness has departed.

Rhoda. The name can also mean danger, warning. For when winter comes, what use is an evergreen except for firewood?

* * *

Some people became jealous of Father's success, of his ability to produce a harvest from the dust and ashes. Others wanted him to become the new Steward of Hamath. Having lost his own family in the war, and with opportunities directing his attention elsewhere, Ïdathor was ready to delegate leadership to another. A man from Girion, Malech, was also being considered for the stewardship. Father suspected that Dwairian had sent Malech and his supporters to Hamath to gain political control. Malech's outspoken ambition fueled many peoples' imaginations with ideas of a strong Illiri future.

Father would accept the stewardship if it was offered to him, but did not really desire the title. He wondered if Malech resented his success and longstanding integrity in the community. Rumors spread about Father's motives, and I assumed that Malech and his supporters were the cause. Father did not like me saying so. Regardless of the truth, the mounting tension had an adverse affect on our people's morale and confidence.

"Hamath needs unity, not division," Father said.

One day, I spotted Malech at the border of our fields. He was accompanied by two armed bodyguards dressed in blue cloaks. They assessed us and our land—making plans, I suspected. I told Father and then followed him as he calmly approached Malech.

"What can I do for you, gentlemen?" Father greeted.

Atop his horse, Malech's grin conveyed haughty assurance. "You can stay out of my way."

"This is my land," Father replied.

"For now."

"Why must this enmity continue?" Father asked. He sounded tired. "Can we not come to an understanding?"

Malech glanced at me. His dark gray, calculating eyes made me uncomfortable. "It's not necessary for us to understand each other."

"We both want Hamath to thrive," Father pressed. "Why not find a way to work together?"

"You're part of an old world, Siméon." Malech's tone suggested both boredom and contempt. He looked away. "The new world needs leaders with unwavering resolve. Only the strongest will survive."

"I just want to live in peace," Father said, "to rebuild my ranch and provide for my family—for our people. Does that threaten to you?"

"You're too shortsighted, Siméon," Malech said. "Your ideals will not survive." He looked at me once again, his attention moving down and up my body. "Yet if it's unity you desire, perhaps an arrangement can be made. As you said, you must think about your family."

"You would do well to stay away from me," I stated firmly, "You and your thugs."

Malech clicked his tongue in disapproval. "Temper, temper, young lady." His expression suggested amusement.

"My daughter knows how to take care of herself," Father said. "Keep your eyes and thoughts off her."

"We'll see," Malech said, turning away. "We'll see."

That autumn, three months before the steward was to be chosen, Father was attacked while tending one of our eastern fields. All the workers with him were found beaten to death, but Father had somehow survived. I still wonder if that was deliberate. His body was covered in blood and bruises. A few of his ribs were broken. His head and back hurt. He could not remember what happened. It took him more than a month before he could walk again, and his right arm never regained its full range of motion.

The Reeve and his men concluded that brigands were responsible. Lawlessness was rampant in those years; it took time before Dwairian's forces were organized in such a way as to enforce consistent order. Some of us in Hamath did not believe the incident to be a result of brigands, however. Once again, I suspected Malech, for the Reeve was loyal to him; yet I had no proof of devious intent that I could present to Lord Ïdathor. So I kept quiet.

I regret that now.

Malech was ultimately named steward without challenge. People grew distant from Father, as if afraid to work for him. Some confessed that if they helped us, their families would be susceptible to antagonism by Malech's mounting supporters. Father tried to manage everything on his own, and I helped him as best as I could. His trusted manager had been killed in the attack, and as no one stepped forward to replace him, it became impossible to maintain our land. Ïdathor said that he could do nothing, but I did not believe him. I think he did not want to get involved.

The pain in Father's legs returned. They had never truly healed. Gradually, portion by portion, our land had to be sold to Malech. Our home, which Father and I had rebuilt, also had to be sold. Thus our dream to restore the ranch evaporated with the mist of a cold spring morning.

What was there left to do?

Father considered taking me east to Yanweri in Rodaním, to Mother's clan. He thought Mother's sister, Corine, still lived there, but Ïdathor said no one from Siligen was allowed to cross the Elentarí River. Political tension was mounting between Siligen and Rodaním. Dwairian did not want his subjects associating with the eastern clans of Illiri because it was alleged that Rodaním no longer supported his kingship. He had the Alöwean stronghold of Tärm Tower rebuilt, and stationed a sizeable force within its walls. The soldiers were to guard the Elentari Bridge, which provided the best way across the deep, swiftly flowing river. Ïdathor explained that only those with written permission from the king could cross, and that permits were difficult to acquire.

Father did not have the strength to travel anyway. Over four hundred miles of open country separated Hamath from the Elentari Bridge. It would be another hundred miles to Yanweri, the town of Mother's people. Thus, with nowhere else to go, we remained in Hamath.

We survived.

Barely.

The money from selling our lands and ranch helped us transition to the outskirts of Hamath, to the poorest district of the city proper. We lived in a small structure posturing as a home. Really, it was just a room. Father's health rapidly declined, and nothing I did improved his state of mind. He seemed to have surrendered. Piece by piece, his life faded. I worked wherever and whenever I could, but there was little to be found outside the fields. I did not want to give Malech the pleasure of seeing me bent over in his domain. Fortunately, I found work with one of Father's remaining friends, Ozath, but it was still a difficult time. That was true for many people.

Bedridden, his graying beard long and unkempt, Father began talking about death. His skin became pale and clammy. The resonance of his voice faded. Sometimes I sang wordless melodies—ones Mother used to hum to me—to ease and cleanse his troubled mind. His body relaxed in response, but that never lasted.

One day, he pulled me close, as if in desperation. "The Dryden," he urged, "Do you see it?"

I looked around, but saw nothing unusual. "What do you mean?"

"It is here." He stared at the fire burning in our small stone hearth.

I did not know what to say.

Still holding me close, he said, "Remember that the Dryden means submission. The Dryden means fate."

Though he was feverish, his expression showed a surging pang of fortitude. His voice was suddenly clearer with the strength I had once known.

"Nature imposes its boundaries on us," he continued, "in this life and probably the next." He coughed. "Yet the mind and body can go farther than we imagine."

He coughed again, more violently, while covering his mouth. His hand came away stained with bloodied spittle. Pulling the blanket closer about his body, curling up on his side, he looked older than his years. It broke my heart. He no longer had the will to sit upright. I wept as I sat beside him feeling helpless. What could I do?

"You are attentive," he said, hoarsely, "a smart girl. You have your mother's spirit, but with a warmer, brighter light. Endure when others do not. . . . Be stronger than me. You are . . ."

"Father, please—"

"It is the truth," he protested, raising his hand. "I am beaten, weak. I have failed—you, your brothers, your mother . . ." he struggled for breath, tears forming, "everyone. . . . I have succumbed to death. The Dryden is here . . . whispering to me." Father looked up into my eyes. "I see it, sitting here waiting."

I looked at the fire again, but still saw nothing out of the ordinary.

"But you are stronger, my love," Father added, "my flower. You will overcome the Dryden. You will find a way."

"Overcome death? How?"

"The Canta," Father replied, closing his eyes. His breaths were shallow, his mouth agape. After a while, he swallowed, licked his lips, and focused his eyes back on me. "Remember the Canta. Seek to know what that name means."

The word sounded familiar, but I could not place it.

"There are some," Father said, his voice weak, "like your mother, or her people anyway, who believe the Canta can guide us away from the Dryden—after we die, to some place of peaceful rest, another life." He tried to take a deep breath, but coughed instead. After it settled, he added, "I wish I knew more. I wasted so much time."

I still did not understand. He and Mother had spoken so little about an afterlife. Few in Hamath spoke about it, or believed in it. Most seemed to think we pass into nothingness, that the Drdyen is more a personification of that nothingness than anything else—synonymous with fate. I did not know what to think. I am still not sure.

"Whatever happens," Father said, taking my hand, "Do not give up. I love you."

He died that night.

The winter snow felt particularly cold from then on. From our one small window, I stared at the white shroud as if in a trance, lost in its blankness for days before being stirred into wakefulness.

I was seventeen years old.

Winter.

Clouds brood, gliding in with chilling wind and flakes of cold.

The body is held closer, but restful warmth is forgotten. In its place is agitation. It shrouds my consciousness, erodes my patience. Abandoned by calm, my body trembles, the tension screaming for me to strike out at something.

Where is warmth? Why has it abandoned me? Am I to now defy it like all the rest?

To live, I struggle on against Nature.

* * *

Winter progressed into a new year. 43-1-12 forgot what it felt like to live outside the prison walls. Yet her memories, and a deeply guarded hope, dared her to remember the good that had preceded such an existence. If only such warmth would feel less distant. The prison cold taunted her with it.

A few of the women in Unit 1 died from sickness. The guards did not care. To them, the inmates were outcasts.

One day, the Captain of Ward 12 explained to 43-1-12, "We received your sentence from the Arbiter of Siligen."

43-1-12 stood between two guards in the captain's office. The office walls and flooring were comprised of plain wood planks. The warmth of the chamber was enviable. She gazed longingly at the fire crackling within its stone hearth. The reality that she would soon be returning outside loomed both in her thoughts and on her skin.

"Due to the severity of your crime," the captain continued, "and the dissident behavior you have shown so far in this prison, this recent year will serve as the first of a twenty-year sentence. Your case will be reviewed at the end of that time, your sentence either concluded or prolonged depending on your conduct."

The young captain said something else, but 43-1-12 did not hear. Instead, she focused on the savory aroma of supper cooking in the next room, which made her stomach gurgle.

As the guards brought her back outside, her body stiffened against the change in temperature. For a moment she would have given anything to be able to remain warm, but quickly thrust the thought aside in frustration. She did not need those men. The gate of Ward 12 closed behind her as she walked hurriedly to the crude barracks of Unit 1.

It was warmer inside the barracks, but the sensation did not last. The wind howled against the outside walls. She trembled. The loneliness of her situation battered against her willpower. The small stove at the center of the room did little to improve her mood. The warmth it suggested seemed to be a cruel charade, absorbing rather than exuding heat. Still, the other women who shared the unit with her gathered around it as if worshipping at an altar. They all seemed to have capitulated to their condition. In the fading half-light of the winter evening, they appeared to be little more than shadows.

Perhaps she was like them. Perhaps she too was fading.

No, she countered to herself. *Not yet.*

She turned away and rubbed some life back into her hands and fingers as she paced along the far wall. She then reached up and gripped one of the roof's many cross beams with both sets of fingers. Settling her hold, she pulled herself up then slowly lowered herself down, repeating this process as many times as she could.

Nineteen more years. The amount of time was unfathomable.

Her heart beat steadily; her arms began to burn. She welcomed the sensation, for there was life within its rhythm. Finally lowering herself to the ground, she reveled in the blood rushing from her chest to her limbs and back.

The other women did not turn their blank gazes from the stove. They had seen her routine countless times before. It was one of her many ways to melt the frost threatening to kill her spirit. Yet winter still waited. Already she felt its hands upon her. She had to fight the allure of death—the Dryden. She had to resist the temptation to surrender.

Retrieving the thick cloak she had taken from the body of a woman who had died a few weeks earlier, 43-1-12 put it on and drew the hood over her head. She stared at the door of the barracks and imagined the terrain beyond being whitened with snow: a blank world.

Nineteen years.

It would not come to that, she resolved. She would find a way to escape.

* * *

Our family cemetery rested amidst a cluster of trees near the eastern border of our old property. Other headstones jutted out from the ground, the older ones leaning every which way. Moss clung to their brittle stone, concealing fading inscriptions. Though the land no longer belonged to my family, Malech allowed me to bury Father with his ancestors.

In the months following, I often went there to stare at Father's gravestone.

51

*Siméon the Horse Master
(569-629 EP
Loving Husband and Father
Loyal Friend*

Ïdathor had paid for the stone, and suggested the last line. I placed Father next to the plot allotted to Mother. Though we never found Mother's body, Father and I had still buried a coffin. We placed a few of her belongings in it: her hairbrush, horse reins, some fresh berries. Father even placed the charred remains of Mother's sword inside.

"I miss her steadfastness, her courage," Father had said on the day we buried Mother's coffin. "Your mother had a warrior's spirit to the end."

Leaving the cemetery that day, he retold the story of how they had met. How Mother had arrived on horseback alone at the border of our ranch, carrying her sword across her back. How his whole family quickly warmed to her strength of spirit. He could not remember how many months Mother stayed with them. She became part of their daily lives, as if she had always been there, helping with chores and ranch work. She agreed to marry him, but first returned to her family in Rodaním. When she came back to Hamath, Father said she was more relaxed than before, but that she also seemed to have buried some weight of grief within her. She did not tell him much about her life in Rodaním. He knew that her younger brother had drowned as a boy, and that her two older brothers had left home at the threshold of manhood to serve the leader of Rodaním, the Rïmon, in his capital of Trïesch. Neither brother had been seen since.

I realized how little I knew about my mother. Had I been blind to her true character, or had she hidden it from me? If so, why? Why, when I would need the lessons of her experience? Was she being brave or foolish by leaving us that final night?

I miss her.

*Hedda
(576-625 EP)*

Tender Wife and Mother
A True Daughter of Rodanim

I recall receiving little tenderness from my mother. Perhaps it was extended more to my brothers because they were older, or because they were boys. Perhaps she did not know what to do with me, a daughter caught between two cultures: Hamath and Yanweri. What exactly were her expectations for my future? What were anyone's expectations of me?

The last line of the epitaph holds my imagination: "Daughter of Rodaním." What does it mean? Furthermore, what happened to that free-spirited traveler from the east? Father said I was becoming like her, that he saw her will in me; but the strength I had observed in her seemed quieter, more contained. She generally acted reserved. Was a fire still burning brightly within her all the while, waiting for the opportune time? Did it only come out in secret? Did I glimpse it that night in our barn when she attacked the Ülak? Father implied that it was so, and that such a spirit had never died. I wish I had known her better, and had sought to better understand her.

Most of my youth was spent with Father, my brothers, and ranch hands caring for our land and horses. Aside from a few scattered moments alone together indoors, most of my memories with Mother involved her overseeing me and my brothers in some practical endeavor; namely, how to defend ourselves. Father did not like me and my brothers fighting each other so much, even though it was supervised, but I assume he and Mother had come to some kind of agreement. She pushed my brothers hard, and me harder. Eventually fed up with her reprimands, I decided to become quicker than my brothers. I might not have been the strongest, but I never submitted without a fight. I often managed to catch my brothers unaware, when their guards were down—when they thought I was contained.

My relationship with Mother began to change when I reached my thirteenth birthday. We quarreled more often. Nothing I did seemed to please her. Looking back now, I think she was trying to prepare me for womanhood, but did not really know how to do so. I did not want to grow up yet. I could not imagine myself becoming like her: a complacent wife tending to a home and family. Such was my perception. I wanted the chance to see more of the world, to explore the lands beyond our home like she had done when she was younger.

"You are not ready," Mother would say. But when I asked why, she would repeat something about responsibility and a woman's place: "Women are meant to provide stability."

I did not understand, and did not want to. Besides, she did not seem convinced by her own words. Her statement about place contradicted other things she had told me. I accused her of forgetting what it is like to be young. Was she trying to keep me from reliving her own journey?

If I can find Aunt Corine, she might help me understand. Thus, the hope of some answers waits in Rodaním.

Some day.

* * *

Since her arrival to Tïrmen Prison, 43-1-12 had generally distanced herself from the other inmates. At first, she did so with a thought of precaution, assuming all the women of Ward 12 to be actual criminals. Yet as time passed, as she overheard the other women's stories of grief, anger, and injustice, she abandoned first impressions. Loneliness gnawed at her spirit.

One day, she noticed a new face in Unit 1. The young woman appeared to be around her age, the only other one in their barracks. She had blue eyes. Her red, wavy hair contrasted her white skin. Such bright, untarnished beauty looked out of place among the muted tones of the prison and its inhabitants. How could such a one be a criminal? 43-1-12 felt compelled to know the woman.

She waited two days, hesitant, watchful.

On the third day, the ground outside was frozen, covered by a fresh layer of snow. The sun shone somewhere above the low, gray canopy of the sky, its light vague and its warmth unfelt. Despite the frigid temperatures, 43-1-12 valued walking around the Ward 12 perimeter each morning, afternoon, and evening. She appreciated how the routine provided fresh air and space for her thoughts, both of which were harder to find inside the stuffy, windowless barracks. She also liked the sensation of warmth, however brief, which met her once she stepped inside after being out in the cold.

Walking back to the Unit 1 barracks at dusk, she noticed the young red-haired woman standing outside beside the door, sheltered from the wind. The woman stared at 43-1-12, all the while keeping her arms crossed against her chest for warmth. 43-1-12's footsteps were muffled by the soft snow as she approached. She noticed that the skin of the woman's right jaw line was reddened where *86-1-12* had been recently tattooed.

"Hello there," the woman greeted.

"Hello," 43-1-12 replied, trying to keep a casual tone. Her heart beat rapidly. She stopped beside the young woman, and leaned back against the wall. "What is your name?"

"Opal," the other said, glancing at her. "Yours?"

"Where are you from, Opal?" 43-1-12's voice sounded gruff in her ears. It had not been used for days.

Opal looked at her curiously. "Winslöri. I was born there anyway."

"In Rodaním?" 43-1-12's interest mounted.

"Yes," Opal smiled. "Mind, I recall little of it. I've lived most my life out here in the west—in Girion. What about you?"

"I grew up in Hamath."

"I've heard tell of it." Opal's expression became solemn. "Were you there when it happened?"

"When what happened?"

"The fire and destruction. Some say there was a dragon."

"I know of no dragon," 43-1-12 replied, bewildered, "but there was certainly death." She glanced out. The atmosphere beyond the walls of Ward 12 looked void of life except for the faint flickering lights of Tïrmen's central keep.

"How long you been here?" Opal asked.

"A year now."

"Have you received a verdict?"

"I have," 43-1-12 replied, "though some of the women here have been waiting four years, and are still waiting. I am not sure whether that makes me fortunate or not—to have an answer already."

"And?"

"Nineteen more years. If I behave myself."

"Mercy," Opal whispered, more to herself.

She watched the steam of Opal's breath dissipate. The comment reminded her of her mother, which sent a pang of grief to her heart.

A gust of wind swept around the corner of the barracks, causing both women to shudder.

"We should go inside," 43-1-12 commented, moving to walk past Opal to the door.

"Wait a moment," Opal said, grasping her arm, the action firm but gentle. "You didn't tell me your name."

43-1-12 felt an ache of hope within her heart, but also sadness. Her name still bore too many confused emotions, memories both lovely and painful. With it were longings struggling to survive. Hearing Ürstus speak it had been difficult enough; she was not ready to be so blatantly reminded of her past by a fellow inmate.

"Call me Friend."

An advantage of winter for the women of Ward 12 was that they did not have to work. A disadvantage was that it left them little to do. Thus, 43-1-12 continued to walk three times a day, regardless of the weather. To feel some life and strength within her, she began to jog the perimeter instead, and convinced Opal to join her. Gradually, they ran twice a day, morning and afternoon. It was not long, for their energy was limited, but provided a landscape, albeit contained, where they felt a kind of unwatched freedom; for few guards lingered on the surrounding ramparts when the north wind blew the fiercest.

She and Opal rarely talked during such activity. Walking or running together, side by side, they communicated through presence and shared experience, reveling in their defiant actions against the cold and their tired bodies. 43-1-12 anticipated the eventual warmth of spring, how she would find ways to be partnered with Opal in their work. Their friendship reminded her of goodness. It nurtured her hope for survival.

During those winter nights, and often even the days, they shared a bed at the back corner of the barracks to keep warm. It had been 43-1-12's idea, the consolation of being together deeper than physical warmth. Over time, a few other inmates mimicked their example. 43-1-12 began to consider other ways the women of Unit 1 could consolidate their resources. Someone needed to take charge, to lead for the benefit of all.

One evening, Opal said, "I suppose you've wondered why I'm here. Or have you already heard?"

"Rumors mean little to me," 43-1-12 replied. "What you may or may not have done—does it really matter?"

"Maybe you're right," Opal said. "True or not, what sent us here marked us as criminals." She ran a finger along the tattoo on 43-1-12's jaw. "Innocence matters not in this place."

"I agree."

The two women faced each other, lying on their sides, wrapped in every layer they possessed. Through the cracks around the barracks door, the light outside was fading. Shadows darkened inside while the warm glow of the central stove enlivened Opal's red hair. 43-1-12 wondered about her own appearance. She felt too thin, that the bones at her hips and shoulders jutted out awkwardly, uncomfortable to embrace. But then, all the women were too thin as a result of being underfed. She felt her hair, grown down past her ears. The volume felt thinner than she remembered. She wondered how long Opal's hair would retain its luster in the prison.

It was best not to dwell on such things.

"Still," Opal said. Lowering her voice, she pressed her head against 43-1-12's forehead, smiling slightly. "Between you and me, that official was a devious bastard. Poisoning him seems a small justice, even if it only managed to make him sick."

"You do not have to explain," 43-1-12 said softly.

"I acted on my own initiative, for what that's worth," Opal added. "It was no collusion with the Rebels, as was asserted; though maybe if I'd been helped by them, I would've known how to make a better poison. I might not have been caught either. I'm not the cleverest of schemers."

"Are the Rebels even real?" 43-1-12 asked. They were said to be Alöwean loyalists, based out of the northern wilderness beyond Dwairian's reach.

"They're real," Opal said. "Of that I'm sure. I know a fella—." She stopped herself and looked around nervously. "I shouldn't a said that, nor talk about it. Promise not to tell anyone. Promise."

43-1-12 was surprised by the fear suddenly clinching Opal's voice. "Of course." She drew Opal closer. "You are my friend."

Opal stared at her awhile longer with a furrowed brow. At last, she nodded and relaxed. "If ever I manage to get out of this place, I'll be sure to find them. I hear they look kindly on anyone who's been imprisoned here."

The guards began to show signs of boredom.

Opal was targeted first.

She did not resist. Standing at the door of the barracks each night, they merely looked at her with an unspoken command, to which Opal followed submissively. She would later come back fatigued, the light in her eyes replaced by shame.

The other women in the barracks acted as if they did not notice. 43-1-12 wondered if some of them had undergone the same treatment, and whether they were thankful for younger inmates like Opal to draw attention away from them. 43-1-12 wondered if she would have to do the same to survive.

Early each morning, Opal would return, wrap herself in everything she possessed, and sink into 43-1-12's arms.

"Why do you go so quietly?" 43-1-12 asked.

"What can I do to stop it?" Opal replied. "Why make it more painful than it already is? They always have their way."

"Only if we let them," she urged, trying to sound more confident than she felt. "We could fight them."

"We can't win," Opal said.

"We could at least make it more difficult."

"I don't know. To what purpose?"

She held Opal close. Was it really that helpless? She looked at the other women in the barracks. Did each have to submit in her own way? Why not at least try to resist?

"It's degrading, Friend," Opal added, tears forming. "I'm ashamed of myself, I am. I feel my body being torn from my—my sense of self, or soul or whatever you want to call it; whatever's at the heart of me."

"I am sorry," 43-1-12 whispered. "I understand."

"Do you?"

"I think so."

She resolved not to submit. She would find a way to assert her power, to take action. One night while Opal was away, she carefully removed a support board about the length of her arm from under their mattress. It would have to do, she thought, hiding it within a long pocket she had stitched into her cloak. The guards would soon tire of Opal and desire someone else. She was surprised they had not done so already.

Signs of the coming spring began to show. Temperatures became milder during the day, warmed by moments of sunlight. Buds formed on the plants lining the outside walls of the barracks. Yet each evening, as daylight receded, the ghost of winter's chill returned.

The women of Ward 12 ventured outside to absorb the sunlight whenever they could. One day, they were brought water and soap to bathe with. At a corner of the ward, the inmates undressed and cleaned themselves in view of the guards patrolling the surrounding walls. Most of the women did not care about the audience.

43-1-12 wondered if the soap and water had been given more for the guards' amusement than for the women's hygiene. Therefore, she decided to only wash her face and then hair, which had grown down to her neck, all the while keeping her clothes on. The wash was refreshing, but she did not want to remove all the grunginess from her body; she did not want to look appealing.

That night when the barracks door opened and a guard called, "Prisoner 43-1-12," her heart shuddered.

The other women glanced up at her. Sitting beside her on their bed, Opal gripped her hand tightly, sympathetically. Standing, 43-1-12 did not look back at her friend, but instead drew her cloak closer, trying to find assurance from the piece of wood waiting ready beside her hip.

She followed the guards out of the barracks into the cool night, and proceeded across Ward 12 toward the gate. Panic pricked her when she realized that a search at the gate would expose her weapon.

What was I thinking?

With her arms already crossed in front of her chest for warmth, her hands inside the folds her cloak, she felt for the tip of the board. If she could lift it out of the inner pocket, she might be able to subtly lower it to the ground as they walked. They were nearly to the gate.

A warden stepped out in front of them. They halted.

She needed more time.

The warden glanced at her with a grin, but addressed the lead guard. "Fresh game, Lavrev?"

"Whores cost too much," the lead guard replied dryly.

The warden laughed. "You boys are insatiable."

"A man's got to eat," Lavrev commented.

"Indeed." Still smiling, the warden waved them through. "Go on then. But save some for me. My shift ends in an hour."

"You'll have to get in line," Lavrev replied with a chuckle.

One of the rear guards nudged 43-1-12 forward. "Let's go."

She would have felt more relief at not having been searched if it were not for the dread churning in her stomach. Once through the gate, they made their way left toward a renovated stone structure, which served as one of the prison guard barracks. Yellow light shone from its windows. As they approached, she could hear voices and laughter. Having been directed through the main door, she was stopped in the entryway.

"You won't be needing that," Lavrev commented, indicating her cloak.

Her heart beat rapidly as she removed her cloak, careful to not let the makeshift weapon show through the motion of hanging the cloak on a wall hook. She was glad the guards let her hang it herself. Two of them waited behind her, watching from the entryway. Meanwhile, Lavrev opened the door, which led from the entryway into the barracks. Trying to control her heart with slow steady breaths, she followed him inside.

The first thing she noticed was the air, thick with heat and body odor. Most of the guards were lounging casually on their bunks or around a few tables at the center of the room. Many looked up at her with lusty expressions; a few made crude remarks. She took in as much information as she could, trying to count how many men there were and where their weapons had been placed; yet there were too many of them. Perhaps Opal had been right: how could she win?

Lavrev pressed her through the main room into a smaller side compartment that appeared to be for storage. Before entering its open door, she glimpsed the young captain of Ward 12 sitting at a desk in a small, neighboring room, presumably his personal chamber. His eyes looked up at her, but then quickly returned to the papers in front of him. The look showed disapproval of the whole affair, but that he could not or would not do anything about it. His passivity worked against her, she realized with despair.

The storage room was illuminated by a single candle flickering from the center of a table. It was supplemented in part by the moon, which shone through a small square window high on the wall. A few barrels were stacked at one corner of the space, along with some wooden boxes. The room was otherwise empty.

"Turn around and remove your clothes," Lavrev ordered, closing the door behind him. He had left his sword belt outside.

Muffled laughter sounded through the wall.

She faced the window, her heart and mind racing. How could she stall? Lavrev's breath was upon her neck. His hands grasped her hips then slid up under her tunic. It became difficult for her to focus. She looked at the moon through the window, and met its gaze.

Defy or submit? The words began to cycle through her mind.

Lavrev's hands gripped the waistline of her breeches, and started to pull them down.

Defy or submit?

Instincts took mastery. Her right foot stepped forward while her left elbow plunged back into the man's nose. He did not have time to cry out. With both feet still planted, she pivoted and brought her right knee sharply into his groin. Gasping for breath, with one hand holding his bloodied nose and the other now holding his testicles, he collapsed to his knees. She grabbed his conical helmet with both of her hands, removed it, and swung it down hard upon his exposed head. He fell to the ground with a thud.

Still holding the helmet, she watched him, ready to strike again. But he did not move. Blood pooled on the wood floor under his head.

The murmur of conversation continued unabated outside the door in the barrack's main room. No one had heard. With her heart still pounding ferociously, she placed the helmet on the table and dragged Lavrev's body to where it blocked the door. She found a small knife sheathed in his boot, pulled it out and placed it beside the helmet on the table.

Looking around, she decided to try the window. Barely able to reach it, she picked up one of the boxes and placed it against the wall. Stepping onto it, she was able to see outside. Relief washed over her as she realized the window had a latch that could be opened, though climbing through would be a tight fit. She unlocked the latch then pressed the glass out until she discovered a clasp that held the window flat up against the outside wall.

A patrol appeared across the street. She ducked down. Remembering the candle, she was about to blow it out when an idea presented itself.

Defy.

She took the candle and held it under the table. Fortunately, the wood was thin, dry, and untreated. As the table began to burn, she lifted it and set it against the door. Someone knocked. "Come on, Lavrev," a voice chided playfully. "That's long enough. Give someone else a turn. We haven't got all night."

Hastily, she placed the candle on the floor beside a barrel, tilting the wax stick at an angle to let the flame lick at the wood. Some hay, which had been scattered on the floor, was added for kindling. She then seized the knife, holding it between her teeth, returned to the open window, lifted herself up and began to crawl through. All the while, the table burned brightly and the knocking at the door persisted.

"Lavrev, open the door."

Once halfway through the window, she shifted to sit on the ledge and face the outside wall. With her hand gripping the upper window frame, she managed to bring her left leg through the window and, using that leg for support, brought the right leg up until both feet were placed firmly on the bottom sill. She held the squatting position a while longer until, sensing no one nearby, she dropped carefully to the ground.

As she crouched in the shadow of the barracks, a dull crash followed by a chorus of startled voices sounded through the window from inside. She glanced up and saw the red glow of the fire reflecting off the storage room ceiling.

"Get some water," someone shouted.

"Sound the alarm," another said. "The prisoner's escaped."

Keep moving.

Cries echoed behind her as she dashed across the road away from the barracks and central keep toward the quiet of the outer city ruins. Hiding behind a pile of broken stones as a patrol rushed past, she tracked the patrol's progress until the soldiers were out of sight. Back up the street, smoke now billowed from the barracks window. Turning away, she continued down a narrow side street, running by the stone shells of devastated city buildings. Five guards stood at the center of a crossroad not far ahead, so she flattened herself against a dark wall.

"Stay alert," one of them said. "She won't have made it far."

Three of the guards went down another street while two remained barring her path. She needed to reach the wall. Climbing over it was her best chance, for the gates would be too well guarded. She crept forward, trying to hide her progress behind walls or piles of rubble, all the while her hand gripped the knife.

One of the guards ahead turned abruptly, looking in her direction. "Who's there?"

Both guards walked with their halberds lowered toward her position. She quickly looked back the way she had come, and panicked at the sight of a larger patrol marching down the street toward her.

Meanwhile, the first two guards were getting close, their halberds leading the way. Trying to ignore her heartbeat pulsating in her head, she hid behind a half-broken wall and waited. The metal tip of the first guard's halberd appeared around the corner. She seized a fist-sized stone with her right hand while the left continued to clutch the knife, blade up.

The first guard's face came into view, but continued to look ahead for a moment before shifting to look in her direction. With all her might she smashed the rock into his face. His skull cracked as the rock made contact. He dropped the halberd and collapsed. She dashed out of the archway aiming past the other guard. He cried out in surprise and lunged at her with his halberd. She felt its tip sting her side, but she did not stop.

The sound of heavy boots and angry commands echoed down the street after her. She ran with all the speed she could muster. It felt like such a long way, and her side throbbed painfully. She covered its warm dampness with her hand, hoping the wound was not deep. The wall was less than a quarter-mile away.

A mounted contingent entered the street ahead of her. She veered right, but then stopped and turned abruptly at the sight of three more guards. She ran back across the street ahead of the mounted soldiers to follow a narrow alleyway. Onward she ran, gasping for breath, while the sound of horses and armored men grew louder behind her.

The pain at her side became unbearable. Her energy waned. Desperation welled within her.

Do not stop, do not stop.

She stumbled and fell with a sideways roll. A soldier seized her arm and pulled her roughly to her feet. As he did so, she brought her knife up into his ribs and pushed him away. As he cried in pain, she ran a few more steps until the shaft of a spear struck her shin. Falling forward on her stomach, her head hit the ground, causing her vision to spin violently. The butt of a spear beat her on the back. Pain reverberated down her body. Angry hands grabbed her arms and pulled her up, causing her to cry out from the sharp pain at her side.

She nearly passed out.

A bag was placed over her head and tightened around her neck, which made it difficult to breathe. Her hands and feet were bound and she was lifted up and tossed over the back of a horse. The horse's every movement made her side hurt, the pain increasing until she could no longer bear it. It was so difficult to breathe.

Sounds diminished.

There was darkness.

The grave: a pit in the earth that swallows goodness; dirt raining down upon the shell that once contained life.

Where are you, Love? Where have you gone?

A figure appears, body blazing with blue flame. The Dryden. Death. "Who are you, child?" it asks, smiling.

I cannot tell if its face resembles a man or a woman.

I turn to look at a crowd of solemn faces. They say that everything will be all right; that I must endure, for in the end strength always comes from pain. But now they are all walking away, abandoning me. Will none of them help me reach the end? Can I do it alone?

Perhaps they were lying. Perhaps they told me to endure as a way to free themselves of responsibility.

Please do not go.

I cannot do it alone.

"You are not alone," the Dryden says, still watching me. "I am here."

"Your life is going round and round, Prisoner 43-1-12," someone said with a tone of mild concern.

She opened her eyes but could not see. Her side ached, but it had been bound. The bandages felt tight around her ribs.

The black bag was yanked from her head.

She grimaced under the light of the lamp hanging above her. She tried to move, but her hands and feet were bound to a chair—the chair. The room. Two guards held her down by the shoulders while a figure stood before her:

Nabilak.

Her heart sank.

He spoke softly, with a hint of incredulity. "You came back." Or was it curiosity?

The Warden of Tïrmen Prison stepped into the light and crouched before her. She stared back at him with all the boldness she could muster. A fist struck the side of her head. Her vision was consumed by flecks of darkness. A moment passed before she regained full sight.

Nabilak stared at her. "It was foolish of you to try to escape." Was that sympathy in his gaze? "The guards want to make an example of you."

She was struck again, this time from the left side. Her cheekbones began to ache. All the while, Nabilak calmly watched her.

Damn you.

"Leave us," he ordered, straightening to look at the guards standing behind her. The gloved hands released her shoulders. Heavy footsteps withdrew, and a door creaked open and shut.

Nabilak's back was to her for a moment, as if he was contemplating his next words. He turned to face her. "Why are you here?" he said, as if the question was a plea to reason. When she gave no reply, he knelt down once again. "Do you not realize the severity of your situation? Two of my men are in fatal conditions because of you. Another is dead. Many more are burned from the fire you started. Their comrades want justice. They want you to suffer slowly, on and on until they decide they have had enough of you, and you are ruined beyond repair. Only then will they cast you aside and let you die alone in some forgotten pit. Is that what you want?"

She trembled, wishing she could hide her fear from him. She wished that she could run. She wished many things.

"No, you do not want that kind of existence," Nabilak answered his question, shaking his head. "For it could hardly be called an existence. No one desires such pain and isolation. Each of us desires warmth, peace, and plenty." He took a few steps closer and placed both his hands on her thighs. "I did not want this to happen. I commanded the guards of Ward 12 not to touch you, but they disobeyed. Now you have given me no choice. Torturing you would be easy to justify. The Arbiter will not care. You are nothing to him, and to no one . . . except me." His voice softened. "I can temper their aggression. I can protect you, sheltering you from the hungry appetites waiting outside. I can give you warmth . . . love. You only need to say one word."

That word again.

She avoided his eyes, but continued to feel them stabbing at her attention. Pain and confusion consumed her. She could not think.

"I admire your strength of spirit," he said. "You are better than them. They are simple-minded men while you are a powerful, beautiful creature. I would not have you destroyed. I would keep you safe, care for you, and love you."

She turned her head away as he drew closer. At this, he hesitated. "Of course, I will not force you. You have to live with your choices—if 'live' is the right word."

He remained pensive for a while. She followed his gaze to the ashes of the hearth.

"I will give you some time to reflect on what I have said," Nabilak remarked. "In the meantime, the Watchman will come . . . to remind you of your place." He raised a finger. "No one will be allowed to rape you, but their actions will be distasteful. I wish it could be otherwise."

Though she had stopped trembling, her heart still pounded in her head. Could she endure what was to come?

Nabilak pressed, "You have a choice, 43-1-12. I can only protect you for a while longer. They have a right to punish you. It is just. King Dwairian would approve. Therefore, you have two choices. You can choose my mercy and remain whole, or you can choose their justice and become something else. The choice is entirely yours."

She thought of Opal. What choice did she really have?

Nabilak knelt before her. "Please, I implore you, do not be a fool." With a hand he turned her head to look at him. "I may not be what you desire, but I can free you from this prison and give you a better life. You need only say one word. . . . You need only say 'Yes.'"

She looked at him, at his brows raised in concern and his pleading eyes, and wavered. Yet in his eyes she glimpsed hunger and lust. He was no different than the others. She saw herself facing the same kind of enemy that she had been defying since her father had died.

Her eyes narrowed slightly as she met Nabilak's gaze. "No," she said. Her voice felt worn, but regained some strength. "You would have me leave one prison to enter another—to be your slave or pet." She shook her head slowly. "No."

Nabilak looked like he was about to say something in protest, but she spat in his face. Stumbling, he backed away, wiping his mouth with his right hand. He studied the hand for a moment then shook his head slightly to himself, wiping his mouth further with his sleeve. Without another word, he walked past her and opened the door.

She heard the heavy footsteps of the guards close in around her. Gloved hands untied her and lifted her roughly from the chair. A tall flat object covered by a faded maroon cloth was placed in front of her. As the cloth was pulled away, she found herself looking at her reflection. She could not see the faces of the two guards holding her arms. Wearing black masks, they bore the semblance of shadows glaring over her shoulder. A third figure, dressed like the others, except a head shorter, strode up next to the mirror and studied the image.

"Take note of your appearance, Prisoner 43-1-12," the figure said with a slight accent. It also sounded feminine—a woman?

43-1-12 looked at herself. Her auburn hair had grown in a ratted mess down below her jaw line. Though her tunic and general attire were worn, she could see and feel that her body had maintained a degree of strength. She stared into her own eyes. Their green depths looked back insolently at the reflection of the two guards, and then over at the third.

The latter grabbed her chin and directed it back to the reflection. "Take note," the figure repeated, "For the next time you gaze into the present, you will not see such confidence."

The figure was certainly a woman.

She released 43-1-12's face. Once the cloth had been placed back over the mirror, the figure looked back at 43-1-12 with a fixed gaze. "I am the

Watchman. . . . Let us begin."

Everything happened quickly. Two guards held her arms while two more came from the shadows and took hold of her legs. She tried to resist, but the guards were too strong. Discerning the helplessness of the situation, she thought to dissociate herself from it as she had done in the past. They carried her to the back right corner of the room, removed her boots and fastened two cold metal clasps around her ankles. Attached to the clasps was a chain, which became taut as she was lifted upside-down off the floor. Her hands were then clasped and chained to the floor. She clenched her teeth as her head swelled with pressure.

With long scissors, her breeches were cut from the waistline up the side of each leg. The tip of the blade jabbed her skin in places. The breeches were removed. The process then began with her tunic.

"Do not remove the dressing," the Watchman commented. "We do not want her bleeding to death."

The scissors moved down the middle of her back, careful of the bandage, until the tunic was also tossed aside. Slowly the musty, cold air in the room clung to her bare skin. She closed her eyes, trying to shut out the image of her vulnerability. The rusting clasps dug into the skin of her ankles. She lost feeling below her knees.

A gloved hand grasped her hair and yanked her head back. The scissors moved greedily across her head. She felt the strands of hair fall away. To finish, the hand continued to keep her head back by pressing against her face. She struggled to breathe.

The hand withdrew, leaving her hanging as the guards sneered. She focused on keeping her eyes shut as coarse gloved hands moved across her body.

"Such a shame," one guard said.

She was slapped lightly on the check. Opening her eyes, she saw the Watchman kneeling down to look at her. "You are fortunate to have Captain Nabilak's favor."

"For now," one guard muttered.

"Will there be enough left to satisfy him once we're through?" another said, chuckling.

"There may." The Watchman moved away. "Or there may not."

43-1-12 felt herself passing out.

Cold water was slowly poured over her groin, it icy fingers running down to her face, returning her to alertness. She cursed them. She cursed them all.

The guards laughed.

She was spun around to face the corner.

"This is for Lavrev," one guard said.

A cane struck the side of her back and ribs. She cringed, gasping for breath. The cane whooshed again, a sound terrible in its familiarity.

There was no more laughing. There were no more voices. The only thing she heard was the whoosh and snap of the cane on her flesh. Sound slowly muted as feeling took mastery. The sting left nothing untouched. It spread across her back. She cried out.

The pressure in her head mounted. She clenched her teeth against the agony, and for a moment there was no more fear. Rage overwhelmed it, though it struggled to hold on.

Then there was blackness.

She awoke lying on her stomach.

Lifting herself slowly, she collapsed with nausea as the movement of her sackcloth shirt tore the fresh scabs off her back. Her body ached, as if fingers dug into her skin and muscles. A whimper escaped her lips. She hated herself for it, barely holding back tears.

She heard the drip-drop of water into a puddle, and looked around trying to penetrate the darkness. A thin light shone from underneath the door. Daylight?

Round and round, Nabilak had said.

She was subjected to cold water or hot water. She was beaten or flogged. Flesh was tormented by fire—not to be burned, but intimidated by the possibility. Once more the night became a curse, the day a limbo. Time did not dwell in the depths of Tïrmen Prison. Time did not care. Life had abandoned it. The prison was a frozen, hollow thing, proclaimed as justice in a world of chaos—a place for those deemed lost and forsaken.

* * *

Ïdathor offered me a faint smile. "How are you faring, child?"

I suspect the expression was meant to be compassionate, but it looked weakened by weariness. The lines in Ïdathor's face were deeper than I remembered. His whitened hair and beard provided another reminder of the strain of recent years. He sat on a gray horse. Behind him, five mounted bodyguards dressed in the white, blue, and gold of Girion remained attentive to their surroundings.

"I am surviving," I replied. I did not know what else to say.

The dimming light of an ochre dusk settled across the grain field. Among other harvest workers, I was preparing to return to town after a day's work.

"I meant to check in on you more often," Ïdathor continued, his eyes lowering along with his smile. "Forgive me."

"You need not worry about me," I said, trying to sound more optimistic than I felt.

I grew up thinking of Ïdathor as an uncle, but had seen little of him during the last few months—since Father's death. Dwairian had made him a general of Siligen. Since Malech's appointment as Steward of Hamath, Ïdathor spent most of his time west in Girion; though he retained some level of authority over Hamath.

"I am glad to see that you have work." Ïdathor watched the other field workers as they left in quiet clusters. He straightened. "It is rare for a young woman to be in such a place these days."

"I have been fortunate," I replied.

While the male population had been directed toward agriculture and building, we women were meant to focus on bearing the new generation: the new empire. Those too old or too young to have children were supposed to support those who could. Children were the future, and we women would bear the future. Those already married were to have more children, and to keep having them. Those unmarried or widowed were to get married and do the same, or to just get pregnant without wasting time on trivialities like love. The population needed to be both restored and increased so as to face threats amassing outside the borders of Siligen. Or so we were told.

I was fortunate that, so far, the enforcement of this ambition had been sporadic and disorganized. Being seventeen, I was also exempted because of my age. Dwairian had decreed eighteen years old to be the minimum age a woman was expected to begin bearing children.

Though most people found contentment in such narrowly focused work, I perceived a shadow hovering over Hamath's morale. The sorrows of war still festered, poisoning our joy. Creative thought waned. Songs were seldom sung. The time was not yet fertile for us to find purpose beyond survival. Since the final months of Father's life, I tried to avoid drawing attention to myself while in town. I particularly did not want to face Malech. I would cross town hooded and travel along crowded streets in hopes of anonymity. As one of the few women working in the fields, that was not always easy.

"Have you been treated well?" Ïdathor asked.

"Ozath has been kind," I replied.

Aside from Ïdathor, Ozath was Father's only surviving friend in Hamath. He tried to keep close to me as I worked in his fields, frequently assuring me that I would not be bothered by anyone. I had a protector in him, his attention suggested. Occasionally, I spotted him eying me. He would look away when I noticed. I wondered how he saw me. Was I like a daughter to him, or something else?

"Just the man we were talking about," Ïdathor stated, looking past me.

I turned to see Ozath walking toward us. He was wiping his face and hands with a faded cloth. "Greetings, my lord," he replied. His voice was gruff. "I trust our work is satisfactory."

"Beyond satisfactory," Ïdathor said, smiling more readily than he had with me. "King Dwairian is pleased by Hamath's progress."

Despite being older than my father by at least a decade, Ozath's bearing remained firm and strong. His beard was graying, but the blueness of his eyes retained an eager light. He paused beside me. "The season has been good to us." He glanced around, avoiding my eyes. "What news from Girion?"

"More of the same." İdathor shifted in his saddle. "We are to continue focusing on basic needs."

"You mean building the new empire, of course," Ozath said evenly.

"For now," İdathor replied. "It gives us purpose." I could not tell if he agreed with this statement or not. "Anyway, our people need to be fed. Their health allows us to build and maintain security. You provide a valuable service in this, my friend. That has not gone unnoticed. The King rewards those who are faithful."

"I do what I can," Ozath replied.

"As must we all," İdathor said, glancing at me, "particularly as things continue to change. For example, King Dwairian is not pleased with the current birthrate. He has decided to lower a woman's minimal childbearing age to sixteen years old."

My body suddenly felt heavy, unbalanced. I had already resolved not to be reduced to a birthing agent for the empire. Dwairian cared little for us beyond what we could do for him. So many lives had been sacrificed for a cause cast upon us without care or warning—by a vision for our people that we did not choose. That is what I believed at the time, yet I was small-minded. For years, there had been warnings. My brothers noticed, even my parents. Some of us just chose to disregard the signs. Great care had gone into planning the overthrow of the Alöwean Empire. Dwairian's rise did not materialize out of nothing.

In the West, most Illiri chose to follow that vision. A hunger has driven the new empire into its new age. Greed for power consumes the imagination of individuals and our civilization like a plague. We have all contributed in some way, whether through action or inaction. At the time, I blamed Dwairian and underlings like Malech. I was not sure how to feel about İdathor. I had my own ideas about the future, about who I could be. I still wanted to explore the world and determine my place in it.

"Women will no longer be allowed to work in the fields," İdathor added. He fixed his attention on me. "No more exceptions, I am afraid."

I should have anticipated such a change to come sooner. Ozath's agreement to let me work in his fields had allowed me to bide my time while evading the mounting social constrictions on my sex, yet I had become too consumed with the present. The West offered little for my future, so it was to the East and the thought of Rodaním that I had to turn. Rodaním's autonomy from Siligen promised freedom and the possibility of a new life. I longed for it, to know and dwell among my mother's people, but I needed to be more proactive about planning my escape.

"We must all accept the dictates of the King," Ídathor said. To me, it sounded like he was reciting words given to him. "We all must come to believe in the new laws. It is for the betterment of our society—for our unity, security, and peace."

"How does the King intend to enforce such laws?" Ozath asked.

"Hamath's garrison will be increased," Ídathor replied, "and the administration of the communes will be reorganized. Malech is already working with our sheriff to ensure that all Hamath's citizens remain aware of the law. Examples must be made. Those who resist the law will be punished, and imprisoned if need be; for those who defy what is expected—what is needed—have no place among us. Everyone must come to understand this."

I needed more time.

"I am sorry, child," Ídathor said, noticing my dejected expression. "Do not despair. There is much to be thankful for. You are young and lovely. You have your health. Hamath has great hopes for women like you."

Ozath muttered something, but I did not understand it. Ídathor looked at him questioningly as well.

The farmer cleared his throat. "She can come live with me." As I looked at him, he focused on Ídathor instead, as if it was a matter for only the two of them to decide. I resented them for that. "My sister, Nelle, could use the help," Ozath continued, "and my children would be glad for the added company. We have the means to accommodate one more in our household."

"That is generous, Ozath." Ídathor turned to me. "It would please me to know that you are no longer living on your own—that you are safe and cared for. What do you say?"

I knew that Ozath's wife and three eldest children had been killed during the destruction of Hamath. His home and barns had since been rebuilt. He was a gentle man, generally liked by those around him. Despite my uncertainty about his motives, I knew there would be more danger being outside his protection. Living and working in his home would at least provide me an excuse to avoid town.

I had heard scattered accounts of some young women, namely those alone without family, being taken advantage of. If impregnated, which I suspect was how their predators justified or got away with such horrible treatment, such women were pressed to live in communes where they could be cared for. At least that dignity was given to them, that worth, for the communes offered shelter and charity. I overheard some people, men and women alike, voice approval when certain "aimless" women chose to get pregnant to improve their circumstances—"At least they're contributing to society" was a common refrain.

The children of the commune came under the direct control of the empire. Each boy born there could stay with his mother until his fifth birthday, at which time he was taken away and placed in Dwairians' newly established Academy of War north of Girion. Thus the empire had begun to further develop its new position of strength.

I grieved for the commoditization of such women, and could not imagine myself being one of them. I would not let that happen, so I agreed to Ozath's offer, grateful for his continued generosity—at least as a means to gain some time. I moved into his household without delay.

The daily rhythm of his home was pleasant. The interior was warmer than the room Father and I had lived in on the outskirts of Hamath. The harvest concluded. Months passed, mixing into each other without distinction. Winter settled.

All the while, I secretly planned my escape. I learned what I could, asking questions about the geography of Siligen and its current affairs, adding to what I had learned as a child and remembered from my mother's map. I entrusted no one with my true intentions.

I knew from earlier discussions between my father and Ïdathor that the most direct route to Rodaním would not work. I would not be able to acquire a permit to cross the Elentari River, and there were too many new Siligen outposts guarding that border region for me to pass through without question. I would be caught and sent back, or worse.

During my midday break, having an hour to myself, I used the pretense of a walk to leave the house and ascend a hill overlooking Ozath's lands. At the summit, sheltered by a rocky outcrop, I would study an old map of Illirium, which I had managed to acquire from a merchant from Rökad. The map was cruder than Mother's, but served my purpose.

I ultimately discerned two options for escape. I could journey into the forest north of Hamath and eventually cross the Ümo River. The river was full of rapids and waterfalls, too dangerous to navigate for long by boat, so I would have to cross the river then traverse the land of Gigor. Though the lands further north were not controlled by Siligen, I doubted I could survive such a long journey by that route.

Instead, taking a watercraft downstream along the Menelmachar River from Gigor to Mirror Lake appeared to be swiftest. But the route was also full of risks. Managing to purchase, steal, or build some kind of craft was one matter, along with the fact that I had no knowledge of navigating a swift river myself. Secondly, Gigor was an uncharted, uncultivated land of wild beasts and legendary creatures. Moreover, too many Siligen vessels used the Menelmachar River. If I was not first killed by some predator in Gigor, I would be caught by a Siligen patrol or drown in the river.

One option remained, but it was as treacherous. I could venture northeast from Hamath on foot, enter Marshwood and follow its southern border to the western shore of Mirror Lake—similar to what Mother had done in the opposite direction many years prior. I was not sure when passage through the marshes would be safest. Would water levels be lower in the summer, or frozen and thus more traversable in the winter? I knew little about such landscapes. I should have asked Mother more about her experience there. The route also left me with the question of how to navigate Mirror Lake without being caught. Still, my chances were higher there than along the river.

Assuming for a moment that I evaded the Siligen soldiers who patrolled the western shores of the lake, I could rest on the island at its center. The island was once called the Tower of the Sky, a stronghold for Alöwean Sky Riders. Since the conclusion of the war, it had been abandoned, or so the Rök merchant who sold me the map had commented. He said that no one ventured there anymore, not even patrols, because the waters surrounding it were full of ghosts. To me, ghosts were the least of my concern; I was willing to risk their presence. From the island, I could continue to the eastern shore of Mirror Lake, re-supply at a trading post called Fumond's Hut, and then travel by foot down to Rodaním's northern border.

In my imagination, the journey to Mirror Lake would take about ten days. I was not sure how long it would take to cross the lake. Growing up, between Mother's lessons, joining Father on a few of his business trips, and spending time with Jed, I had learned the basics of hunting, foraging, and surviving in the wilderness. I would have a better chance in the summer, I thought. I needed to gather enough provisions for the initial journey, and then wait for the warmer season to come. I thought it was a good plan, relatively simple. It was my only plan, but it motivated me to rise each day with some purpose.

One winter morning, Ozath acted more tense than usual. I had just finished serving him breakfast, and was about to wake his children, when he said, "Come sit," indicating a seat across the table. "We need to talk."

I sat down, but then he hesitated.

"Go on," Nelle encouraged her brother, standing behind him. Her right hand remained on his shoulder while her left rested in a fist against her hip. Though she was older than Ozath, her hair had not yet lost its brown hue. She generally treated me well, especially when I listened without comment to her rants. When she was young, after just a year of marriage, her husband had run off with some barmaid. The only man Nelle still respected was her brother.

Through the kitchen window, the sky beagn to lighten.

"You know . . .," Ozath said, addressing me. He stared at his calloused hand, which fidgeted on the table. "You're a hard worker, and I appreciate your help to my family. It hasn't been easy these last years. You know this better than any."

"You have been generous to me," I offered, wondering where this conversation was going. Ozath was usually a quiet man. We rarely spoke at any length, for he relied on his sister to direct my tasks.

"It's been difficult," he continued, "since my wife died." He glanced up, but then quickly averted his eyes. "I mean . . . You know you're a beautiful woman: young, strong . . . Every day I've seen you, since you began working for me last spring, I . . . I've wondered . . . I mean, I've thought to ask . . ." He looked up at me like I could understand what he was trying to say.

"He wants you to be his wife," Nelle said.

"My children love you," Ozath went on, as if to explain. "We have a good life here together, all of us. With you, we could be a whole family again, even have our own children." He stood, but then appeared to forget why he did so. He stared at the ground, and then at me.

"So what do you say to that?" Nelle asked me.

I felt rigid in my chair. I should have been more prepared for this. "I am thankful for all you have done," I said. I looked at Ozath. "You are a good man; but forgive me, I cannot marry you."

Ozath's shoulders slouched as he nodded quietly.

"Why not?" Nelle demanded.

I could not imagine marrying a man older than my father, even one as kind as Ozath. "I have my own goals, my own plans." I hoped to sound confident, authoritative.

"What plans?" Nelle pressed. "Your place is in a home, bearing children. It's the law, and you've been neglecting it long enough. My brother is offering you a good life here, secure and with rising means. What other goals can you have, or what else can you do?"

"Is caring for motherless children not enough?" I protested. "What about you? You have no children of your own."

Nelle's expression hardened. "You know I can't bear children. You know this. It's why he left."

"I have work to do," Ozath mumbled, moving to retrieve his cloak. "Forget I mentioned it."

"No, she must learn her place." Nelle continued to glare at me. "She must learn gratitude. We've sheltered her from being a responsible woman long enough. It's more than a responsibility, in fact. Managing a household and bearing children are a privilege and a gift."

"It is a gift," I agreed, trying to remain calm. "But it is not for me. Not yet, anyway."

"Don't be so selfish," Nelle said. "Who do you think you are? You're not a girl anymore. The King demands that you fulfill your duty. We all demand it. It's for the good of Hamath."

As he stood there, wrapped in his cloak, Ozath's eyes were downcast. He shook his head to himself. His voice was quiet. "That's enough, Nelle." He looked at me and raised a timid hand. "Please forget this conversation."

He strode out of the house.

Nelle had not moved from her original standing position behind Ozath's chair. She crossed her arms in front of her chest. "Shameful girl. Selfish. Shortsighted."

"I need to wake the children," I said, not knowing what else to say or do. I rose and proceeded to walk around the table toward their bedchamber. I wanted time to think.

"You'll not speak to them," Nelle replied, moving to block my way. "You'll not touch them, corrupting them with your disrespect and disregard. You're finished here. I'll have no girl like you in this house, troubling my brother's thoughts. I don't care what he says. Pack your things and leave."

"What?"

"Now," Nelle said.

"Fine." My heart pounded with rage, fear, and anticipation. I left Nelle to do as she said. This was the moment to execute my plan, I realized. I had no other choice.

Nelle called after me. "Malech will hear about this, and will know what to do with a spoiled brat like you. I'm sending for him at once." She opened the door and called to one of the farm workers.

In my small room, I hastily removed my outer work dress and changed into trousers, a tunic, and belt that had all belonged to my father. I had already adjusted the waist and length of the trousers to fit me, but left the remainder loose. With the addition of a hood and hat, I hoped to pass as a boy, at least at a glance—to call less attention to myself as I traveled. Over Father's tunic, I wore a sheepskin vest for insulation. I owned little else aside from the old map I had acquired, and a small knife I concealed in my boot. I put the map in my side satchel. Lastly, as I wrapped myself in the deerskin cloak, which Ozath had made for me, I wondered if I was being a fool for rejecting his kindness. Was I indeed being shortsighted?

No. I would not second guess myself. To marry Ozath would be to submit the rest of my life to living in Hamath under Dwairian's empire. It would be like giving away the key to lock me in, all without a fight. I would not let myself be locked up, not if I had any choice in the matter.

All the shouting had awoken the children. Ignoring me as I passed by her, Nelle hushed them and told them to dress for breakfast.

Without her seeing, I grabbed the two loaves of bread I had baked the day before, as well as some apples and dried venison—whatever was easily within reach—and put them in my satchel. I wished to say goodbye to the children, but could not stay any longer, especially if Nelle had sent for Malech.

I went out the side door, walking as calmly and quickly as I could. The dawn sky glowed violet, but I had little mind to appreciate it. A thin layer of snow crunched softly beneath my feet, and the cold morning breeze brushed against my cheek and chilled my nostrils. Thankfully, Ozath was nowhere in sight as I left his property.

An hour later, I came in view of the northern forest, a dark, quiet mass. I recalled standing with Jed on the bank of its bordering stream years earlier. It was all frozen now, buried under the present. To reach it, I needed to walk across a field of black, firm soil glazed with snow. A barn stood on the other side of the field, at the edge of the trees. It belonged to a farmer named Rumford, I recalled—or it used to, anyway.

I adjusted the strap across my shoulder, and proceeded.

When I reached the far end of the field, three men suddenly stood and came out of a ditch. I slowed my pace. They were hooded, dressed in identical blue cloaks. Clubs hung from their belts. Judging by their attire, they were some of the Sheriff's men. I recognized one of them, for we had grown up together. He was around my age and had light blonde hair.

"Good morning, Rello," I said to him, trying to sound calm while I shifting away from them.

"Hold for a moment," he said, raising the palm of his gloved hand. Vapor escaped his mouth as he spoke.

I stopped, feeling increasingly uneasy as they took a few steps toward me.

Rello's expression remained stoic. I was not sure he recognized me.

The oldest of the three, a middle-aged man with black hair, stepped forward. "Where're you going in such a hurry, boy?"

"Just an errand." I tried to keep my face partially concealed under the rim of the hat.

Looking at me closer, the man's eyes widened. "Wait, you're no boy."

My heart froze.

"What're doing dressed like that?" he continued. "It's dangerous to be out walking in these parts alone. Where're you coming from?"

"I am part of Ozath's household," I replied.

"I see," he said, looking up and down my body. "How old are you?"

"Fifteen," I lied.

"She's seventeen," Rello stated. "I recognize her now. She's Siméon's daughter."

"The Horse Master?" The older man raised a brow. "I never knew him." He indicated my satchel. "What're you carrying there?"

I scrambled for an answer. Seeing the barn, I said, "Farmer Rumford lets me care for his horses."

"Oh does he now?" The man considered this with a frown. Rello and the other young man glanced at each other, but I could not read their expressions.

"Yes," I replied. "I am bringing them some treats."

"Well then," the older man stepped aside. "Lads, we should let the lady continue on her way." He smiled, holding his arm out as an invitation to pass between him and the other two.

I wondered if I could outrun them.

"No need to be shy, missy," the older man urged. "We're your humble servants, here to ensure your safety." He looked at his two companions. "Boys, give her some space; you're making her nervous." As the other two stepped back, the older man shifted his gaze back on me. "Come on. Best not keep Rumford's horses waiting. Your master'll be wanting you back soon, I should think."

I inhaled slowly. "Yes." I needed get away from these men. The forest was not far.

"What're you waiting for?" The older man still offered a smile.

My heart beat ferociously as I stepped forward, but I kept my head high.

Rello seized me as I passed. I tried to scream, but he covered my mouth with one hand while wrapping his other arm around my neck. At the same time, the other young man took hold of my legs

They carried me to the barn, which took a while because I resisted the whole way. Once inside, the older man closed the door behind us while the two younger ones continued to hold me.

"Trying to be clever, little bitch?" the older man commented, securing the door. "This isn't Rumford's barn. It's mine. It seems you need a lesson in, shall we say, honesty."

There were a few horses within the barn. A cow murmured as the two younger men pulled off my cloak and vest and shoved me into an empty, neighboring stall. As I lay there, momentarily stunned, I recalled being in the stable with Father and Mother as our ranch burned. I remembered Mother's fierce expression, how she had defied her assailants.

"Since you know the girl," the older man said to Rello, "you go first." Shifting his attention to me, he added, "There's no need to make this too hard on yourself." His grin widened. He waited with the other man at the entrance of the stall, watching.

Rello unclasped his belt and took a step forward. "This could be nice if you let it."

I crawled away from him, but found myself trapped in the corner of the stall. My heart raced. I took a deep breath, and my mind became clearer. I thought of the knife concealed in my boot.

Taking my ankle, Rello pulled me away from the corner. "Don't move."

Resting on his knees, he fumbled with my belt. I grabbed his hand to pull it away, and tried to strike his face with my other hand, but he was too quick and strong.

"Be still," he urged.

The others chuckled.

Releasing one of my hands, Rello slapped me. I continued to resist, but he managed to remove my belt. I fought harder, but still could not push him away.

He struck me again, this time with his fist.

Ignoring the pain, I brought my right knee up into his ribs. He clenched his teeth, focused on keeping my left thigh pinned with the weight of his leg. I clawed at his face, seeking his eyes. Seizing my wrists, he pressed my arms back. He called for the others to assist, but they merely laughed.

"Come on, Rello," the older man called. "You're nearly twice her size."

Rello did not seem to know what he was doing. He tried to press my right leg down with his free knee, but it made him more unbalanced; so with all the strength I could muster, I twisted right toward the wall. He kept hold of my wrists, but his legs were forced to move off me to catch himself from falling over. That was the moment I needed. I brought my right knee up hard into his testicles. He grimaced, but maintained his grip of my wrists. So I brought my knee up again, and then again, until he finally collapsed onto his side.

Free, I stood and leapt over the opposite wall of the stall. I landed hard, but pushed through the pain. As I dashed toward the barn door, two hands seized my right arm and jerked me back. I turned and punched the man in the face. He let go, but the older man was suddenly beside him with a wooden shovel. He swung it and struck me on the side of the head.

The world spun.

I felt myself land on the cold earthen floor. The two of them picked me up by the arms. I heard Rello murmuring something; spotted him half-crouched leaning against the entrance of the original stall, his hands covering his crotch. They dragged me back to him, and pulled off my tunic. The winter air quickly seeped through the thin cloth of my white undershirt.

One of them kicked me in the stomach. Bent over, I gasped for breathe and clenched my teeth to detract from the pain. Rolling onto my side, curled up, I managed to pull my knife free before my boots were pulled off. The second man, who leaned over me trying to pull down my trousers, did not realize the blade was there until I thrust it up into his stomach.

He shuddered, looked at me in surprise, and then screamed in agony as I pulled out the knife.

The others were too startled to respond at first. I kicked the first man away. He buckled over with both hands pressed against his stomach. Standing up, I pointed the bloodied blade at the other two as a warning.

"You little whore," the older man said.

He came at me with the shovel, swinging it wildly. I stepped away just in time and, before he could bring the shovel back, seized its shaft and pulled him close. Blood splattered onto my face as my knife sliced across his neck.

I no longer thought about my actions. Instincts prevailed: action and counteraction. Defiance.

The man with the stomach wound was curled up on the floor moaning faintly. The life of the older one was quickly leaking out where he lay choking with gurgled sounds. I glared at Rello as I knelt down to retrieve the shovel. He was still bent over slightly, clutching between his legs.

His eyes widened. "Please." He extended his hand. "Mercy."

I glared at him in indignation. "Mercy?" Confusion and rage overwhelmed me.

I swung the shovel with all my might. He fell to the ground, but I was not finished. A part of me awoke that I did not know could exist: fury. For too long, I had tried to contain it. I do not know how many times I brought the shovel down on Rello's head.

When I stopped and realized what I was doing, his disfigured skull lay in a thick pool of blood and pulp. My legs trembled, and my vision blurred. Turning away, I stumbled as I saw the entire front of my body stained with blood. I dropped the shovel, leaned against a post for a moment to try to steady my nausea. Dropping my knife, I went over and opened the barn door. The fresh air helped a little, but it was very cold, so I retrieved my warmer clothes and satchel, all the while trying not to look at the three bodies.

I left the barn and ran.

I should have stolen one of the horses, but I no longer thought clearly.

Soon, I was captured. They dragged me by my arms to Hamath, down its streets to the main square; all the while, remaining deaf to my pleas of having defended myself.

"Insolent, wretched thing." Malech looked down on me where I lay on the cold cobblestone of the square. He addressed the amassing crowd. "She's stolen that which is most precious to us. Two of our men are now dead because of her. The third may not survive the night."

"She must be executed for her crimes," someone shouted.

A man lifted me by my shirtsleeve and punched me in the stomach. I gasped for air while an old woman struck my shins with her cane. The pain consumed my lower leg, causing me to collapse. Others pressed close. A fist struck the side of my head. A hand slapped my face. On my knees, bending over, I shielded my head with my arms as more people struck me. I still struggled to breathe. I got knocked onto my side. Bitterness repressed through years of hardship had found another outlet.

"Stop," I heard a firm voice shout. "Move aside," he said more forcefully. "Move aside and leave her be."

Rolling onto my back, I saw Ïdathor's white-cloaked bodyguards materialize from the crowd, pressing people away from me with shields or the threat of their spears.

"Control your people," Ïdathor commanded Malech, stepping into the center of the circle.

"We can handle this, General," Malech replied, his voice losing an edge of ferocity.

"Then do it." Ïdathor turned his head to me with a strained expression. Was that regret, or uncertainty? "You should bring her to the central hall before someone else gets hurt."

Blue-clad Hamath soldiers came and brought me across the square to the steps of the central hall. With their spears and halberds, they kept the crowd back. At the top of the stairway, I was pressed to my knees before Malech.

My skin and undershirt were stiff with dried blood. I felt so cold.

"Good people." The steward raised his hands to quiet the crowd. "Justice will be declared, here and now. This foul woman, whose name no longer deserves mentioning, has committed the most heinous of crimes."

"Kill her," someone cried.

Another woman sobbed, "My son is dead because of her."

Malech raised his hands again. "The rebel will be punished, but let it be slow." He looked down at me with contempt. For a brief moment, through my tear-blurred eyes, I saw a glint of satisfaction on his face. The trace of a grin formed at one end of his mouth.

He looked back at the mob. "Hear me, good people of Hamath, as I declare her sentence."

Ïdathor pulled Malech aside. "Remember your place, Steward. You cannot execute her without the Arbiter's authority."

"I know the law, General," Malech replied calmly, loosening his arm from the other's grip. "You needn't worry; the Arbiter will know everything. Or do you intend to impede the King's justice with your personal feelings for this girl?"

Ïdathor stared at the steward, but said nothing.

Meanwhile, the crowd quieted.

My attention wandered down to the blood on my clothes and hands, and to the frayed cloth around my knees. One of my eyes was beginning to swell shut. My body throbbed, as if still being struck.

Malech addressed the gathering. "There's no leniency in such affairs. The law is clear." He paused to let the words settle among the crowd. "As the rebel's crimes are too severe for her to stay here, I shall send her to Tïrmen Prison."

The people murmured agreement. By now all sympathizers had left or been pushed away.

The steward continued. "Amidst those ruins, the spirit of insurrection shall be purged from her. Rather than death, let the rebel live long and remember the bountiful opportunities once offered to her—opportunities she has scorned. As she has taken life, so shall life be taken from her. That is my decree."

The crowd shouted in approval. "It is just."

Malech looked down at me. "It is finished."

* * *

"Why are you here?" Nabilak asked.

Prisoner 43-1-12 shivered as a cold puddle formed at her feet, and beads of water slid down her bare head and neck. Her soaked, baggy tunic clung to her body. She felt its weight against her with every breath. She tried to loosen her hands and feet from the cords binding them to the chair, but failed.

Something hard and flat struck the top of her exposed thighs. She could not help but whimper as the pain coursed through her body.

"I asked you a question, 43-1-12."

Her eyes tried to focus on the man crouched before her.

"This cycle continues needlessly." Nabilak said. "Why do you persist?" He glanced behind her. "The Watchman is relentless. Believe me when I say that no one has been able to resist her methods. In the end, everyone breaks . . . everyone."

He looked down at the blue bruises on her thighs. Delicately, he placed a hand over one of the larger marks on her left leg. "This abuse can stop." His voice remained soft, his eyes lingering on her bruises. "Please, let me protect you from their cruelty. Say the word and it shall be done."

She tried to stop shivering, but could not. A draft was coming in from behind her. She turned her head to look back, managing a glimpse of the shadowed archway scowling in her periphery.

Nabilak sighed. Even as his hand slid away from her leg and he stood, she did not return his gaze. A light flickered through the archway. Something else was watching, something unseen. There was a sense that the room smiled as the warden walked past her and out through its open maw.

The guards returned.

They freed her from the chair and lifted her up, but she could not stand.

Her legs cried out in protest, and she collapsed to the ground. The guards picked her up by the arms and dragged her back to her cell.

By the time they reached it she felt half conscious. They wrapped a blanket around her before laying her down, yet it only offered a veneer of warmth. The struggle between warmth and cold tormented her dreams and disrupted her sleep, loosening her grip on consciousness.

Jed.

Gently touching my cheek, lifting my chin up as his face draws near.

"Rhoda."

A kiss. A smile. A longer embrace. Birdsong all around. The warm sun. Trees whispering with their thick shrouds of leaves. A cool stream lapping merrily around our feet. Life, free and hopeful.

The Watchman.

A glowing hot iron coming closer, reaching out to touch my neck. Arms and legs bound. Head held firmly at a angle by two sets of gloved hands.

"43-1-12."

A kiss. Heightening pain. A cry. Powerful hands that do not let go. The crackle of a fire. The echo of a hammer. Metal. Harsh voices. Stale air. Cold sweat dripping down my face. Life, imprisoned and slowly suffocating.

* * *

My memories faded. The plague called life carted them away to be buried. Everything I once knew as good had proven frail. Comforts deceive, thinly veiling the harshness of reality. Why? Why must it be so? Why can there be no lasting meaning? Why must it all lead to suffering?

Weakness crept into my thoughts. My resolve faltered. Some may question why I was not stronger, or why I did not submit sooner, but I do not need their understanding.

I just want compassion.

Or something deeper.

* * *

The blanket was pulled off her curled-up form, the chill in the air causing her to tremble. The guards stood her up—she was surprised she could stand, she felt so weak—and led her out of the cell down a hallway, a blur of shadows and torchlight. A door opened before her; beyond, blinding whiteness.

At first, the fresh air was a relief. Yet it did not take long for the teeth of frosted air to snap at her flesh. They reached the base of a square tower. Upon entering, she felt a trace of warmth return to her limbs. Passing a large cave entrance to her left, she noted runes marking its stone. She could not see where the cave led, but felt strangely clear-minded as she gazed into its black depths.

They left the room with the cave behind, proceeded through a small door, and ascended a few flights of stairs. The last was more a wooden ladder than a stairway. At the top, the guards opened a trap door and brought her onto the pinnacle of the tower.

A small, rusting cage hung expectantly from a gallows. They lowered the cage, opened its door, and forced her inside. In it, she could neither entirely sit nor stand. The door clanged shut.

Suspended by a pulley system, the cage was lifted back into place. It rocked heavily above the center of the tower for a moment. The arm holding it was then turned until the cage hung beyond reach of the tower platform. Hundreds of feet below, the snow-laden ruins of Tïrmen looked like the gaping orifices of giant faces waiting to devour her. Or were the mouths open in the horror of death?

The guards derided her as a frigid wind blew through the cage. She tried to ignore both, focusing instead on wrapping her arms around her chest, yet the action did little to help. She felt her limbs going numb. The guards returned down the trap door, the last one closing it behind him.

Winter surrounded her, cold and mute.

Were they going to finally let her die? She felt some relief at the thought. Her body trembled, warmth like a tormenting memory.

For distraction, she observed the surrounding landscape. A few snowflakes glided down, the air otherwise clear under high gray clouds. North, beyond Tïrmen's walls, slept Lake Valon under a sheet of ice. Further still, on the far western shore, the yellow lamps of Girion were being lit. The lights contrasted the brooding forest beyond the city. She did not want to think of Girion, however. Dwairian dwelt there, a man whose self-proclaimed kingship had brought her death and suffering.

Rocking the cage to turn away brought a semblance of life back to her limbs. As the cage creaked right, the shores of Lake Valon were replaced by an eastward stretching forest. Not far beyond that horizon was Gigor, and farther still Marshwood and Mirror Lake: landmarks of an old escape plan. Still turning in the cage, she observed the land descend south from Tïrmen to the plains. She could identify each landmark, having studied her old map well in Hamath—little good it had done her.

She recalled Hamath, her hometown beyond the eastern horizon. Did anyone gaze toward her now? Did anyone still speak her name?

Her knees ached from pressing against the rusted bars of the cage. Her back begged to straighten. The heat within her flickered, soon to be snuffed out entirely. She longed to sleep and never wake. Perhaps then her body would stop shaking. The breath of winter saturated her, body and mind. Thoughts died one by one.

She closed her eyes.

Perhaps there could be peace in death.

She shuddered with a convulsion. Every muscle hurt. She cursed her body. Why would it not go quietly? She was weary of trying to resist.

"Just let me die," she cried. To what? The emptiness around her? Within her? She clenched her eyes shut, wishing to ward off all sensation.

But then warmth caressed her skin.

She opened her eyes.

In the west, the clouds had parted, allowing the sun to spread its smile over the landscape. Snow-covered terrain glowed with soft, crimson light. The green fir and brown bark of the coniferous trees appeared richer. Even the ruins of Tïrmen looked enlivened, the silent stones emanating a former glory. All gazed at the sun. All seemed pleased.

Her heart quivered with an emotion she could not name. Tears caressed the borders of her eyes. Perhaps all had not yet been claimed, and the land would one day be warm again. Did she dare hope her life could be the same?

It was a fleeting thought.

The sun disappeared from view as if uninterested in what was happening to her. She wanted to curse it, but could not bring herself to do so because her spirit had been nourished by its brief presence. She watched the clouds slowly adorn themselves with yellow, red, and violet light. Though the sun had passed, the sky was still alive: a visual poem to the light's passing.

What did it mean? What could she do?

She closed her eyes again. Her jaw tightened as her body continued to fight, her mind telling her not to surrender.

The trap door opened.

The guards came out and looked at her with expressions of amusement shifting to disdain. They brought the cage back over the tower platform and lowered it, unlocked the door and brought her out. She felt the tension in her back and legs crack loose as two of the guards held her by the arms. Her hands had turned a pale shade of blue. While the first two guards continued to hold her arms, another guard lifted her by both of her legs. Thus they carried her down from the tower into the illusive warmth of the prison corridors.

Her head pounded, and her throat felt parched. It all seemed like a feverish dream from which she longed to wake.

Cold, warm. Warm, cold. One passageway, another. One room, another. Indoors, outdoors. Exposed, unexposed. Confined, unfettered.

Was there ever anything more to existence?

Someone was slapping her face lightly. "Wake up." A woman's voice.

43-1-12 felt herself propped up on either side by two sets of firm arms. Her eyes flickered open, but struggled to recognize the person looking back at her.

"See what you have become," the woman continued with her mild accent,

91

indicating the reflection in the mirror.

The person in the mirror looked like famine: gaunt with pallid skin. The eyes were familiar. There was life within their green depths. Somewhere behind their gaze was a girl picking white flowers in a lush field warmed by the sun. Behind those eyes was the support of a father, mother, two brothers, and friends. There was spirit still, though it had withdrawn to the deepest and most guarded place of her being. Her aggressors had not found it. They could not claim it.

She tried to smile defiantly, but lacked the energy.

"Yes," the Watchman said. "Continue resisting. I like the challenge. I admire your strength." She stood in front of 43-1-12. "The Captain believes you will eventually beg for his protection." She brought her face closer. "Either way, I will not be beaten. Either way, you will submit to me."

The Watchman turned away, stared into the burning light of the stone hearth.

43-1-12 realized she was back in the room. She could not recall how many times she had been brought into it. Days? Months? A year? Time was a sadist.

"You have nothing left to fight for," the Watchman whispered into her ear. "I know your brother came to you; yet whatever promises he made, whatever hope he offered, they no longer matter. . . . He is now also gone."

She looked up at the Watchman, unable to hide her bewilderment.

"Yes," the Watchman replied, a trace of triumph in her voice. "I have followed the reports from the Kurshemnt Campaign, including its casualty lists. Your brother Ürstus was killed in some nameless part of the mountains fighting some nameless Boldei. He has abandoned you. You are alone."

43-1-12 looked away, grief besieging the walls that remained around her heart. Could it be true? The thought that all her family was now truly gone drained what little hope she had left.

"Say the word and this will all stop," the Watchman said softly. "Say what the Captain wants to hear. You have nothing else to protect yourself with."

43-1-12 felt so utterly exhausted. Swaying, she could not will herself to speak.

Let me give you rest, Death whispered.

With a gloved hand, the Watchman brought 43-1-12's face to look at hers. "Maybe we have not been convincing enough. Maybe we have been too kind."

The Watchman nodded to the guards. They brought 43-1-12 to the table in the left corner, and placed her on her back. While her arms were bound above her head, her legs were spread so that her ankles could be fastened at the two corners of the table. She saw the Watchman pull a thin straight wire from the fire.

"There are women who cannot bear children," the Watchman said, "even if they wish it. Something has scorned them, some unseen power; call it Fate or Nature, it does not matter. Such women are cursed. Yet some must endure a worse pain. They conceive, but cannot deliver the child alive." The Watchman's attention seemed to withdraw, her voice softening. "Life can be pitiless."

From the side of the table, she looked down at 43-1-12 through her black mask. "You have not known real pain." Her tone was bitter. "You have not born children only to watch them come out suffocated." She rested her hand on 43-1-12's stomach.

43-1-12 shuddered, bracing herself.

"Do you know why you are really here?" the Watchman asked. "You withhold life. That is the seed of your rebellion." She shook her head. "I do not understand why the Captain wants to have such a woman."

The hot wire was brought close to 43-1-12's face. "So I will destroy your seed." The Watchman glanced at the tip of the wire then back at her. "I will take your choice, and prevent any more rebellion from growing inside you. Who knows . . ." The Watchman turned away. "I am no physician. I have not done this before. My hands can be clumsy. This could cause other damage, changing the Captain's mind about you. He might decide to turn you over to us completely."

The Watchman looked at the other guards. "Hold her still."

The guards pressed their weight on 43-1-12's arms and legs as the Watchman walked to the foot of the table. 43-1-12's meager tunic was lifted up to the waist. The glowing wire was lowered toward her vagina.

The significance of what was about to happen struck her. She struggled against their hold. *No.*

"Hold her still," the Watchman commanded.

"No," 43-1-12 cried, fighting against them with all the strength she could muster. "Damn you, no!"

Her thoughts sped furiously. They were going to ruin a piece of her, an aspect of choice, the meaning of which she had not yet determined but did not want to lose. She could not let them take it from her. She could not let them have the satisfaction.

It would end with one word. One word. But would such a word truly save her? And what would it cost? Or would the gains overpower the cost? Could she defy them with her life, her survival—by any means necessary: defiance through survival? Was there not power therein?

The heat of the wire came dangerously near.

Could she survive and find a way to live again? Could everything be made right?

She felt her skin beginning to burn.

Clenching her teeth, she closed her eyes to drive away the humiliation and, instead, concentrate on saying the word. Saying it took everything within her, required her to open a gate to a different kind of unknown, a different kind of vulnerability.

"Yes," she said.

The Watchman stopped and withdrew the wire. She came around and leaned her head close. "What did you say?"

"Yes." Tears broke through the barriers around her heart.

"Say it again," the Watchman urged.

"Yes."

"Louder."

"Yes."

"Louder."

"Yes, damn you," she shouted, barely containing her sobs.

The Watchman said something to the other guards, but 43-1-12 did not hear it. She did not hear anything. Her spirit collapsed. Already, she doubted her choice.

The guards pulled down her tunic and unbound her limbs. The door of the room was opened. She turned onto her side and curled up as tightly as she could. Someone stepped out quickly. She could hear the sound of the boots receding down the corridor.

With one of her hands between her legs, shielding herself from the thought of what had nearly happened, the other hand covered her face. She ran her fingers across her scalp. The hair felt less than an inch long. Had it only been a month? Had it been less? Had she capitulated so quickly?

It did not matter anymore. Who could judge her?

She withdrew into a shell of herself, her feelings draining out the cracks. Unable to will any further thought or action, she cradled one last idea: she would be the one to decide whether she survived or not. Through the preservation of that choice, she would fight on.

Let them think they had broken her. Let them lower their defenses in the self-assurance of victory. She would be patient. She would adapt. And at the opportune moment, she would find a way to hurt them. Then they would learn the true nature of strength.

Part 2: Wilderness

"No, no, no, no, no." Nabilak approached the bed where she lay. "This is all wrong." He knelt beside her, looking over her emaciated figure as if in shock. He felt her burning head, ran his fingers in disbelief across the canyons of starved flesh between her ribs. "It went too far," he whispered, resting his forehead against hers. "Why did you let it go so far?"

The room was warm. The bed felt soft, its sheets gentle to the touch. 43-1-12 noticed the sensations, but struggled to comprehend their blessing. Abuse had deadened her body. She could barely see Nabilak leaning over her, and keeping her eyes open made her head hurt. She had no more strength left for it. Finally allowed respite, her vigor crumbled.

Light dimmed. Shapes blurred, and their color faded. All except the bright, blue figure crouched before the fireplace at the opposite end of the room. The Dryden, Keeper of the Dead.

Her heart shuddered at its presence.

The Dryden's human-like form flickered with white-blue flame. Thin black eyes watched her. A voice spoke like the breath of wind through a roaring fire. "Are you ready to die?"

No one else seemed to hear or see it.

The Dryden smiled. "Follow me, child."

Panic threatened. She gritted her teeth and looked away, gasping for breath, trying not to drown in the doom of such a presence. She resolved not to give in. She was not ready.

Another voice drew her consciousness back to the present. "What happened?" The woman spoke to Nabilak. "No doubt you're responsible."

Nabilak straightened, addressing the newcomer. "You have work to do."

"I recognize her," the woman said. "She's a prisoner, isn't she?"

"She was," Nabilak replied.

"What's her name?" the woman asked. "If I'm to tend to her, I won't be calling her by a prison number."

Glancing back at 43-1-12, Nabilak said, "Call her Namél. She is going to live here now."

"Well enough," the woman conceded.

Namél. Another name, another movement. What did it matter if it was given to her by an oppressor? Had she not decided to submit to Nabilak's authority? To survive, she needed to adapt. For now, discarding her prison identity offered a kind of liberation.

Nabilak spoke again, trying to meet her searching eyes. He said something about removing the number tattooed on her jaw, so that few people would know her true identity. She tried to focus on the warden, willing her spirit to resist—only this time directed at death itself. The Dryden could call her, but she did not have to follow.

"That is it," Nabilak urged, his voice becoming clearer. "Breathe. Yes, keep fighting, Namél. Do not give up." He stroked her head, and wiped the sweat from her brow. "You are safe now. You will recover. That is what I love about you. After all that you have endured, you still defy death."

Without looking away, he curtly beckoned to someone with his hand. A middle-aged woman approached with a solemn expression. "Ida is a skilled healer," Nabilak continued. "Once more, she will guide you back to health. Now, you can rest in peace."

He withdrew. As he did so, Ida came to the bed, adjusted the pillow under Namél's head, and drew the covers over her naked form. The healer then gave Nabilak a stern glare. He nodded and left the room. Returning her attention to Namél, Ida helped raise her head so that her lips could receive a wooden cup.

"Here, drink this," Ida said. "Hold the water in your mouth for a moment before swallowing."

Namél felt the cool liquid moisten her mouth, but then almost choked as it rushed down her parched throat. As the water's caress reached the core of her body, she felt a brief pang of renewal.

"Yes, that's it," Ida said. "Good girl. Let the water restore you. It's the source of life, after all." She placed a cool wet cloth over Namél's forehead. "Rest now. Ida is here."

The Dryden continued to watch. "Yes," its voice echoed. "Rest. . . . I am here, always near, always patient."

Months flowed by, a limbo of dreaming, waking, drinking, eating, and dreaming again. Like a mother with her child, Ida tended to Namél, gradually rehabilitating her body. Most of the time, Namél was too weak to speak. Ida fed and bathed her, changed her clothes and linens. Once Namél's hair had grown long enough, Ida brushed the knots from it.

Nearly a year passed before Namél's body rediscovered its full vitality. At last, days regained meaning. There was light: outside the room, through the lone window. There was sound: tools clanking on rock. And there was dark: inside her mind, images of the past and present—hope and heartache—real or imagined.

All the while, the Dryden waited. "What of the future?" it asked. Its light had faded, but its voice remained clear. Stranger to Namél was the Dryden's alteration. Where before it appeared neither male nor female, it now looked like a woman; its face even mirrored her own. Was it mocking her?

"What do you want from me?" Namél asked

The Dryden smiled. "I want to know what you will become."

Nabilak came once Namél could walk again without Ida's help, when she at last felt her body reclaimed.

Ida warned Namél that he would come, that he was growing impatient. "I'm sorry," she said. "Some predators prey on the sick and weak. I fear the Warden preys on the resilient."

Later, waiting alone in her room, Namél told herself that she was ready. Yet she struggled to sustain such conviction. She did not really know what to expect, and was anxious to move past speculation—to get it over with.

Though she had buried her spirit before, it was difficult to convince herself that rape would be a less formidable barrage against her body than torture. It would be another kind of torture. What would Nabilak's lust demand?

Feeling her jaw line, she ran her fingers along the scar that had replaced the tattoo of her inmate number. It was not the only surface reminder of her suffering. She had many scars. What did Nabilak intend to convey by having the number removed? True, there was a sense of anonymity in its absence. The number on her jaw was easier to read than her scars, at least from the perspective of others. Without it, she was less obviously an inmate of Tïrmen Prison. Had he removed the tattoo for his own protection? While originally considering the loss of *43-1-12* a step of freedom, she suspected that Nabilak meant to mark her deeper than the surface. The sign of his power over her might remain invisible to the eyes of an outsider, but she would know. It would be within her. Could her spirit evade such a branding? Could her body somehow resist impregnation? If not, what would she do with his child—what would she do with herself?

Through the window of her room, the last light of dusk dimmed to gray.

Behind her, the door opened. She turned as Nabilak stepped inside.

"I am glad to see you well," he said, closing the door. He wore a white tunic. She could spot no weapon.

Someone locked the door from the outside.

"Ida has been a patient healer," Namél replied. She felt her heart rate increasing. Dressed in a plain, pale green gown, she stood as tall as she could before him. The last image of her mother flashed across her mind: her calm, strong demeanor facing the invaders of their home.

Namél realized with mild amusement that she was taller than Nabilak, for this was the first time she faced him unfettered, standing on her own.

"You are such a beautiful woman." With a scarred, grimacing smile, Nabilak slowly approached, looking over her body. "How fortunate I am."

He stopped in front her. His brown hair looked freshly trimmed. She smelled herbs and oil. Was it meant to attract her?

"But it is not just how you look," he continued, brushing a strand of hair away from her shoulder. "It is your courage and robustness that I admire."

He touched her cheek with his hand. "That you, a strong, independent woman, have said 'Yes' . . ." He stared at her mouth. "To me."

Still, she did not move, wanting to appear unafraid and in control of herself. She hoped he did not notice her trembling.

Suddenly, he seized her jaw. "Never forget that." Though his voice remained quiet, it carried an edge of sternness. "You have given yourself to me, Namél. You are mine now. Remember that obedience welcomes kindness, but resistance demands punishment." He released her face. "Is that clear?"

A wail sounded from the hearth as a gust of wind blew in. The flames flickered. Was the Dryden laughing at her? She glanced at the fire iron.

"Take it," a voice whispered. Was it Nabilak who had spoken?

She could fight, perhaps even kill him, but what good would it do? Not knowing where she was in the central fortress, she did not think she could escape—and the cost of capture would be too great. She reminded herself of the choice to defy her enemies by survival, by adaptation; that to do so for now, she had to submit. What was the body anyway? It was the spirit that mattered.

Right?

If only she could stop shaking.

"We do so much to hide our intricacies," Nabilak said, "all the while wanting to be known. A strange paradox, I think." His eyes rose to meet hers. "It is time to stop hiding. Remove your clothes."

As she obeyed, she met his eyes, which did not shift. They seemed to search her, amused by her. Or was it mystified?

Finally, he looked down.

"There is something awkward about the naked body," he commented. Slowly, he removed his boots, belt, and shirt. His trousers remained. She found herself staring at the mangled web of red flesh that comprised his left chest and shoulder.

"Yes," he said, noticing her gaze. "I too have been marked."

The chair creaked as Nabilak sat, leaning back. She felt the cool of night seeping through her bare skin. What was he waiting for?

He watched her until the firelight began to fade. "It is better this way," he said softly. "We can bear only so much light."

She said nothing.

He smiled. "That is what I like about you, Namél. You stand before me in the most vulnerable of circumstances, yet still strive to maintain an aura of bravery. Let us be at peace with each other. Let us be equals."

"We are not equals," she said. He had ensured that it was so.

As he stood, a hammer of fear struck her heart.

"We will be," Nabilak said. He approached, took her wrist and led her to the bed.

She tried to breathe fully, slowly, all the while withdrawing her thoughts from the present, but it was difficult.

"Relax," he whispered.

She closed her eyes, not wanting to see what he was doing on top of her, and tried not to think about it. It became difficult to breathe.

Nabilak exhaled heavily into her ear. "Run your fingers through my hair."

She did as he asked.

Eventually, he tensed and inhaled in a few shallow gasps. Rolling onto his side, he assumed a fetal position with his back to her. "Hold me."

She shifted to face his back, but became distracted by how much her vagina hurt. She reached down to touch it, and noticed some blood on her fingers.

"Hold me," Nabilak repeated, louder.

She brought her arms around him.

"Keep stroking my hair," he added.

She did so, wondering if this was the extent of his desire. Was it so bad? She recalled her mother telling her that sex was an expression of intimacy; that it bound two people together more powerfully and mysteriously than anything else. This could not be what she had meant. Surely, intimacy was more than a physical act.

Nabilak lay still. Namél resolved not to be bound to him. There would certainly be no intimacy.

Nabilak came to her often, but only at night: the continuation of a haunting journey. Only now it was more a wilderness of vague shadows and doubts than physical torment. Nabilak's lust was as hungry as the dark, and as empty. He was a silhouette in the doorway; a ghost that breathed yet rarely spoke, except to tell her what to do.

Despite trying to console herself with the idea that the warden's form of domination could be worse, she could not dissociate from the fact that he was claiming a part of her. Was it just her body, or also her will—could his power extend that far? Was it foolish to think her survival could be a form of defiance? Or was she being passive? Should she do more to resist? Despair caressed her, eroded her confidence, and filled her with self-contempt.

The fear that she might become pregnant, that her body could betray her, haunted her every morning. Trying to separate her mind from it would not be enough. Though she did not want to linger on such a thought, something substantial happened every time Nabilak raped her. There was coldness in the loss. She tried to convince herself that it was preferable to the torture from before; that one day she would reclaim what was lost, and remove the mask of submission.

Nabilak's tenderness was likely a façade that would not last. He would tire of her eventually, and cast her aside. She braced herself for that day, not sure whether to hope for or dread it. Until then, she would continue to play the role he wanted, even if it meant living like a creature caged in a pretext of independence. She would take care of herself: welcoming the food and drink brought by Ida, cleaning and grooming her body when needed, keeping herself fit during the long hours confined to her room. She was not doing it for them, but for herself—to be ready. Nabilak thought she had been tamed, that she relied on him, but he would come to realize his mistake.

Or so she kept telling herself.

"Burn," the Dryden said, sitting inside the fireplace. "Burn them all: the forests, the fields, the foes."

Wrapped in an ivory-colored sheet, she sat on the stone windowsill of her room and studied her faint reflection in the window. She could not comprehend the face looking back at her. It could be anyone's face.

Shifting her focus to the woodlands beyond the walls of Tirmen, she observed the crimson leaves of the trees brightly contrasting the gray sky. She forgot what it was like to touch and hear the signs of autumn, forgot the soft whisper of falling leaves and the crunch of their brittleness underfoot. All that was now a distant, drying memory—a last vein of light separated from her by glass and stone walls.

Her right hand slid over her exposed left shoulder to feel her scars. She imagined their pattern to be like the interplay of thin tree branches, their color like the fall. Ida had told her that the wounds had healed, that only the scars remained. But had the wounds truly healed? She glanced down to where the sheet curved away from her bare knees, and rotated her foot to observe the marks on her calf. It was true that the scars did not cause her physical pain. In a way, her body had healed. Yet it had also become numb.

Two months had passed since her first night with Nabilak.

She noted the strands of long auburn hair resting on her uncovered collarbone. She had little recollection of those months, including the period of recovery that preceded them. Round and round her life went like a fever dream, an unprogressive fugue: so many movements offering so little meaning. They had absorbed each other without any real sense of change—a vague blur of images, words, and actions.

The prison had taken much from her. Nabilak had taken much. Perhaps it was best that she not remember. Perhaps there was a trace of mercy in that kind of forgetfulness, even some peace. Yet the days felt like links of a long rusting chain bound to her spirit.

The Dryden appeared next to her.

Startled, she lurched back as it grew to her size from the flame of the candle she had placed on the table next to the windowsill. The Dryden had never come so close. Though its blue form rippled with flame, she did not feel warmed by it. In fact, she felt colder.

Its face resembled hers. Seeing it smile was strangest of all, for she could not remember when she had last smiled.

"You need not be afraid, child," the Dryden said with its airy voice.

"I do not fear you," she countered, though she felt her tone falter.

"I was referring to you." The Dryden leaned closer. "You fear yourself, your own weakness and strength."

She was fed up with the Dryden's presence, real or imagined. "What do you want from me?"

"You decide," the Dryden replied.

"Stop mocking me," she said. "Go judge someone else."

"I judge no one," the Dryden said. "I do not have that kind of authority. I merely wait and observe. You make the choices."

"Choices? What choices do I have left?"

"Many."

"I know of only two," she replied, "destruction or survival. One demands submission, and the other defiance."

"Is it so simple?"

"I do not possess the freedoms others enjoy, or take for granted."

"Let those who judge examine their own graces." Still smiling, the Dryden placed its hands behind its head. "So what will you do?"

Namél stared into its black eyes. "Do you not know?"

"I am not omniscient," the Dryden replied. "I can only guess your mind."

If that was true, she was not sure it made her feel any better. "Why should I tell you anything then?"

"Do what you wish."

"I am condemned to attrition, either way," she replied. "But I will not surrender to you. That is certain."

"Surrender to me?" Shaking its head, the Dryden chuckled. "All are dying, and must one day surrender. Death prowls this world with insatiable hunger."

Her father had said that once, in his last days.

"Are you not death?" she asked.

"The temperament of this world keeps me here," the Dryden replied. "A cycle of decay: you began in your mother's womb, and end in the Mother's womb. Your people tend to call that cycle Nature. So think of me not as Death, but as Nature's midwife." The Dryden smiled. "She produces nothing without my help. With my hands, I cradle her offspring. I cleanse the world, sometimes slowly, other times abruptly. Who can say which is better?"

"I do not understand," she said. "A midwife helps bring about life."

"There is a kind of life in death."

"Do you mean the Fields of Gedáron, and the hope of transcending death?"

"Hope does not survive." The Dryden's black eyes narrowed. "No matter how fervent the belief."

"What about goodness and love?"

"Do not tell me you still believe in love, that most fickle of hopes."

Indeed, she did not know why she had asked. Survival was difficult enough; hoping for more only made it harder. A future of freedom remained out of reach while past goodness continued to retreat, transforming the present into a limbo of oblivion. What did she really want from love anyway?

"Does survival amount to anything in your world?" she asked. "Does Nature honor the resilient?"

"Nature does," the Dryden replied, "but only to be cruel. Survival is just another hope that delays the inevitable. Why punish yourself with it when there is no victory in the end?"

"There must be some kind of relief," she pressed, "even if it only comes from delaying death."

"Death is the only relief."

Was it her upbringing that urged her to seek and fight for more, or was it something intrinsic to being human? Or did the desire come from something else, something outside her?

"You may be right," she said. She looked at the trees outside, in the distance, heralding the fall. "Hope can be treacherous, leading us to cling to ideals—ideals that may be bright and soft at first, but inevitably dry up and crumble in our hands."

"Yes." The Dryden offered its hand. "There comes a time to let fire consume the fragments. Why not embrace it? Let it wash over you, cleanse you."

"But what if you are another illusion," she countered, staring at the Dryden's hand, "no more real than love."

The Dryden smiled. "Find out."

"Can a person love death?" she asked.

The Dryden's hand lowered. "The longer you cling to love, the longer you know pain. Love is like water on your dry autumn leaves. It only prolongs the burning, and blinds you with smoke."

Her father would argue that to press on toward ideals was to defy the oppressive nature of reality. He believed that goodness was intrinsic to all people, even nature. Her mother had spoken of evading the Dryden through some form of self-assertion in the afterlife. But how? Why had her mother not been clearer? Was hers a vague faith, or merely self-deception?

Anyway, was death the true enemy? It had been people who attacked, imprisoned, and abused her. It had been life. No, her outlook was not yet so dark. Not all people were her enemies. Her parents had loved her in their own way; they had died to protect her. And what of others like Jed, Ozath, Ida, and Opal? Surely, they were real—their actions were real. Despite the brevity of their presence, their goodness had to have been real—at least as real as death. Death was as much an abstraction as love.

"If you really are the Dryden," she said, "tell me what happened to my mother."

"She is dead."

"Did you see her?"

"Yes."

Her heart sank at the thought. "Where is she now?"

A light struck the periphery of Namél's vision, distracting her attention. Squinting, she looked through the window to the east where the rising sun shone through a small gap in the clouds. Though her mind was weary, the touch of warmth filled her with a glimmer of peace. She almost smiled.

Returning her attention to the Dryden, she found only smoke slithering up from the candle wick.

She was grateful for the day.

During the day, as Nabilak tended to prison matters, she experienced a semblance of freedom. Though confined to her room, she did what calisthenics she could to keep her body strong and her mind focused. Her failed escape over a year earlier haunted her; now well-fed and rested, she resolved to be better prepared for the next opportunity. She knew there would be only one more chance, but could not decide whether she was meant to orchestrate it or wait for it to present itself.

Meanwhile, new prisoners arrived to Tïrmen every week, most of them purportedly from the south. From her room's high vantage point, she watched distant lines of downcast postures plod into the city through the southern gate. The prisoners were led along barren streets to their allotted wards and units. Many came. Few left.

She overheard guards outside her door talk about how poorly the campaign in the Kurshemnt Mountains was going—the Great Boldei Purging, they called it—and how new leadership was being sought. She smiled to herself at this news, glad to know that Dwairian's new empire did not always get its way. At the same time she also felt a pang of grief; the thought of those mountains reminded her of her dead brothers, how both had fallen in the campaign.

She wondered about the Boldei. Who were they, and was she meant to hate them like the Alöweans? On a few occasions, she had noticed prisoners with bark-like skin. She had later learned that they were Boldei prisoners. Though she only ever observed them from a distance, their large stature and red-brown, bark-like skin was unmistakable.

As Namél watched from above, she spotted a lone Boldei prisoner looking up at her window. His eyes were not dark like the others, but white. Pressing her hand against the glass, she wondered if the Boldei prisoner saw her. He placed his hand against his chest then slowly turned away to focus on his labor. As he did so, she noticed an intricate, black design like a tattoo covering his back.

The moment reminded her how little she knew about Illirium. It made her feel small. Prior the war, no one believed the Boldei existed. They were a people of legend, from another time. It was said that they had never before interacted with the Illiri, nor anyone in Illirium. There had to be more to it than that. There had to be so much more to the world.

The door of her room opened.

"Good morning," Ida said, entering with a tray of food held on top of fresh linens. Behind her, a guard closed and locked the door from the outside.

The healer came at least once a day, working efficiently and routinely. Her attention remained downward on her labor, leaving a slight slouch in her posture. The lines extending from her hardened gaze conveyed a mounting weariness; yet when her eyes caught the light, their hazel color retained a youthful brightness—as if Ida drew her strength from an invisible well. Namél wanted to know the source. More so, she missed Opal and having a friend.

The will to keep her body ready for escape sometimes felt suffocated by the grip of loneliness. The initial months after she had been released from the central prison had been comprised of feverish nightmares, painful waking, and endless hours of half-consciousness. All the while, the healer's presence had grounded her in the present. Ida had been patient and gentle, tending Namél's wounds, feeding her, whispering comforting words to steady her spinning thoughts. What was there to live for if she could not trust someone like that?

Ida placed the tray of bread and fruit on the table. Her whitening, gray hair was gathered back in a single braid. "Come, young lady. Sit and eat."

Now conscious of her hunger, Namél left the windowsill and sat at the table. She bit into an apple, its crisp succulence waking her senses.

As she ate, Namél considered a question that had been churning in her thoughts. If she did not ask, the prospect of connection would only remain a formless hope—and hope built upon anticipation alone would not last. She needed something more tangible.

"Ida," she said.

The healer did not turn from changing the bed. "Yes?"

"Can you sit with me for a while?"

Having finished the bed and gathered the used linens into a mound, Ida turned to Namél. "What was that, dear?"

Namél motioned to the table. "I would like to talk with you."

Ida appeared bewildered for a moment, but then put the linens down. She came to the table, pulled back the extra chair, and relaxed into its embrace. "What can I do for you?"

"I want to know you better," Namél said.

"Really? Why?"

"I would like your friendship." Namél had resolved to be frank, but hesitated. "That is, if you are willing."

"Willing?" Ida laughed. "That's a strange way of putting it. Of course I'm willing. But you've been so quiet all this time. Why now?"

Namél glanced away, but then felt Ida's hand rest consolingly upon hers.

"It's all right, child." The healer's voice became soft. "You've been through a lot, and I can't imagine the strain. I'll listen, if that would help. Is that what you want?" She offered a faint smile.

Namél was not sure. "You carry yourself with such strength." She realized that the healer reminded her a little of her mother, older but with a kindred spirit. "How do you sustain it in this place? I want to hear about a life beyond these prison walls. For example, what brought you here?"

Scratching her nose, Ida's expression conveyed a hint of skepticism. "You really want to know?"

"Yes." For so long, Namél had felt trapped in her own narrative. Hearing another person's story might provide some relief, even if only a brief distraction. She also wanted to discover more about what was going on in the outside world.

The healer inhaled slowly. "Well, there are a few parts to that answer."

"I have nowhere else to be."

Ida stared out the window. "The war changed my life, as it did everyone's life, I suppose."

"Yes."

"I'll warrant that yours was one of the more desperate struggles."

Namél shrugged.

"Whether by your choice or not, I cannot say. Nor will I judge." Ida raised her finger with the last point before settling her hands back on her lap. "I suppose I should count myself fortunate, in a way."

"Fortunate? How?"

"Well, for one, there are few from my clan left. The fires of the war and that cursed dragon destroyed everything. All my family was slain." Ida straightened herself in the chair and rubbed her eyes. "But you needn't hear about that grief. You've enough of your own."

"Please go on," Namél said, hoping her attentiveness conveyed her genuine interest.

Ida crossed her arms and stared back at the window. "Anyway, I left Sedwarke a long time ago, before the war. I was tired of its ways, you see, and wanted to live at the center of progress, so to speak—to leave the warrior mentality behind. I thought to do so in Girion, where I studied and trained to be a healer—as women were permitted to do at the time. But I'll not burden you with those details.

"In Girion, I met Franór. He was a captain; had broken his leg during some night patrol in Wéswood. I was charged with mending the leg and caring for him."

Ida smiled faintly, her eyes distant. "We talked often during those times, especially when I was off duty late in the evening. Once Franór recovered, we often walked together outside the city among the fields. Eventually, we were married. Those were warm times, optimistic I'd say. That seems so long ago. . . . Have you been to Girion?"

Namél shook her head. She had no desire to see Dwairian's capital.

"Well, it's not what it once was," Ida continued. "Pity you missed it before the war. Now the dust of empire-making covers everything. I can't breathe there any longer. I abhor violence, you see—now more than ever. So I try to use my skills and lingering strength to counter its affects. I love our people, and I believe there's still reason to hope for a peaceful future. We mustn't give up, I say."

"But the violence is surely greater here in Tirmen than in most places," Namél said. "Why come here?"

"You're right, of course." Ida frowned, though more to herself. "Violence is everywhere these days. Do you know what ended the war?"

Namél shook her head. "Not really."

"Well, what happened in the end influenced why I came here. Franór rose quickly in the ranks of Lord Dwairian's army. By the time the war began, he'd been promoted to general. Franór led a host from Girion against this city, in fact." She quieted. "But after the Alöweans had been defeated, while the city of Anaríl still smoldered, he was killed. That's when our forces turned against the Küllka, our so-called allies. On a plain called Prothílaüm, my husband fell fighting them, his head cleaved by some Küllka chieftain's broadsword."

"I am sorry," Namél said.

Ida rubbed her eyes again. "Prior to that, our eldest son, Ríon, was killed defending Pernor. Our youngest son, Bram, died taking this very keep." She stared at the stone floor. "So you see, one of my loves gave his life for the Alöweans while the other two died conquering them. And if I'm to be honest, I stand somewhere between accepting and hating King Dwairian's vision, the creation of this new empire." She shook her head. "In that tension, what matters most to me is what I can do to honor the fallen. I came here because this is where my loss began, I suppose. Here, I perceive their presence. That probably doesn't make sense. It's hard to explain."

Namél did not understand, not entirely anyway. But in Ida she saw another woman as much a prisoner to grief as her. "Well, I am glad you are here."

"Thank you," Ida replied. "The world isn't as clean as we healers would like it to be, and not everything can be mended. Split in our loyalties, maybe my family was dying before the war even started. Maybe part of me thinks my work here is a way of reuniting them. I can serve both Siligen and its enemies, its wardens and prisoners. It's baffling sometimes, but I don't know what else to do."

Namél thought of her own family, about the disparities of their views and deaths: how her brothers had left to support Dwairian against her father's wishes, ultimately dying for the former. "I know how it feels to be stuck in between," she said quietly, not meeting Ida's eyes.

"I feel no ill will toward the Alöweans," Ida added.

"Nor do I."

"The war was about power and control," Ida commented, "from all sides. Considering the presence of those demons from beyond the mountains—those Ülak and Küllka, and Boldei—maybe it also had to do with the spread of some kind of evil. Something greater was behind it all, something

111

none of us could comprehend. I don't think King Dwairian understands the consequences of his war, nor do I think his new empire will bring lasting peace. I hope I'm wrong, of course, but it all seems too fragile. This new world is more susceptible to evil than ever before. Don't you sense it?"

Namél had not thought about it that way. Still, she nodded. There was no denying that, in her life, cruelty had become more pervasive since the war.

Ida sighed. "With Pernor and the Guardians gone, there may be little left but the egotism of our rulers to protect us." She leaned forward, lowering her voice. "Do you believe in Gedáronith?"

The name sounded familiar. "Is it related to the Fields of Gedáron?" Namél asked, also quieting. "My mother spoke of it."

"They're the same," Ida said. "Did your mother also tell you about the Dryden and Canta?"

"I know of the Dryden," Namél replied. She glanced around, wondering why she had not seen it for weeks. "*Canta* sounds familiar." She suddenly recalled something her father had said. He had urged her to seek an understanding of the word; that it could guide her away from the Dryden.

"The signs of death are all around us," Ida said. "Yet there must be more than what we see, more than this existence. If it's true that there's a world beyond our own—call it Gedáronith, the Fields of Gedáron, paradise, or whatever you want—if there are powers unperceived by human eyes, then I'm led to wonder who or what is really in control. It sometimes makes me afraid, if I'm honest. Many claimed to have seen a dragon during the war. Surely, that can't be a coincidence or delusion. Evidence of its destruction was everywhere—fire greater than anything we or the Alöweans could harness, I'll wager. And consider this: King Dwairian shouldn't have been able to defeat the Alöweans so easily and so quickly. Something must've helped him, maybe something we can't see or don't understand."

"What are you getting at?" Namél asked, keeping her voice just above a whisper.

Ida's tone remained hushed. "What if it was the Dryden who entered the world as a dragon of judgment? Or what if the dragon was the Dryden's pet? Either way, the Spirit of Death longs for us all. But against such power, there must be balance. That is where I believe the Canta comes in. If there's more to the Dryden than people remember, maybe there's more to the Canta as well. The Alöweans seemed to know about such things. Pernor had a great library of ancient texts. What if the answers were contained within them? I think it was a mistake to let Pernor fall and its Guardians perish. It even may have been unwise to drive the Alöweans away." Ida shook her head. "So much has been lost. To me, the world's become stranger, larger and more unwieldy."

"But where do these ideas come from? What gives you such conviction?"

"I thought you said your mother told you the old stories," Ida replied.

"I am not sure which ones you mean."

"About the afterlife. Where did you say you come from?"

"Hamath," Namél replied.

"Ah." Ida appeared to consider this. "That makes sense. Your clan's beliefs have generally been more akin to Girion, I think. Things are changing now, but the Girion Clan traditionally disregarded belief in the Dryden, let alone the Canta. They believe death is a drifting into nothingness, and that's all. Yet in Sedwarke, our views were more like those of Rodaním."

Namél wished that she had talked to her parents more about such views. "My mother said it is difficult to find the Fields of Gedáron, but that they can be reached if one is strong and cunning enough. Do you know anything about that? She never mentioned the Canta, though she came from Rodaním."

Ida scratched her chin. "I'm not sure whether our ideas of strength and cunning mean anything in the world beyond. No doubt, some details have faded in the passing from generation to generation. *Canta* is just an old word that means 'guide' anyway. I was raised to think of the Canta as another spirit like the Dryden, except one that comes to our aid. That makes more sense to me, anyway; for how else would the Dryden be overcome? The Spirit of Death is formidable. It's said to seize most and bring them to its cave, a shadowed oblivion for all eternity—a place of wandering or servitude—all the while it feeds on their souls."

"But if the Canta exists, why would it not help everyone?"

113

"That's a good question," Ida replied. "Honestly, I don't know. My grandmother taught me that the Canta only chooses those it deems worthy, those good in heart and deed. Maybe that's what your mother meant, though I should think more people than not would therefore qualify. Maybe a person must be resilient as well as good. I'm not sure."

Namél also wondered if it was just a tale used by parents to coerce obedience from their children. After all, how could abstract ideas like goodness and resilience be measured? It all seemed too speculative.

"I know what you're thinking," Ida commented. "I used to consider these beliefs too simplistic. That was part of the reason I left Sedwarke in the first place. Yet the war brought these ideas back to my attention. They helped me make sense of what had happened, I suppose. Death feels more powerful now. What if other creatures dwell in the Dryden's cave, and were released? How else can we explain the phenomena of the demons and the dragon? Something changed during the war, something unnatural."

Though Namél admired the healer's passion, and thought her views interesting, she needed something more practical. "Have these beliefs changed how you live?"

"Yes," Ida replied, "in subtle ways, anyway. I still have many questions. There must be fragments of the old stories we're missing. I want to find out more. Before I get too old, I'll journey east to learn what I can from the Alöweans. Captain Nabilak promised to get me a pass."

A pass to the east? Namél became more attentive. "Where will you go?"

"To Hamrothél," Ida replied, brushing a loose strand of gray hair from her face, "the last Alöwean city. I hear they allow some Illiri visitors, at least those who seek to study in peace. Or maybe my skills as a healer could gain me access. The Alöweans I've met are remarkable healers. I could ask to study with those who live in Hamrothél, if they're not too secretive about it. That way, even if I learn nothing more about Gedáronith or the Canta, I would at least return better equipped to serve the needs of our people here." She stared out the window for a while.

Namél respected that outlook. "I imagine you could use an assistant."

Slowly, a smile rose from Ida's lips. "Now that you've mentioned it, I've meant to ask the Warden for more help; for this place keeps an old woman very busy—and I'm only responsible for the central fortress." She studied Namél. "I'm not sure what the Warden has in mind for you in the long term, but I'll speak to him about your helping me. It's worth a try."

"Thank you," Namél said. Dared she hope? "When has he promised to give you the pass?"

"When the summer comes, I'll be free to go."

Another nine months seemed like an eternity. Could she endear herself to Nabilak in order to get what she wanted? Even if he permitted her to assist Ida, he was unlikely to let her accompany the healer east. Still, for now she could at least learn from the older woman. Perhaps she could even get hold of the pass, hide it away to use when the opportunity was right. Ida might come to understand.

The healer reached across the table with both her weathered hands and grasped Namél's own, squeezing them firmly but tenderly. "I want to do what I can for you."

"Thank you."

"I know you've suffered; and though I don't know what brought you to this place, I can tell that some cruel injustice was at the bottom of it."

Namél nodded slowly.

"However you've managed to survive," Ida continued, "whatever you're doing, don't stop. Keep aware, with both eyes open. Let in what light you can. It exists, even if only in small reminders—in colors and sounds. That's the spirit of the Canta, I think. It reminds us of good, and keeps us going."

Light.

Sound.

There was a chance they were mere illusions, but what if Ida was right? Despite how distant such sensation seemed to Namél, there were moments when they returned with undeniable clarity, however brief. She looked into Ida's bright, hazel eyes: light. Yes, a pang of life. For a moment, Namél no longer heard the healer's words, but only the resonance of her voice: sound. Like music. If these were not real then nothing was. Namél could believe in that. She had felt it before.

115

Yes, survival depended not only on enduring, but remembering. Like Opal, Ida reminded Namél that a person could embody goodness—a crescendo of light and sound. She wanted to trust in that, in another person's sincerity, despite how much others had given her reasons not to. Survival alone was not enough. She needed to believe that her suffering would one day end, and to keep remembering that goodness was real: to follow the glimmers and echoes wherever they might lead.

Nabilak said he would think about letting Namél assist Ida in her healing duties. In the meantime, Namél's trustworthiness would be tested by being given access to some areas outside her room. Though she was not allowed to leave the central keep, she could roam a few of its halls and courtyards under guard.

Outside one day, she leaned upon the crenel of a wall, enjoying the warmth its stones had absorbed from the sun. Far below, the wind agitated the surface of Lake Valon into frothing waves. As the sun dropped below the horizon, she turned away and studied the tower she had hung from over a year before—the tower with the cave inside. Her eyes climbed the flat side of the structure until she spotted the top of the cage dangling at the tower's pinnacle. She wondered if anyone was up there now. More so, she thought of the cave, wishing she could go inside to look closer and discover where it led.

A hush of footsteps crossed the lawn of the small courtyard behind her.

"It's time," one guard said, halting a few steps away. He and the other had been watching her from the shade of the tower.

She glanced down from the battlements to the rocky shore below. It would not be difficult to jump.

"Come on." The second guard took another step forward. "Let's go."

Namél nodded in acknowledgement, and turned away from the wall to follow them back to her chamber. Behind her daylight faded. Ahead loomed the night.

A silent forest.

Like an apparition, smoke slowly floods the area, rising around me. I cannot see where to go. There is nothing around me but trees drowning in swirling gray shadows. No air. No breeze. Just suffocating ash and chill.

Hooded figures as gray as the atmosphere materialize between the trees. I try to flee, but everywhere there is unchanging wilderness. The figures are always around me, closing in. I run again, but it is useless. The figures continue to draw closer.

I collapse to the ground. The figures stand over me, looking down with pale faces. Their cold hands seize my limbs, lifting me above them as they carry me deeper into the void.

"Did you hear what I said?" Nabilak had been speaking to her.

From her pillow, Namél looked blankly up at him, her dreams slowly dissipating. Outside, through the window, the sky brightened: morning. Why was he still with her? He never stayed to the dawn.

The temperature from the previous day had dropped little overnight. It would be another hot autumn day. While the warmth was a relief from the memory of cold, it did little to warm her spirit. She pulled the bed's ivory sheets closer around her naked flesh.

Nabilak watched her intently as he finished fastening the collar of his shirt. Staring into his gray-brown eyes, Namél felt nothing but contempt for the warden. He reached for his sword belt. For a time the only sound heard was that of the leather strap sliding into the buckle frame and then being secured with the prong. Her eyes lingered on the sword waiting expectantly at his left hip. She did not remember him bringing it in the night before. How had she missed such an important detail?

"I am leaving Tirmen Prison," he said, looking up from his belt.

Her eyes rose to meet his, while her peripheral vision noted his left hand resting on the butt of the sword hilt.

Nabilak's attention remained fixed on her. "After six years, I am finally being awarded for my services."

"Services?" she said, not bothering to conceal her skepticism.

Nabilak diverted his gaze to the view outside the window. "I did not seek to be Warden of Tïrmen Prison." He walked over and leaned against the table. "When I returned from the war, I thought I was going to be stationed somewhere within the capital. After all, I led the company that took Tärm Tower. Yet when I was finally brought before King Dwairian, he commanded me to oversee the work here in Tïrmen, building a prison from its ruins. 'It is a job of the utmost importance,' he said." Nabilak looked over at her. "I had to accept."

He straightened and came to sit at the foot of the bed. As he did so, she brought her knees up closer to her chest while at the same time holding the sheet tighter about her. Nabilak's eyes did not meet hers, but instead stared blankly at the shape of her shins beneath the sheet.

"I have never liked it here," he commented. "It is a lonely place." His hand rested on her knee for a moment. "Until you arrived, that is."

He shook his head as if to ward off a thought, took a deep breath, and then stood up. "Anyway, I have been offered an opportunity to leave this dreary existence. The King has given me command of one of the new Barorian units. I will finally do something to be proud of again."

"Why are you telling me this?" she asked. He had shared little of his affairs with her before.

"I will leave once the new prison warden arrives." The warden walked casually to the door and knocked. It was unlocked and opened by one of the guards posted outside. Pausing under the archway, Nabilak looked back at Namél. "And you will be accompanying me."

The door closed.

She watched it with a sinking heart.

Eventually she rose, keeping the sheet wrapped around her body, and walked over to the window. She studied the prisoners below as they marched in lines to begin their labor for the day.

At least eighteen years remained of her prison sentence. While Nabilak had removed the tattoo on her jaw, she had not anticipated leaving the prison walls with him. What future did he envision for her?

The prison city came fully awake. The clanking of iron on rock began to chime throughout—as it did every day. Heavy stones were broken then brought to the masons for fashioning. The city was being rebuilt in greater strength than before. In time it would be complete: an impenetrable fortress against those inside. To the left, at the eastern end of the city, she glimpsed the small women's ward. She imagined herself back there. She imagined the cold, and what the guards might do if Nabilak released her to their authority and whims. At the thought of Nabilak taking her with him, no matter what arrangements had been made, the day seemed to brighten.

Leaving the prison would be her next act of defiance, and might be the only chance for her defiance to survive. She looked past the city walls to the unfettered countryside beyond, and imagined herself walking amidst the soft warm grass with the autumn breeze blowing through her hair. She imagined many things, but knew she first had to get beyond the walls. A rare opportunity had presented itself.

Six days passed before Nabilak's replacement arrived. He did not come to her in that time. Though she was grateful for that, she slept restlessly each night.

On the afternoon of the sixth day, she learned from Ida that the new warden had overseen a smaller facility in Zirgalath, a place for punishing military deserters. The older woman had been introduced to the new warden the day before.

"His name's Nül," Ida said. "He's known to be very cruel to prisoners."

"Should I be worried?"

"About what?"

"I have not seen Nabilak for days. Has anything changed?"

"I know little more than you do, I'm afraid," Ida said. "There's probably much the Warden must do before leaving."

"I wish you could come with me."

The healer offered Namél a faint smile, and drew her into a hug. "I wish I could too, but my place is here for a while longer." Ida kissed her on the cheek then took a step back, holding Namél's shoulders with her hands. "There are others who need my help, as small as it may be."

"You are a light in this place, Ida. Never forget that."

The older woman looked away, tightening her lips. Her eyes briefly glistened. "You're a good girl."

"We will meet again one day," Namél offered.

"I hope so. Maybe in the east."

Namél tried to mirror Ida's wry smile, but it felt weak. "Maybe."

"In the meantime," Ida added, lifting Namél's chin so that their eyes met. "Don't let them bring you down."

Embracing the other woman once more, Namél said, "Would you be willing to do something for me?"

"Name it."

"Do you have access to Ward 12?"

"I think I can manage."

"There is a young woman there," Namél explained. "Her name is Opal. She has red hair. Can you give her a message for me?"

The healer met Naméls gaze with a knowing grin. "I'll find a way."

The next morning, before dawn, Namél sat alone on the bed, already dressed. She had been awake most of the night with troubled thoughts.

A key slid into the keyhole of her room's door, and the lock was released. She leapt out of bed and backed away toward the window, retrieving a candlestick as she went. If Nabilak had changed his mind, she would not return to the prison cell below. Gripping the candlestick, she was prepared to break the window and leap outside to her end. It would be useless to fight the guards.

The door opened.

Three silhouettes filled the space of the hall outside the room. Upon sight of her, they hesitated. A woman took a step forward. She was not dressed like the two guards. Her more rugged cloak and gear suggested a long journey ahead. She was shorter in stature, with hardened facial features, and skin a shade darker than anyone Namél had met. Strands of braided black hair were gathered up in a bun on top of her head.

The woman watched Namél with dark, calculatingly eyes. "It is time," she said, with a slight accent. "Are you ready?"

The voice was familiar. The eyes were familiar.

"The Captain is waiting," the woman added.

Where had Namél heard that voice?

The woman watched her calmly, her hand resting at her side, gripping the hilt of her sword. If the moment of their leaving Tïrmen Prison had truly come, Namél did not want to hinder it. So she slowly put the candlestick down and stepped away to retrieve her cloak from its place over one of the table chairs. She put the cloak on while the woman waited at the center of the room with eyes that never left her movements. The two guards remained at the door. With the cloak secured, Namél grasped the single strap of her bag, which was waiting on the table. Ida had helped her pack it days before.

"Please." The other woman indicated the bag. "Allow me."

Namél passed the woman her bag. Receiving it, the latter then stepped aside to provide a path to the door. With her heart pounding, Namél walked toward the waiting guards, who stepped back to make room for her in the hallway. Once in the dimly lit hall, she paused between them and turned to look back at the room as the other woman exited, promptly closed the door, and moved past her.

"Come," she said.

Namél followed her while the two guards walked a few steps behind.

Outside, the sky had lightened to a bleak gray with a hint of pink shortly to come. Twelve mounted knights waited in the central courtyard. Servants moved between them, carrying gear and provisions. Most of the knights appeared ready to depart. Nabilak stood next to an unclaimed mount, stroking its neck while talking with a man she had never seen.

Doubt penetrated her thoughts once again. She prepared herself for the worst. Yet when they reached the gathered company, Nabilak greeted her with a reserved smile and motioned her toward another available horse.

"Ketash, help her up," he commanded Namél's female escort.

"Yes, Captain," Ketash replied, offering Namél her hand.

Namél ignored it and mounted the horse expertly on her own.

Ketash said nothing, but studied her a while longer before securing Namél's bag behind her saddle. Seeing that gaze and watching the woman's movements, Namél realized why she was familiar. She remembered the room in the central prison, and the long nights. She remembered the Watchman. Having secured the bag, Ketash glanced up then walked away toward her own horse.

Yes. Here was the Watchman.

"Ketash is accompanying us," Nabilak explained, noticing Namél's gaze. He mounted in one fluid motion and settled himself on the saddle with the reins between his fingers. He looked over at Ketash, who nodded in readiness, and then back at Namél. "She will keep you safe, making sure you do not get into trouble."

Namél shifted her attention away from Ketash, who had noticed her staring. The Watchman's presence concerned her, but more so it angered her. She had not forgotten the pain inflicted. She could not. The scars would not let her.

"Are you sure you want to bring this whore with you?" The stranger stepped between Nabilak and Namél. He was a large man with a grim demeanor. She guessed that he was Nül, the new prison warden. He raised an eye to look up at her in cold appraisal. "She'll only become a burden. Why not leave her here? I'll see to it that she's not forgotten."

"We have already discussed the matter enough," Nabilak replied, not looking at Namél or the new warden. "My mind is set. She comes with me."

"But who gave you permission to do so, I wonder," Nül persisted with the trace of a sly grin. "I know who she is."

Namél's heart began to beat furiously. She looked ahead, past the courtyard to where it led across the drawbridge, down a ramp, and became a winding road to the city's southern gate. She wondered if she could make it the whole way on horseback without being caught. Probably not, she concluded with an edge of despair, recalling her last failed escape. There would be too much distance to cover.

"I have served Siligen faithfully," she heard Nabilak say. "Namél is mine, to do with as I will. King Dwairian would not disapprove." He leaned toward the other man. "You would do well to remember that he and I have a certain . . . understanding."

Nül nodded, but was clearly unconvinced.

"She is coming with me," Nabilak stated, "and that is the end of it." He tapped his heels into his horse's side and began to move forward. Ketash followed closely behind.

Just before Namél did the same, she saw Nül watching her intently.

"We'll see," he said.

She glanced away and urged her mount forward. The knights followed in two columns behind. The company passed through the inner and outer ward gates. The red orb of the sun shone just beyond the eastern hills to the left as the dull clapping of horse hooves echoed across the drawbridge, down the ramp, and onto the lower city streets.

Namél kept her eyes forward, not looking back at the central keep as the morning rays rose to warm its weary stone. She had seen the keep plenty of times before. Its images, sounds, and smells were burned into her memory. She was tired of it.

In the city, groups of prison inmates began their daily labor. She noticed a group of tall figures with bark-like skin: the Boldei. She saw them and dared to hope that she could leave such a regulated, contained life behind—that she could be free. Ahead, the road turned and revealed the final hundred yards to the outer city gate.

It was so close.

As the gate creaked open, something cracked within Namél's heart. The company rode through the gatehouse to the open dirt road, which cut across the plain. Her eyes moistened for the first time in years. No tears fell, yet a door had indeed been opened. A weight fell from her as she went. She knew it was just the beginning, but it was a beginning she had long hoped for. New opportunities awaited her. She had merely to be patient and attentive.

Slowly, the looming presence of Tīrmen diminished behind her. All the while it watched, called to her even, but she did not listen and did not look back. Its history was marked on her skin, even inside of her. While she knew she might never be free from its memory, she would at least be rid of its presence.

There are songs of the open country that have been forgotten:
  The delight of sunshine amplified by the dancing melody of a stream,
  The chorus of leaves accented with the whistle of birds,
  The groaning of tree boughs in a warm breeze,
  The quiet of night under the serenity of moonbeams.
  Between the spaces there is the howling of a wolf. Are you distant or near, lone
wolf? Do you call to me, weep with me? What do you say?
  I will come and follow you. Just give me time.

The company rode at a steady pace, reaching Hamath in seven days. Having not ridden for years, Namél felt sore the first few days, but gradually reclaimed what had once been second nature. All the while, warm days of riding and cool nights of being wrapped in her cloak beside a fire merged as a new kind of temporality.

She kept her hood down low as the company approached the outskirts of her hometown. From the shadow of the hood, she watched the townspeople going about their work. She recognized some of them, but most faces were unfamiliar. Much of the town had been rebuilt, and more was under construction. Though Hamath had not yet reclaimed its former beauty, it appeared to be approaching a time when it would exceed it. Its walls and streets, even its people, now felt foreign to her. She realized she could never live there again.

Flanked by his personal guard and a few attendants, Malech welcomed their company in the town square. To Nabilak he said, "Let us know how we can make your stay as comfortable as possible, Captain."

"Thank you, my lord, Steward." Nabilak dismounted then indicated his companions. "This is Ketash Masanor, my personal bodyguard."

Standing beside Nabilak, Ketash bowed her head.

As Nabilak indicated Namél, she felt her heart tighten with disdain. Malech's hair had grayed, and his skin had weathered, but the firm haughtiness in his eyes remained unchanged. Before she could protest, Nabilak drew her hood back. "And this is my mistress, Namél."

She focused on maintaining a courteous demeanor, bowing her head as a façade of respect. All the while she concealed the scar along her jaw with the edge of her hood. She did not want the steward to have any reason to think she had been a prisoner of Tïrmen. She did not want him to remember her.

"My lady." Malech took her hand and kissed it. It was difficult not to recoil from his touch. He looked at her thoughtfully for a time, his eyes searching. "She's as beautiful as any I've ever seen," he said to Nabilak. He took a step closer to Namél, lowering his voice. "You seem familiar." He assessed her further. "Have we met before? In Girion perhaps?"

"My lord, you are too kind." Nabilak calmly guided Namél's hand away from Malech's.

As Namél brought the hood back over her head, Malech watched her a moment longer before returning his attention to Nabilak. "But of course. Pardon me, Captain. You're all tired from your journey. Accommodations have been prepared for you in the central keep, and your knights will find space prepared in our barracks. I'm afraid it's nothing as grand as you're used to in Girion, but the rooms are warm and the food is good. My chamberlain will show you to your quarters."

"We appreciate your hospitality," Nabilak replied.

The next afternoon, Nabilak's new command of Barorians arrived. Their lieutenant was frustrated by the delay, having expected to arrive a few days prior. He was a gruff man named Zürishek whose attention seemed entirely bent toward military matters. His brown beard gathered beneath his chin in four different braids only added to his hardened demeanor. He never spoke with Namél, and hardly looked at her. She did not mind.

They left Hamath early the following morning.

Her heart sank as they passed the land that once belonged to her family. She did not recognize it at first. A small military outpost had been constructed where her family's home used to be, the fields around it muddied by activity. Perhaps it was better that way. She was not sure how she would feel if she saw a new ranch bustling with the peaceful prosperity she had once known.

Nonetheless, the heaviness of grief lingered within her for many days.

She tried to focus on the long journey ahead. As they rode, she overheard Nabilak and Zürishek talking about how the company would follow the road down to the Talus West, which descended the high cliffs known as the Bulwark of Enisön. From there, they would cross the Storming Plain toward the northern stretches of Dunwood until finally reaching the city of Zirgalath. Though she was not yet sure what their destination would bring, with each step and each mile, there was a sense of growing possibility as a new world introduced itself.

She had heard only a few accounts of Siligen's southern vassal kingdom, most from Ida. The people who comprised its three clans were said to be a tougher breed of Illiri, more akin to Rodaním than Siligen—more crude than cultured. Yet despite the opinions voiced by soldiers in Nabilak's company, she was resolved to form her own conclusions. The reputation of the southerners appealed to her, for she thought of herself as no civilized creature. She had been called an animal, and had been treated worse, so resolved to scorn Siligen's so-called refined ways.

"Only two clans remain of the original three," Nabilak explained to her as they ascended the road to Zirgalath. Zürishek and the company of Barorians followed close behind them. "Sedwarke, the first clan, which dwelt south of here near the middle stretch of the mountains, was destroyed early in the war because it refused to join our cause. Now only Zirgalath and Magog remain." He glanced over at Ketash.

Ketash's eyes remained fixed on the road, her expression mournful.

Not far ahead, the citadel of Zirgalath came into view. Soon, Namél saw the entire city contained within the embrace of its outer wall. Chapped snow patched the shaded areas of the surrounding hills and forest, while just beyond the city loomed the tall Kurshment Mountains. Thin clouds swirled and glided lazily over the ridges and peaks. She had never seen mountains so close before.

One could disappear in such a place.

"Look to the left." Nabilak pointed. "Do you see the gap between those two peaks?"

Namél nodded. Zürishek, who was riding beside them, glanced at the spot with mild interest then returned his attention to the progress of the company.

"That is the Northern Pass," Nabilak explained. Since leaving Tïrmen, he spoke to her more often about general matters. "Beyond it, on the other side of these mountains, lies a vast desert we call the Wasteland. Perhaps one day I can bring you up to have a look."

"I would like that," she replied. Yes, opportunities for escape were increasing with every step.

They rode up the final rise to the main gate, passing a few columns of soldiers marching on foot or horseback. Nabilak's company was halted by a group armed with halberds. Over their chain mail they wore black tunics lined with white.

Nabilak and Zürishek rode forward to speak with the group's leader, but Namél could not hear what was being said. Assuming that it was all a matter of preliminary formalities, she returned her attention to the mountains to consider how to vanish within their high rocky folds.

Days passed into weeks, during which Namél was confined to a room with one small window. A guard always stood outside the door. Most often it was the Watchman, who did so diligently, quiet in her obedience, though not without a shade of resentment. Namél wondered about the true nature of Ketash's relationship with Nabilak.

Nabilak came to her only twice during their first weeks in Zirgalath, little more than an apparition in the night. She asked about his work, trying to gather any information she could, but he shared little that was helpful. The third time he came, having returned from the Northern Pass, she decided to try another approach.

"Why is the Watchman here?" she asked.

In a half-conscious, muffled voice, Nabilak replied, "Ketash keeps us safe."

Namél stared at the silhouette of his face. When the room suddenly brightened with moonlight, she saw that his eyes were open and staring at the ceiling.

Inhaling deeply, he sat up, rubbed his face, and exhaled slowly. "If you must know, I saved her life—during the war, outside the walls of Tärm Tower.

She led a company from Magog that fought alongside my unit." He yawned. "She claims to be indebted to me. I have tried to release her from such a pact, but she will not be swayed. She says her honor will be measured by the fulfillment of her vow."

"Is that why you have her guard me so closely?"

"You are precious to me."

"Why?"

After a moment of silence, he replied, "My mother."

She was startled by the response. "What do you mean?"

"Mind you, I hardly thought of her as my mother." He settled back against his pillow. "To me, she was just Fenna. She said my father was a military man, some noble, but I never knew him. I tried to find him once, which is what brought me to Girion—to King Dwairian." He glanced at her. "Fenna was a prostitute: lusted after, abused—mostly for money, but sometimes by her own choice. She tried to live a normal life with a few of them—there was a lord, Goreb, and later a baker, and then a blacksmith—but it never worked. Fenna and I often found ourselves a step away from living on the street. I did what I could to support her, to defend her against the cruelty of men like Goreb, but she considered me a nuisance. She claimed to want nothing from me, yet was always quick to take what I had."

Namél did not know what to think of this sudden openness. She was not sure she liked it.

"Fenna had quite the appetite," Nabilak continued, pensively. "She was not tender with me, except when she felt lonely . . . or hungry. . . . She used me to . . ." He shook his head. "At the threshold of manhood, I finally came to recognize her manipulative behavior, and left." With his forefinger, he traced the thick scar descending from the corner of his mouth. "She is probably dead now. I tried to find her after the war—out of guilt, I think. A part of me grieves that I could not save her; for she was strong, resourceful, a survivor. She could have been a great woman if circumstances had been different." He looked at Namél. "I do not want you to end up like her."

"Like her?" Namél sat up, pulling the sheet to her chest as a barrier.

Sitting cross-legged, Nabilak shifted to face her. "You both have endured so much." Gently, he took Namél's hands into his and studied them.

It remained difficult for her not to recoil from his touch.

"Fenna believed in the Canta," he said, "in the idea that she could defy death. No matter what happened, she asserted her freedom—that no one could claim ownership of her."

Still confused, Namél asked, "And you think I am the same?"

"Yes," Nabilak replied, "and that is what I love about you. King Dwairian has helped me see the truth. He is more than a king; he is a prophet. What has long been dead in the minds of our people is being reborn, yet with new understanding. It is not about the afterlife, but the potential of the present. The Canta and Dryden are symbols, you see. They represent the spirits of man and woman."

Namél had not expected their conversation to shift in this direction. It recalled her talk with Ida, though Nabilak's fervor rooted itself in a far different motivation.

"From the legends," he continued, "Dwairian has helped us understand that women embody life and prosperity, a kind of liberation. Such a beautiful vision has long been associated with the Canta. Yet her power is limited; her knowledge must be protected by a greater force: the Dryden, the spirit of mankind."

"But what about death?" she countered.

"Death is the natural order of the world," Nabilak explained. "We are learning to control such order—to control ourselves and overcome death. Too many people interpret the legend of the Dryden and Canta as a message of some supernatural conflict in the afterlife, but the legend is meant to point us to immortality in *this* life.

"Dwairian is reconciling Illirium, which begins with each of us—each man and woman. The relationship of the Dryden and Canta is about creating unity through order and balance. That is the way to Gedáronith, to paradise, and it is something we can attain in *this* life. If each of us fulfills his or her role, the mysteries of nature will be unraveled and the secrets of immortality found. You are knowledge, Namél. I am strength. Together, we can overcome death. It has already begun. Dwairian has found a way."

Namél was astonished by Nabilak's conviction, and more so by the strangeness of his views. While she knew that the changes in Hamath, including the new expectations placed on her sex, were a result of Dwairian's kingship, she now began to understand how he justified his purposes. Could there be a more compelling vision than a means to conquer death, whatever that meant? She thought of Nabilak's words to her in the central prison. Did he truly believe he had saved her, despite the fact that he had been the instigator of her torment? What knowledge did he want from her?

"What does all this have to do with your mother?" she asked.

"You are not listening," Nabilak said sternly. "Like you, Fenna longed for liberation. But liberation is founded upon stability, and she failed to find a truly stronger force. The men she knew were weak. None was worthy of her. Do you not see? That is where you and I can be different. I saved you from destruction." He caressed her cheek. "Now, you have to do something for me. . . . You have to save me."

Save you? The thought baffled her. "How am I to save you?"

"I have only been with one other woman." His tone grew eager. "But you are purer than her, more resilient. You embody the fullness of the Canta's potential. You can cleanse me of the past—free me from my own frail ignorance." His hand slid up to rest at the base of her neck. "I have made you a new woman. Now you can make me a new man. Together, we can be whole." His grip tightened. He pulled the sheet away, pressed her back, and shifted his weight onto her. "Hold me."

Stiffly, hesitantly, Namél placed her arms around Nabilak. Guessing that the other woman had been his mother filled her with a new level of uneasiness. What did he really want—to continue an abusive relationship, except with a reversal or roles; or to purge himself of it?

His breath was hot in her ear as he whispered. "I was not sure before, but I am now. You can provide me with the knowledge of eternal life. You can give me a son, the first of a new line. That is how we foster immortality, for a child provides an identity that can be carried from generation to generation. Bear me a son and you shall go free."

What?

Was this another game, or would he really let her go? More importantly, what would a child mean to her? She had resolved not to be bound to Nabilak; a child would change that irrevocably. Even if she willingly gave him what he wanted, and even if he released her afterward, he would retain a tangible part of her. There would be a kind of everlasting imprisonment in that. Her child would be his, theirs. Could she bear that? Could she abandon her child to him? And what if she bore a daughter? No, she could not let the cycle of abuse continue. Nabilak could not be trusted. She would not be his savior, mother, or whatever he wanted. She would be the one to decide her future. She would resist.

She pressed against his chest with her arms, trying to push him away, but Nabilak was powerful. He struck her into submission, to the point that she nearly lost consciousness. She cursed life for not making her physically stronger.

"It is time for change," he growled, holding her wrists above her head, pressing one of his knees into her thigh. "We must redeem each other."

The present had to be surrendered once again, she realized, like before in the prison cell. So to save her strength, she went limp. What else could she do? If she resisted too fervently, Nabilak might return her to Tïrmen Prison. She had sacrificed too much to be free of its walls. She would not undo that progress. Unable to resist Nabilak's external power, she prayed that the life inside her would repel his advances. Somehow, she had managed to do so during the previous months. Could she not do it again?

Something new appeared in Nabilak's eyes as he raped her. There was hunger, like a torment that he sought to satiate by physically overpowering her body. Or was it her will that he wanted? She began to perceive a kind of helplessness in him, a lack of control. Could she use it against him?

Still, with every blow, every defeat, the light outside diminished. She tried to console herself that Nabilak could conquer her body, but not her spirit; yet she perceived that the light, her window to freedom, was being further closed off, brick by brick, doubt by doubt. That her spirit was dying. Against this fear, she wondered if giving Nabilak a child would be so bad after all. She had already abandoned her dignity; could she not also abandon a child for her own sake? Or would the cost to her conscience be too great?

What power did she have? There no longer seemed to be a choice between defiance and submission. To survive, there was only submission.

How much longer? she cried to the silence. *How much longer before there is nothing left?*

Months passed, but she did not trace time beyond a chain of half-conscious nights and days. She found that the less she resisted, the less violent Nabilak's domination. Day after day, exhausted from the night, she slept. Yet it was not a restful sleep.

Though Nabilak had not come to her for about a week, the ghost of his fists still struck her. The initial bruises had healed, but the ache remained. Nightmares replayed her suffering. Even death had abandoned her. Only a narrow pillar of light from the outside lingered. She reached for it desperately, kissing its feet, pleading for mercy.

The door of her room creaked open. Nabilak stood at the entrance, watching her with mild disdain. Rising from where she lay, she looked back at him with as much fire in her eyes as she could muster. Yet she felt so tired.

Ketash stood behind Nabilak, but there was a third person as well. Nabilak shifted to let him enter while Ketash remained outside the doorway.

The old man wore white robes. The wrinkled lines of his face pointed to blue eyes that beamed with compassion. He approached Namél slowly, with his hands folded together at his waistline. At her bedside, he knelt to meet her gaze. She sat up, leaning back against her pillow, while keeping her attention on his hands as they came to rest on each of his legs. While he continued to study her, she just watched his hands.

"I am not going to hurt you," he said. His voice sounded quiet and gentle. He extended a hand to touch her head. As she tensed, his hand withdrew with a gesture of assurance. "I will not hurt you, child."

Nabilak took a step forward, but faltered as the old man firmly motioned for him to stop.

"My name is Diachtoris," the old man said, not averting his attention from

132

Namél. "I am a healer. I was born in Girion, but live and work here now."

"He is the best in Arizaleth," Nabilak said.

"I understand that you are unwell," Diachtoris continued, ignoring Nabilak. "Your husband has asked me to examine you."

Her eyes glanced at Nabilak for a moment. *Husband?* He looked at her sternly, threateningly even. She looked back at the healer, noting the shimmer of his white hair drawn back loosely behind his head. Kindness resonated from his tan, beardless face. She nodded in assent.

Diachtoris turned his head partially to the side, addressing the other two. "Wait outside, please."

Nabilak appeared ready to protest, but the healer turned his head completely, his face so stern that Nabilak nodded and withdrew.

"We will not be far," Nabilak said, closing the door as he went.

When the door clicked shut, Diachtoris returned his attention to Namél. Once more, he extended his hand toward her face. As she strained to not jerk away from his touch, he again assured her of his intentions. She closed her eyes as his hand came to rest against her forehead. The coolness of his palm felt enlivening against her throbbing head. He removed his hand from her forehead, lowered it to her bruised cheek, and then guided her head to turn slightly. He studied one of her eyes, turned her head once more and studied the other eye. He then took her left hand in both of his to inspect. When he was finished, he placed her hand gently upon her knee, inspected the other hand, and then focused back on her eyes.

"You have a mild fever," he began. Though immensely weary, she was transfixed by the brightness emanating from his seasoned eyes. "With some rest you will recover soon."

"I have been unable to sleep," she said. Her voice sounded hoarse.

"I can give you something to help with that. It is a simple herb. Dissolve it in hot water then drink it to help relax your body." He straightened his posture. "Could you lie down for a moment?"

She hesitated.

"I know that Captain Nabilak is not your husband," Diachtoris said. "I can guess what you are to him, and what you have endured."

She looked at him pleadingly. "Help me."

He sighed. "I wish I could do more, but my efforts would be futile. I am old and you are exhausted. There are too many soldiers and too many guarded passageways. To say nothing of the challenges winter poses in this region."

She lowered her eyes. She had reached the same conclusions, but hoped for more.

"Let me at least treat you, child: help you recover—see that you are made well. Please." He motioned to the bed. "It will take but a moment. I just need to fully assess your condition."

She relented.

He helped make her comfortable, placing a pillow behind her head as she leaned back. "Please lift your gown up to your chest." Noticing her questioning glance, he explained, "I know that Captain Nabilak desires a son from you, and that you have been unable to conceive. I must give him some kind of explanation. I can help you in that."

She nodded, pulling her gown up to expose her bare body. At the sight of her, the old man's eyes winced slightly. His jaw tightened. She wondered what he thought of all the scars and discolored spots that decorated her skin. As he carefully felt around her stomach and upper groin, his eyes stared ahead as if picturing what he could not see—what was underneath the skin. Finally, he nodded and helped her pull the gown back down. She rose to a sitting position as he sat near the foot of the bed with a hand holding his chin in quiet consideration.

"You have suffered more than I first imagined," he said with a weight of sadness. "I am ashamed of my fellow man." He looked back at her. "I hope you find a way to escape, and that you can one day forgive us and find peace. There is strength in you yet."

Hope meant little to her now. What strength was there left? "Is something else wrong with me?"

"Remarkably, it appears that only the surface has been damaged," he replied. "I do not know how you have managed to avoid becoming pregnant. It may be a result of the strain your body has endured. I have examined Captain Nabilak as well, and there is nothing wrong with him—not his body anyway.

I do not think you are barren, though it is possible. Perhaps there are other forces protecting you, helping your body resist. I wish I knew. But I pray that you find the means to keep enduring, and that you find what you are looking for."

She did not understand. "What I am looking for?"

"We are all looking for something, child," Diachtoris replied. "May the Canta guide you."

She studied the healer's pensive expression, listened to his words, but did not know what to say.

He placed a hand on her knee then rose and strode to the door. With a hand on the door handle, he paused to glance back at her. "Truly, I will pray for you." He looked away. "Forgive me for not doing more."

He opened the door and shut it behind him. She watched it close as if time had slowed: the dull sound of its creaking hinges reverberated in her ears, the sharp sound of its wooden edges abruptly stopped by the stone doorframe. She felt her heart shudder; felt a pang of hope, but also a chill of despair. Then she felt nothing. Emptiness returned to enshroud her. It brought a sense of calm.

She heard voices being raised outside the door.

A while later, the door opened. Nabilak entered while Ketash waited silently in the hallway. As the captain approached, Namél gathered her knees tighter before her.

He looked at her with a blank expression, save for a hint of firmness. "The healer told me to be gentler with you; that the stress you have endured has kept your womb closed—that I am to blame." He shook his head. "Very well, I say. I will give you another chance to give me what I want. I will even do it on his terms. 'She must be allowed to recover,' he said. 'Her body must heal. She must be allowed more fresh air and exercise. She must, she must, she must . . .'"

Shaking his head, Nabilak grinned scornfully—or so his scar made him appear. He drew closer to her and, with a hand lifting her chin, brought her gaze up to meet his. "Very well." His voice was quiet, but fierce. "One. More. Chance. Fulfill what I expect of you—what the world expects of your sex. This is not about pleasure. It is about legacy, about a new beginning—a new order. King Dwairian has decreed it. You have been defiant, Prisoner 43-1-12, and you have been punished. I gave you a new name, but you have only shown contempt for it. This is your last chance to atone for your crimes."

He released her chin and stood back, turning away to speak to Ketash. "See to it that she is ready." Nabilak glanced back at Namél. "We leave before dawn."

"Where are we going?" she asked.

"You will see," Nabilak replied.

She glanced back at the Kurshemnt Mountains only once as they descended from Zirgalath. The mountain range was like a wall dividing her from a distant unknown. She regretted that she had not been allowed to see the potential of the Wasteland's vastness. Had she missed an opportunity?

Nabilak and his new second, Lieutenant Gamon, a young man with blonde hair, rode in front of her, while Ketash rode behind. Zürishek was to remain in Zirgalath. She listened to the sounds of the company's progress—the steady rumble of horse hooves and wagon wheels. A thin haze of dust churned around them, bronze in the morning twilight. Its dry smell encouraged her somewhat: the scent of a journey—the prospect of freedom.

Yet with it there was a growing unease within her heart. She did not know where they were going. Were they returning to Tirmen Prison? She thought of Nül, the new prison warden, and imagined a slow wasting away. She would not go back.

She determined to be more aggressive in seeking a way of escape. But the thought felt vague, weak. It seemed too intangible. She could no longer survive on the prospects of the future. She had to focus on the immediate, to take all she could from its grasp. She would steal more from the present, even if only the crumbs beneath its table—any opportunity. Though it might not be much, it would sustain her until the time of liberation. She had to keep her resolve sharpened: fangs that would strike first at the master's heel and then at his throat when he bent over to crush her.

She would be free, she vowed.

One day soon.

Sunlight swiftly, almost imperceptibly, flooded the Dunwood Plain. As the company descended from forested hills, the open space stretched out before them like an ocean of hazy gold. Namél glanced back at Ketash who studied her with solemn eyes. Namél sometimes felt like the Watchman could perceive her thoughts; so she turned away, burying her hopes deep within the untilled fields of her heart.

Days later, the company stopped at the northern rim of the Divide, a long rocky ridgeline that separated the Dunwood Plain from the Storming Plain. As they made camp, Namél noticed a young woman guiding her horse to where the other mounts were kept. Wearing a white cloak lined with silver fur, the woman looked out of place among the grim, dirty warriors all dressed in black and gray. Namél considered her beautiful, but hardly more than a girl. Though the young woman's long blonde hair and white skin were elegant, hers was not so much a beauty of appearance as that of youthfulness—freshness. The young woman gave little attention to the armed men moving around her—as if unaware of their true, destructive power. Her expression and mannerisms suggested that such things were part of life and not to be examined or questioned. That each element had its place; one could do nothing more than accept them and carry on with the few pleasantries life offered.

Nabilak appeared beside the young woman and helped tether her mount. He smiled as she offered him the harness. The smile lingered as they spoke. The young woman acted shy in his presence, but presented her own smile. It all looked so innocent, a mockery of the truth that Namél knew about Nabilak. Having tethered the horse, he took the young woman's hand and led her away through the camp.

"Who is she, Ketash?" Namél asked, knowing her bodyguard had been standing behind her the whole time.

Hearing no response to her question, Namél glanced back and was surprised to see in the other woman's gaze, which followed Nabilak and the young woman, a shade of disapproval. Yet it was only the hint of such emotion. Her eyes quickly darted back to focus on Namél. She stepped aside, indicating with her extended hand that Namél proceed.

"Your tent is ready." Ketash's other hand remained, as it always did, fastened around the hilt of her sword.

Namél walked beside the black-haired woman toward the center of camp where a small canvas tent had been prepared. A guard stood outside, and drew the flap back as she approached.

"We depart at sunrise," Ketash commented.

Namél nodded and ducked under the open flap.

While Namél removed her dusty outer layers, shaking them out before placing them over a single chair at one corner of the tent, she listened to the sounds outside: horses grunting, men talking quietly, metal pans and wooden utensils clanging against each other in anticipation of an evening meal after a long day's ride.

A gentle breeze stirred. Daylight diminished. Namél walked to the entrance of her tent and lifted the flap back just enough to glance outside. A violet glow lingered across the land, warming the tents and faces in the camp. She released the tent flap just as the guard stationed outside looked back at her.

She washed her face and neck with water from a bowl, and then approached a small, iron fire pit, which was fastened to a stand and ground plate near the center of the tent. Inside the cauldron-shaped framing danced the flames, their speech playful and crackling. Sitting down on her cot, she removed her boots, and then pulled off her breeches and tossed them onto the chair. After massaging some of the stiffness from her thighs, she straightened her long ivory undershirt down to her knees and crawled under the blankets of her cot.

Lying back against the pillow, she stared once more at the amber flames in the fire pit. They seemed to be looking at her—like the face of some lambent spirit.

"Is that you?" Namél said, though the presence did not feel the same as before. Had she imagined the Dryden, or was it mocking her in a new way?

A different voice whispered to her thoughts. Its presence felt warm and encouraging. "Patience, Rhoda," it said. "Patience. You have a long road ahead."

"Who are you?" she asked, all the while her eyes became heavy. She felt herself welcoming sleep.

"Rest now," the voice said, mixing with the gentle whisper of the flames. "Rest. . . . A time is coming."

When Namél awoke, her heart pounded from a dream she could not remember. She also longed to be held, cradled with real love, to not feel so alone against the night. The thought of night filled her with images of Nabilak, however. His treatment had nearly overwhelmed all previous memories of touch—from her parents, Jed, Opal, anyone good.

She no longer wanted to be held.

Rubbing the sleep from her eyes, she sat up and listened. A stream trickled nearby. Tree boughs creaked in the breeze. An owl hooted. Gradually, the memory of the last few days returned to her: vague hours covering vague distances. The company had crossed the Storming Plain, passed through the heavily-guarded Talus West of the Bulwark, and entered Enisön Forest. Northward they journeyed. Soon, they would pass near Tïrmen Prison.

The thud and sizzle of collapsing firewood drew her attention to the fire pit at the center of her tent. Her heart leapt as she saw a figure sitting cross-legged beside it, carefully stirring the embers with a stick.

"What are you doing here?" Namél demanded.

The Watchman did not acknowledge her, but focused on reviving the flames. Gradually, the light in the tent grew, pressing back the shadows from her profile. Her thin sword rested on the floor in front of her.

She turned to Namél. The two women stared at each other, for a moment locked in quiet focus. Namél would not let herself retreat from other's steady gaze. Eventually, Ketash lowered her eyes, returning her attention to the fire.

"Where I come from, in Magog," Ketash began, "discipline is the highest virtue."

What?

"It is not a cold thing," Ketash continued, "like a mountain of rock and snow, but grows full of life. Like water to a tree, discipline allows us to reach toward the limits of the sky. Discipline is the wellspring of my culture: our habits, craft, even dreams. Yet I see from your expression that you do not understand. Let me share with you a saying among my people; perhaps it will provide clarity. Discipline, we say, is dictated by duty, while duty is dictated by discipline. It is a balance of choice and perspective."

"Did Nabilak send you?" Namél asked.

"No," Ketash replied. "Yet I see my words still trouble you. Consider then obedience: it is the highest discipline, duty in action, therefore the highest form of virtue—to family, clan, ruler, or any who gives us life. It is how we find serenity. Without obedience, the tree of possibility dies from decay. Without it, we lose our way of life." She looked at Namél. "You have lost your way, 43-1-12." She returned her gaze to the fire. "That is why I punished you. That is why you are still a prisoner."

Namél did not know what to say.

"No matter what you think of the Captain," Ketash continued, "he offers life, only asking for obedience in return. Before he saved me, I looked to death for salvation; but life desires more from me, and I must obey. I know it can be cruel. No matter what a person gives, life takes more. It picks at and removes the scabs before wounds can heal. I know this, for I have given . . . and lost. I have buried so many; none are left to bury me."

"What do you want?" Namél asked. She recalled something the Watchman had said over a year ago in the central prison, something about stillborn children. What kind of grief had this woman been forced to bury?

"I now struggle to meet your eyes," Ketash replied, "Not for shame, I think, but because I see you will never understand. You are infected by ignorance."

"Why are you speaking to me like this? Why are you here?"

"Yes," Ketash said with a brooding tone, "why. Why, after so few words have been shared between us, and those few muffled by a mask of torment." She straightened. "I am trying to tell you, 43-1-12. It is because you and I each have a duty to serve the Captain until proving worthy of the life he has saved. His command is our obedience. Therefore, stop robbing life, and fulfill your duty. You can free us both. Balance must be maintained, and if I must fell another beautiful tree to do so—another woman reaching beyond her limits—then so be it."

Namél could not dissociate the Watchman from the room of torture in the central prison. Too well, she remembered the endless anguish. She could still feel the marks on her body.

A word took form in her mind. She spoke it with cold composure: "Leave."

Ketash's eyes wandered to the ground as if to deliberate, but then she nodded and stood. "I do not expect you to pardon my actions." Her voice hardened, conveying a kind of defiance. Or was it grief? "Nor do I need your forgiveness. . . . I did what discipline dictated."

"Get out," Namél urged, firmer than before.

Ketash watched her for a while longer without moving, as if wishing to say more. Namél stood from her cot to threaten the other woman, trying to emit more courage than she felt. Ketash remained calm, but alert, her left hand gripping the sheath of her sword. Her eyes rose to meet Namél's, but then lowered again. She backed away to the entrance of the tent, not raising her eyes—as if in reverence, and finally turned sharply, ducking through the tent flaps to disappear into the night.

Namél's heart beat furiously, and her legs trembled. She sank to the ground and leaned against the frame of her cot. She wanted to cry, to release the tension of confusion and pain, but could not. Defenses kept her from breaking down. She would not give anyone the pleasure of hearing her weep.

The cold air and ground saturated her bare legs and thin undershirt. She pulled the blanket from her cot, wrapped it around her body like a cloak, and crawled closer to the fire. Its warmth slowly saturated the blanket and moved around her like a tender arm. She welcomed the warmth, yet knew it would not last.

She could trust nothing.

Letting the blanket drop away from her shoulders, she reached back and felt the scars through the thin cloth of her undershirt. She could never forget

141

what had happened. She must not. Memory would serve as armor against attack, allowing her to survive.

Yet had Ketash done the same? Had pain pressed her to not only fortify her heart against the ache of grief, but against any feeling at all? The woman from Magog had become a cold thing, bound by duty—an impersonal, abstract concept with little humanity left. Furthermore, she had hurt Namél, and who knows how many others, to consol herself and claim some form of purpose. Was that the inevitable outcome of defiance born from rage? Did it suffocate any goodness that survived the trauma? Was Ketash a warning of what Namél could become?

Namél thought about the men she had killed, and how she had killed them. Had she gone too far? Was she indeed lost?

What way was she meant to follow?

The tension in her stomach eased when she realized they would not pass by Tïrmen Prison. Even fifty miles seemed too close. Though she never saw it, its proximity haunted her like a predator roaming the shadows beyond a ring of light. She sought distraction by observing the landscape, yet the mist-shrouded woods at either side of the road did little to warm her spirit.

She did not know what to expect of their destination. Some soldiers were overheard talking about a new military outpost—Valon Fortress, they called it. Nabilak had not spoken to her since leaving Zirgalath. She wondered why he wanted to bring her along. If she could not bear him a child, what use was she to him? Unless he only kept her to fulfill some base urge. But if that was true, why not pursue the variety that prostitutes could offer? Not that she wished them such a fate.

A white-clad figure caught her attention. Namél had not seen the young woman for many days. She marveled at how immaculate the woman looked. Her posture conveyed refinement and confidence, whereas Namél felt slouched and haggard. She looked down at her attire, at the worn fabric of her gray cloak.

"Hello." It was a bright woman's voice.

Namél looked up to see the young woman addressing her, offering a friendly smile.

"My name is Vera."

Did the young woman know anything about her?

"My uncle is King Dwairian." Vera continued to look at her expectantly. "What is your name?"

Namél stared ahead for a time, wondering how to answer. At last, she said, "Just call me Namél."

Ketash rode close behind them. Though the Watchman looked elsewhere, she was clearly listening to their conversation. Well, let her listen, Namél thought. Most of the company rode ahead of them, while further back, the supply wagons lumbered on noisily.

"I have wanted to meet you," Vera commented, reclaiming Namél's attention. She seemed about to say something more, but then quieted as if thinking better of it.

"How old are you?" Namél asked.

"Seventeen."

Seventeen. So much had happened by the time Namél entered that cursed year. Had four years really passed since then? "I was orphaned at your age."

Vera received this information with a blank expression, as if unable to comprehend it. Namél studied her evenly, and felt a rising resentment. "This is no place for royalty" she added. "Why are you here?"

If Vera noticed the belligerent tone, she did not show it. Her self-assured, smiling demeanor continued to thrive, much to Namél's annoyance. Yet Vera hesitated to speak, as if unsure how to protect her inner bastion of innocence against the harsh prospect of Namél's reality. "My uncle, the King," she began, "wants me to marry Captain Nabilak. He wishes to reward Captain Nabilak's faithful services rendered during the war, and for the many years given to Siligen since. They are close, my uncle and he."

Faithful services, Namél thought bitterly. She glanced back at Ketash, but the other woman did not notice. Instead, she was looking to their right, scanning the misty ridgeline of an adjacent hill.

A horn sounded ahead, startling everyone to attention. The company was called to a halt.

143

Namél watched Lieutenant Gamon ride from the front of the column halfway down the line to where another officer awaited instruction. The latter nodded then turned his mount and rode down the remainder of the line to the rear.

"Bring the wagons together," the officer shouted to the drivers. To other riders present, he added, "Form a perimeter."

"What is going on?" Vera asked to no one in particular.

Ketash rode up beside the two women and directed them toward the gathering wagons. Meanwhile, Namél noted that the foremost company, about a third of the entire Barorian contingent, detached itself and followed Nabilak swiftly ahead down the road. Another third, led by Gamon, had left its horses on the road and was moving with spears or notched bows up the surrounding hillsides. The remaining soldiers encircled the supply train.

"What is going on?" Vera whispered again, this time to Namél.

"Quiet," Ketash said. Having dismounted, she helped Vera down off her mount. "You too," she added to Namél.

Ketash indicated that Vera and Namél leave their horses and crouch beside one of the wagons. The mounted Barorians surrounding the wagon faced out with their shields and spears held before them in anticipation. An inner circle waited with readied bows.

"We're too exposed," an archer commented, but was quickly silenced by his commander.

A light rain began to fall, still bearing a cold touch of winter.

Namél drew her cloak closer about her, wondering whether her chance for escape had come.

Vera's expression was wide with fear. She spoke to Namél with a hushed, urgent tone. "There are rumors of increased rebel activity in this region. They have been resisting my uncle's northern expansion." Trembling, she watched the forest. "Many Alöweans refuse to acknowledge that the war is over, or else they seek retribution. I hear there are even Illiri among them."

"Be silent," Ketash urged.

The soldiers on foot reached the crest of the bordering hills. There they stopped and looked around, uncertainly.

Namél listened, focusing left to where the road continued around the base of a darkening hill. For a moment, she thought she heard the distant clang of metal, but it was muffled by the sound of an approaching rider. The officer in charge of defending the supplies rode forward.

The rider said, "Lead the wagons on toward Valon Fortress. There's a lesser road branching off from the main just ahead. If you hurry, you should be able to reach the fortress before midnight."

"Is the way safe?" The officer asked.

"It's the safest route available," the rider replied. "Captain Nabilak will keep the enemy away from the road as you pass, and Lieutenant Gamon will direct a second force to protect your flank. There are a lot of rebels in the forest ahead, and it is getting too dark to locate their positions in the trees. Hurry. More of them may be moving to outflank us as we speak."

"Understood," the officer replied. He turned to the waiting Barorians. "Let's move."

As his riders reformed their column, with some falling in line at either side of the three wagons, the courier turned his mount and rode hastily back the way he had come.

It was not long before the supply column was progressing steadily. The officer sent a few scouts ahead to mark their way. Meanwhile, the sky's last light faded. When the column reached the point where the side road split from the main, they found three dismounted Barorians—from Nabilak's command, Namél guessed—waiting to direct them.

Her heart beat expectantly. It would not be difficult to disappear into the wilderness, she realized. Yet the Barorians were all around her, and Ketash rode particularly close, keeping attentive to her movements. Could she break through their line unnoticed? Was this indeed the right time?

She hesitated, and then cursed herself.

Maybe I am just a coward.

Vera continued to tremble beside her. To someone like her, the journey to Valon Fortress might have felt like a limbo of heightened senses and imagined enemies in the darkness, but to Namél it was only a breadth of time. To her, it was a night brighter than any she could remember, filled with an anticipation of the end, of imagining all that could be if she dared to believe and actually act on it. That was the true challenge. In a way, she was calmer than everyone around her; yet in another way, she was more apprehensive. It was not the rebels she feared. No, her fear was more elusive. Her fear had been present far longer. She began to wonder if she feared freedom.

She glanced at Ketash's stoic, watchful gaze.

Perhaps it was the fear of a finalizing failure. She could not risk it. Not yet.

They arrived well past midnight. The terrain of the lesser road was difficult for the supply wagons. One had to be abandoned due to a broken axel, but the soldiers managed to quickly disperse its stores to the other two wagons.

In the darkness, Valon Fortress appeared to be a dark and lifeless place. It was mostly comprised of wood, its outer wall surrounded by a narrow, flowing moat. It was not a large outpost. As the castellan welcomed Vera, Namél overheard him mention King Dwairian's plans for its improvement. Apparently, the fortress was meant to guard the Valon Bridge, the main crossing to the untamed land of the north, a land still contested by the so-called rebels.

While the castellan escorted Vera away, Ketash brought Namél to her room. The room was plain, containing little more than a crude bed, small table, and chair. Namél only wished there was a window. She felt uneasy in confined places.

She had been in the room for half an hour or so, staring absentmindedly at its single source of light—a large flickering candle contained within a metal lamp on the table—when her door opened abruptly. The noise of its shuddering startled her.

Nabilak stood motionless in the doorway, his expression grim. She had not expected to see him so soon. As he strode forward, coming further into the light, she noticed that he was covered in dust. The black tunic worn over his chain mail was torn in a few places. A splattering of dried blood stained his chest, but did not appear to be his. She glanced at his sweat-stained face, his expression still hard, then down to his bloodied hands. One hand rested instinctively around his sword hilt. He stank.

Calmly focusing on his face, she asked, "Why are you here?"

"What?"

"Why come to me instead of your young lady?"

"Do not call her that," he growled. He turned away, but then seemed confused.

"Why are you here?" she repeated softly, mockingly.

Nabilak turned around and struck her across the face. Her vision blurred and she hit the ground with her back against the bedside. Her cheek stung, but she did not raise her hand to it. Nabilak knelt down and pressed his hand roughly against her neck. It became difficult to breathe. She tried not to panic as his grip tightened around her throat.

"Never mock me." His eyes bore into hers. "*Never.*"

He suddenly relaxed his hold, as if checking himself, but then pushed her back against the bedside. "You contaminate me." He rose and took a step away. "You are like a disease, or a weight at my ankle. Why did I bring you here?"

Calmly, she held his gaze of contempt. "I have wondered the same," she replied.

"I have a company under my command," he said, looking away, "and now this entire garrison. I lost good men tonight, caught a glimpse of the enemy's ability to hurt us. Yet returning here and seeing you . . ." He shook his head and clenched his fists. "All that I could think about was you—whether you were being watched, whether you could escape. Some of my men are dying from their wounds as we speak, yet I had to make sure you are secure." He continued to stare at her. "Damn you Namél, Prisoner 43-1-12 . . . or whatever you are."

She tried to rise, but became lightheaded and could only lift herself onto the edge of the bed. Sitting there dizzily, she tried to keep her attention on Nabilak. Seeing him remove his belt and place it resolutely on the table, she felt her heart sink, engulfed by a weary dread.

He approached and shoved her onto her back. Like a frenzied animal, he pulled her clothes off, ripping them in places, desperately surrendering to his actions as if wanting it all to be over as much as she did. Sweat, dirt, dried blood—everything mingled together. She did not bother fighting back. Doing so would not purify her, she concluded.

Instead, she focused on the revelation that she was a wilderness in which Nabilak discarded his detritus. His escape to the shadows was a means to temper his fury, to do what even he could not accept in the light. To him, she was not a real thing, but some well of wickedness. The well did not come from within her—he did not seek her true self, what she could really offer—but sought to dig his own space in which to store his corruption. Perhaps by that, he also sought to obtain some kind of freedom. But he was addicted to wickedness, or knew no other source of meaning, returning to it again and again as if to be quenched. She felt a sudden sense of power in his helplessness, in how he looked to her for liberation.

But there was also emptiness.

What was she to do with such power? Was this surviving anymore, or just the final erosion of her spirit? Had she survived the prison only to die slowly in a wasteland? Would immediate death have been a mercy?

She struggled to contain the pressure of despair within her heart. Tears filled her eyes. She could not think clearly, could not find the resolve to keep her spirit from collapsing. The tears flowed, but only for a short while. Then even they were no more. There was nothing left. She felt Nabilak's weight lifted away; felt herself lying there exposed, bare of dignity and hope. She no longer had the will to move.

"Damn you," he said over his shoulder as he stepped away from the bed, adjusting his trousers. He retrieved his sword belt and walked to the door. She heard it open, saw him pause, lean his head against the left frame, and then walk away.

Before the door closed, Namél glimpsed the silhouette of Ketash watching her from the hallway.

The walls of Namél's room could not keep out the brightness of the day. She felt warm air seeping through the narrow spaces between each thick, horizontally set log. After a moment of delirium, she sat up and realized that she was lying under the covers of the bed; furthermore, that she was wearing a fresh undershirt. Her body even felt clean—at least superficially. The clothes from her journey were nowhere in sight. She looked around and noticed fresh clothes set over the chair next to the table. Drawing the covers back, she slid to the edge of the bed, and placed her feet against the cool wood floor. She actually felt somewhat revived, a surprising sensation, though not without a sense of bewilderment. Shaking the thought aside, she walked over to the chair and got dressed.

At her door, she was more startled to find no one guarding her room. The door was unlocked and the outside corridor vacant. She proceeded uncertainly, choosing the direction that offered the most light at its end.

Somehow it all seemed familiar. She passed a few servants who ignored her. She passed an armed guard wearing a black tunic lined with gray, but he also ignored her. At the end of the hallway an open door waited, saturated with white light. She could not see what lay beyond, but stepped through undeterred.

Coming out onto a porch, she felt immediate warmth cover her body. She closed her eyes against the blinding light and stood there for a while, reminding herself what the summer sun felt like. The fragrance of fresh life stirred all around her. Were those flowers nearby? She listened to the joyful clap of leaves singing with the soft breeze, heard the rush of a waterfall and the flow of a wide river.

Opening her eyes, she saw a land bathed in sunlight. To the right, beyond the lower gatehouse of Valon Fortress, a grassy plain descended to a hill of tall conifers interspersed with deciduous trees. She noted a few birds flying happily by. Their song nearly brought a pang of joy. To the left of her position rested a sizeable body of water: Lake Valon. She traced its shores to where it flowed down into the Menelmachar River.

A stone bridge connected the river's northern shore with its southern twin. Across the bridge, a stone tower guarded its entrance. Its counterpart was the fortress surrounding her. The bridge appeared inactive save for a pair of guards walking away toward the keep.

149

Drums sounded nearby. Someone pushed passed her and descended a stairway connected to the porch, which was built halfway up a central tower made of stone and wood. It stood at the center of a palisade-protected motte. Guards patrolled the wall walk of the encircling palisade. The sound of drums came from within the bailey where most of the fortress' activity appeared to be focused.

Descending the stairs, she walked down the motte, through the stone gate and across the lowered drawbridge into the bailey courtyard. Surrounding the courtyard were stables, a barracks, and a few other workhouses and living quarters. Most of the inhabitants' attention was directed toward the center of the courtyard. She walked forward, but kept behind the crowd.

Nabilak stood on a large platform. Two naked bodies rotted in small cages, which hung from gallows at the far corners of the platform. One of the bodies clutched at life, its eyes exposing the man's faded spirit. Namél's stomach tightened.

The drums became silent. Four black-hooded figures held a pale limp form between them. Nabilak asked the man for information about the rebels. The man said nothing. His breaths were shallow, his eyes tired. The crowd was mostly comprised of Valon guards and Barorian riders. Many called out angrily to the man. Some mumbled to each other bitterly about the state of the campaign against the rebels, how many had lost friends, brothers, or fathers in the conflict.

"Punish the traitor," someone shouted. "Give him justice."

Others in the crowd voiced their agreement, but most watched with an air of detachment; for they had seen the spectacle countless times before.

Namél shuddered at the memory of being held before the mob in Hamath.

As the prisoner ignored Nabilak's questioning, the captain nodded to the four hooded figures and turned away. The limp prisoner was placed on a blood-stained table, his limbs secured. Horses facing opposite directions stood idly next to the platform. Namél felt her heartbeat rising. She spotted a table of cruel-looking tools and devices. She had seen this happen before, she realized—numerous times, and in various forms. She felt her limbs going numb.

How long have I been here?

She felt sick and turned away, stumbling back toward a nearby well, the rim of which she grasped for steadiness. A pitiful cry erupted behind her. The crowd murmured approval. The cry became a scream of agony. It continued and was followed by gasping sobs. She plugged her ears, but it did little to muffle the echo that remained in her mind. She collapsed, wanting to vomit, but could not.

Hands suddenly held her shoulders and helped her to rise. She turned to face the source, but retreated when she saw who it was.

"Get away from me," she mumbled.

Ketash held her hands up reassuringly. "I am not going to hurt you."

"Do not touch me."

Namél did not care that others were beginning to notice. She saw Nabilak saying something to Gamon. The lieutenant motioned for two guards to follow him as he approached her. Ketash noticed them coming, turned and spoke to them.

Meanwhile, Namél backed away. Before anyone could stop her, she turned and ran unsteadily back up toward the central fortress, not thinking about where she was going.

Someone called after her.

A stairway appeared. She ran up it, yet the palisade stopped her from continuing any further. Leaning over it, she gasped for breath, staring at the water that lapped against the rocks below. She thought about jumping, but then a hand grasped her arm and pulled her away. Collapsing, she did not look at the Watchman's face.

She could not think, and could not breathe. Invisible hands covered her ears, silencing her world. Black clouds swept into view. She felt herself sinking. Then there was darkness.

A dense forest.

Someone calls. Hope? Goodness? Love?

I try to shout, but cannot form words.

Where are you? Do not go. I must find you, must know that you are real. Please.

151

Do not leave me here alone. I need you.

Wait.

I am coming.

"It is time."

Nabilak's face came into focus. There was a trace of concern in his eyes, but it was quickly lost in an expression of firm resolve.

Namél found herself lying on her bed. Nabilak sat at the edge near her feet. She looked at him blankly.

"I cannot have you here any longer," he said. "You only complicate things: all that I wish to be and do. . . . Vera is pure, and offers me what I seek. With her there is hope of a new beginning. I am going to marry her, Namél. It is what the King also wishes. He knows about you now. It may have been Nül who told him, but that no longer matters. You and I are done."

"What will you do with me?" she heard herself ask. The words seemed distant, as if spoken by someone else.

"A few think you should be sent back to Tïrmen Prison, while others . . ." Nabilak shrugged. "In a way, I think you have paid for your crimes; however, I lack the authority to declare such a verdict. That is why I sent an appeal to the King. You are fortunate, Namél. He has chosen to be merciful. You will return to Hamath and serve Lord Malech."

An ache accompanied the thought of returning to Hamath, especially Malech. It would be like returning to the start. No, she would not go. It was time to be rid of them all. She had delayed long enough.

"You leave early tomorrow morning," Nabilak concluded. "Ketash will ensure that you reach Hamath safely." He looked at her with a glance that seemed marked by grief, reluctance, and relief all at once—all at war with each other. "This is the last time you and I shall speak." His voice staggered somewhat, his posture slouched. "This is my farewell."

He stood and stared at her for a while longer. She did not meet his gaze, but instead stared blankly at the foot of the bed. He moved his hand out to touch her foot, which protruded beneath the covers, but then withdrew it, turned, and walked away.

She neither thought nor felt anything as he closed the door behind him.

There was a knock on the door.

She did not reply.

It was early morning, and she had slept little. Her mind had been restless, disregarding the weariness that permeated her body. She could not stop thinking about escape. Considering the nature of her confinement the last three years, she wondered if it would be easier to escape from Malech in Hamath than Ketash. Yet Hamath was deep within Siligen's growing empire, and a long way from Rodaním. Once again, there were few options.

The door opened.

Ketash stepped inside, wearing black attire. "Are you ready?"

Already dressed, Namél retrieved a small satchel that contained a winter cloak and extra undershirt. Holding the strap with her right hand, she brought it up over her shoulder.

Ketash indicated the trunk of clothing, which Nabilak had given Namél. "The Captain wants you to take it."

Ignoring the remark, Namél strode forward to the door where the Watchman waited. Keeping a hand on her sword hilt, Ketash nodded and backed through the doorway into the hall. Two armed guards were waiting outside the door. Namél followed them.

With the guards in front and Ketash behind, the four of them walked down the silent corridor. A few burning torches mounted on the wall were the only source of light. At a nod from Ketash, the guard at the end of the hall opened the door then moved aside to let them pass.

Outside, the air was warm. The indigo sky brightened in the east, causing a few scattered clouds to glow red. To the north, the waters of Lake Valon were as still as a mirror. A bird's lonesome call echoed across the lake.

They descended the steps from the central tower and continued down the motte. The crunch of their footsteps on gravel sounded intrusive to the pre-dawn serenity. The drawbridge was lowered for them, and they crossed over to the bailey. As they proceeded toward the stables, Namél tried to avoid looking at the new bodies hanging from the gallows above the courtyard platform.

Ahead, horses were held ready. Five Barorians had already mounted. They conversed in groggy tones, but quieted as Namél approached. Three stared at her, while the others did not even look. Gamon stood nearby with two guards at either side of him. Namél wondered if he was relieved to see her go—an excess presence, a distraction.

Ketash offered Namél a hand, but she ignored it and mounted herself. Unfazed, the Watchman climbed onto her own horse and motioned for the small company to move. Gamon nodded to Ketash in farewell as they passed. Once they reached the outer gate, it took a few moments for the bridge to be lowered, and soon they were descending open countryside. A breeze blew.

Namél glanced over her shoulder as the bridge rose back into place. A silhouette atop the gatehouse caught her attention. He did not move. Like a sentinel of the night, Nabilak stood there somberly watching her depart. Looking away, she continued to feel his eyes on her until the road brought them into the cover of the woods. Only then did she begin to feel some ease, though a feeling of emptiness lingered. A piece of her had been taken, and could never be reclaimed—three years of her life lost behind her.

The company proceeded swifter than she had anticipated. In the late afternoon on the third day, she heard the guards talking about their intent to reach the Enisön Plain by nightfall. "We shouldn't camp in these woods," one said. Ketash agreed.

Namél decided that it would be too risky to wait until she reached Hamath. What if Malech kept her as confined as Nabilak? She was done being a prisoner, and would not give Malech the pleasure of her servitude. Escape had to occur before they left the protection of the forest. Recalling her old map, she guessed that the wilderness of Gigor was not far to the north. If she pushed herself, she might be able to reach its river border in two days on foot. The country along the way was said to be rocky. It would be difficult to pursue her on horseback. Considering the threat of the rebels, how far would they dare pursue her into the northern wilderness anyway?

She would wait until the sun had set, hoping that darkness would aid her for a change. It would end that night. One way or another, it would all end. She prayed for more strength than she felt.

The sun seemed slower in its descent than ever before. For hours it appeared to hover over the horizon, keeping the sky bright above them through the trees. But at last, the shadows lengthened.

The company stopped to water their horses at a pool beside the road. Ahead, the way bent around one last hill. Beyond that, Namél glimpsed the forest's final descent to the Enisön Plain. They had gone farther than she had anticipated, and would leave the forest before dusk.

There was no more time to delay.

She glanced around with her eyes, trying not to draw anyone's attention. Two of the guards were stretching their legs ahead while their horses were being watered by a third. The other two had already done so and stood watching the road behind them. Meanwhile, Ketash cared for her mount. For the moment, no one was looking at Namél.

Her heart pounded.

Was this the moment?

Now, her instincts urged. *Now!*

Her heart nearly burst as time slowed. For a few steps, she did not breathe and her muscles did not respond. But then time returned and, without looking at anything else, she ran away from the pool into the darkening forest.

Someone shouted behind her.

Time became a progression of breaths and quick decisions. She ran faster, focusing on the terrain ahead—focusing all her strength on each step and drive of her arms. Her lungs burned at first, but soon found a rhythm. The movement felt invigorating. She could not recall when she had last felt so free.

She ascended a hill and briefly relaxed her stride as she descended into a small dell, which then rose again into an adjoining hill. She maneuvered over and around rocks, heard commotion behind her, but did not dare look back. The light now faded quickly, details becoming consumed by shadow.

Turning left, she ran along the gently-curving ridgeline of a hill. An arrow whistled by her ear and thudded into a tree. Startled, she increased her pace, surging ahead with all the power she could muster. Her limbs began to tire, yet still she ran.

She nearly tripped, first from a root and then a rock, and then almost lost her balance after failing to anticipate a dip in the ground. She countered the pain by telling herself that it was nothing, nothing compared to what she had already endured—to what she would suffer if caught. Yet fatigue crept into her consciousness. Her mind was strong, but her body was not conditioned for such a prolonged effort.

Move, she pleaded with her body. *Do not stop.*

The sky shone bronze and violet overhead. She cursed the sun, wondering where the night was, which had come so quickly and often before.

As she reached a meadow bordered by white aspens, pain suddenly gripped her right calf. She collapsed, gasping for breath, but forced herself back up using her arms and good leg. Limping for a few steps, her vision spun and she fell again; her chest pounded unmercifully, and her thighs cramped. Gritting her teeth, she grasped the shaft of the arrow protruding from her calf, intending to pull it out, but the effort made her entire right leg throb with pain. Pressing her face against the grassy earth, she cried out in agony.

Footsteps grew louder behind her. Ahead, the sound of horses' hooves entered the meadow.

Two sets of gloved hands seized her arms and lifted her to her knees to face the Watchman.

"That was very foolish," Ketash said, the sweat on her brow glistening in the twilight. She gave her bow to one of the dismounted Barorians. Another crossed the meadow toward them, leading the four other horses.

Ketash struck Namél across the face.

Namél looked at the other woman while the sting lingered on her left cheek.

Ketash shook her head, sighing. "I do not understand you. You were given a way to fulfill your duty and restore your name." She stared at the sky. "What should be done?"

The Barorians glanced at each other warily.

The Watchman looked back at Namél. "I know what it is to return home without honor, and how difficult it is to depart the past." She exhaled slowly. "The Captain told me that after I leave you in Hamath, I am free to return home—that I will have fulfilled my vow." She tilted her head. "Maybe it is so, but what now? There is nothing for me in Magog."

"What are your orders?" One of the Barorians asked, nervously adjusting his grip of Namél's arm.

"We need to get out of here," another said.

Ketash inhaled deeply then turned around. "Break the shaft."

The arrow was swiftly broken. Namél clenched her teeth against the pain, but could not stifle a cry. Nausea overwhelmed her.

"Bring the prisoner," Ketash said.

As they brought Namél toward the horses, an arrow hissed past her head and struck the throat of one of her holders. With a startled, gurgling cry, he released her.

She hit the ground.

The horses neighed. Another guard began to shout something, but his call ended abruptly. Namél looked over and saw the first Barorian lying next to her grasping at the arrow lodged in his throat, choking on blood. Another Barorian lay beyond with an arrow protruding from between his shoulder blades. He tried to rise, but collapsed and did not move again.

Dark shapes flooded the meadow from every direction. Most bore notched bows aimed at the one Barorian still standing. Namél could not locate the other two.

"Surrender," someone said. Namél heard other voices speaking Alöwean.

Swiftly, as though gliding through the grass, Ketash approached her nearest assailants. Her thin curved sword was drawn, both hands holding the hilt up at her shoulder. A swift stroke cut one figure's bow in two, and a second cut the breath from his throat. She turned to her next target—four more figures, all wielding spears—yet each fell before the woman from Magog.

More rebels materialized from the shadows—all hooded and masked, many of them a foot taller than Ketash. Namél wondered why they did not shoot the Watchman, until she saw them motioned back by a lone figure who strode to the center of the darkening meadow. He held a short sword in his left hand. Ketash turned to face him, her thick black hair undone and flowing. The tall figure removed his cloth mask, revealing his faint red complexion, pointed ears, and eyes as silver as the moon.

Ketash calmed her breathing, assuming a battle ready stance with her sword. The Alöwean continued to advance, but stepped to the side as if to circle around and measure his opponent. The Watchman did not wait, but lunged forward. Apparently anticipating this, the Alöwean parried the thrust of Ketash's blade and proceeded to divert every attack. After a while, Ketash's movements began to slow, her initiatives growing more desperate. Long black tresses shifted around her shoulders with each movement. Thin strands stuck to her perspiring face. All the while, the Alöwean remained calm and precise in his movements.

Ketash attacked anew, but the Alöwean's blade deflected her sword downward and sliced sideways faster than she could retaliate. She tensed then fell to her knees as the Alöwean took a few anticipatory steps back.

Namél felt something tremble within her as she watched it happen—almost like grief. She could not control the emotion, not even as her mind clung to hatred of the other woman under whose gaze she had suffered so much. Namél felt a pressure in her throat, her breaths shallow.

On her knees, unsteady, sword blade stabbed into the ground as if to hold herself up a while longer, the Watchman slowly turned her head to meet Namél's gaze. As the last light of day shone from Ketash's gray eyes, Namél thought she caught a trace of contentment. But then the light faded. The woman from Magog fell onto her side and lay silent, one hand gripping the hilt of her sword while the other grasped her stomach. The glint in her eyes was gone. No more would she be watching.

Namél suddenly felt exposed, vulnerable. She lowered her head to rest on the ground, dizzy with pain and confusion. The Alöwean knelt down beside Ketash's body and studied it for a moment. He then glanced up over to where Namél lay staring at him.

"Barenen shé," he said quietly to the shadowed figures gathered around her.

158

Namél felt hands gently lift her off the ground, felt herself slipping into a current of diminishing sensations. Pain reverberated from her calf, but she was drawn more to the sound of soft voices. Floating, she perceived the woodland swaying around her; felt the threads of the present coming undone as she passed out.

Soft footsteps over damp earth. Hushed voices: quiet, louder, and then quiet again. A wider silence lingers—not empty or belligerent, but peaceful.

Wilderness, will you let me sleep a while longer?

Birdsong: whistling staccato—joyful sounds, forgotten sounds. Little birds, I envy your wings: cheerful things of color and summer.

My heart no longer believes. Every root has been pulled out. Only dried soil remains: black night fading into bleak oblivion.

I cannot see.

I feel paralyzed. The air is damp, but warmth caresses my face. It comes from somewhere ahead. I try to crawl; it is all I can do. Through a stone cave of shadows I crawl.

"She was sleepwalking," a muffled voice said.

She felt herself being carried by many hands.

"What are you going to do with her?" another asked.

Her eyes flickered open, but she only perceived vague shapes looming above her in a dimly lit space. They were moving her down a passageway of jagged rock, a few dim lamps lighting their way. She closed her eyes. Her hands and feet felt cold. Her leg throbbed.

She felt herself lowered onto a soft surface. A heavy blanket was laid across her and tucked up to her chin, her hands and feet warming under its embrace. A hand held her head up while another carefully guided a cup to her lips.

"Drink this," a woman's voice said.

The warm liquid flowed down her throat and dispersed into her body. She opened her eyes to see someone crouched down beside her. The woman's face was little more than a silhouette, but Namél could trace its smile of compassion.

"Rest now, friend," the woman said with a kind tone.

Namél tried to lift her head.

The woman guided her head back. "You are safe. Rest now, and dream in peace."

Namél closed her eyes and let her body relax. She felt the softness beneath her, the embrace of the pillow. She felt a hand upon her forehead. Its cool touch lingered, calming her spirit.

If more awake, she might distrust it—she could not trust it, for goodness did not last. A hand that offered kindness could also take it away. For the moment, however, Namél let herself receive its comfort. She was too tired to do otherwise.

The darkness returned, but she felt no malice in it. From somewhere beyond echoed the song of a waterfall dancing upon rocks. For the first time since she could remember, she slept without dreaming.

"You may remove that from her eyes."

The cloth was untied and lifted away. Darkness was replaced by blinding brightness, which dimmed to rich colors: blues, greens, and browns. Gradually, details came into focus. Namél stood in a clearing surrounded by what appeared to be a labyrinth of tall, white rock formations. Moss and vines covered the rock. Gray trees towered all around, some growing from the rocks. Clouds hovered above, visible through the canopy of green leaves. The air felt warm, but dampness lingered with a breaking mist.

At least a hundred people surrounded Namél. Most were men, but some women stood among them. They were all clad in colors that resembled the forest. Many wore cloth masks. All appeared to be scrutinizing her, some standing with their arms crossed. She recognized Alöweans among them, a head taller than their Illiri peers. Their red-tinted skin and pointed ears also provided a marked contrast. It was difficult to guess their ages, for Alöweans were said to live many centuries. She wondered how much these ones had endured.

"Welcome."

She turned to face the speaker, and recognized the Alöwean who had slain Ketash. He now sat on a crude, high-backed chair fashioned from a large tree stump. His white-blonde hair was gathered behind his head with a cord, and the color of his eyes now seemed to match the clouds in the sky. Though his face was stern, it was also gentle. His crimson brow furrowed as he studied her.

"You may sit." He indicated a mat on the ground in front of her.

Namél remained standing, despite the ache in her calf.

"You were in Tïrmen Prison, were you not?"

She did not answer.

"Though the number on your jaw has been removed," he commented, "the scar suggests as much. Marked like livestock." His jaw tightened for a moment, and he glanced away. "Shameful how the living can devise such cruelty." Focusing back on her, he leaned forward. His voice softened. "What is your name?"

My name? She hesitated, avoiding his eyes. Caution arose. "I do not know." A pang of defiance returned. "It does not matter," she added, her voice growing stronger. She felt like an empty vessel, with nothing to lose. "As you say, my scars speak louder than any name. Whatever I once was, I am no more. . . . I need no name."

The Alöwean leaned back. His hands pressed against each other, the tips of his fingers held in front of his lips. "Do you know who I am? Who we are?" He motioned toward the others.

She looked around to note the expressions in the crowd, expecting distrust and scorn, yet really there was only curiosity. Had something changed, or had she merely misread them earlier?

"You are the rebels," she replied, returning her attention to the main speaker. "You resist the kingship of Dwairian."

"Indeed." The Alöwean smiled faintly, though his eyes bore some sadness. "Yet we are much more than that. We are Pernor Hunters, Illiri soldiers from the Bulwark, and citizens from every end of this vast land. We fight to preserve what should not have changed—that which cannot change. We fight to contain the violence, to prevent it from consuming Illirium and beyond." He indicated her with his hand. "We fight to prevent more people from being branded and scarred. And what is more, we fight to heal the wounds of the war, which will not happen if that false king's ambition is allowed to expand. In short, we are the new Guardians."

He stood and began to approach her, but she stepped back. He paused and raised a reassuring hand. "I do not think you are an enemy, nor do I think you are merely a victim of what we strive against. I discern power within you, and that encourages me." He motioned around him. "It encourages all of us. Those who have been subjected to Siligen's retribution, sent to places like Tïrmen Prison, rarely survive. Even those who manage to leave its walls often come out broken beyond mending. But you . . . yes, you give us hope. How do I know this?" He offered Namél a smile. "A friend of yours has told us much."

"A friend?" Namél felt her heart stir. "Who?"

"Opal," the Alöwean replied. "You will see her soon." He returned to his place on the tree stump.

"She escaped from Tïrmen Prison?" Namél pressed.

"She was released. But I will let her share her tale. Her memory has served us well. Despite her abuse, Opal remained attentive while imprisoned. There is much we have learned about the Tïrmen of today, though there is much we already knew—that not even Dwairian knows. After all, the city was once ours."

He stared past her for a while, but then shook the thought aside. "Yet this is unnecessary talk." He stood again, placed his hand on his chest, and bowed his head in respect. "My name is Hectiliath." He indicated an Illiri man who stepped forward with a limp in his right leg. "And this is Theanor. He will ensure that you have all you need."

Theanor's eyes were dour, lined with weariness, but his posture stood firm and commanding. His black hair and beard were lined with gray.

"You may move about the camp as you like," Hectiliath added. "But you may not venture beyond its border alone or without permission. Trying to escape would be foolish." His tone lightened. "Now, I must attend to other matters." He bowed again, turned, and walked past the tree stump out of the clearing. A number of others followed after him. Everyone else murmured to each other, shifting their attention to various tasks.

All the while, Theanor watched Namél, not having moved since his first appearance.

A younger man came beside him, and whispered something in his ear. He appeared to be around Namél's age. A thick scar began at his left hairline, passed through what remained of his left eye and ended at the base of his chin. The scar formed a line through his mustache and beard. He watched her expectantly from his remaining eye, brown in color, as if he knew her. It made her uncomfortable, so she followed Theanor as he walked over to sit by a fire.

"Are you hungry?" Theanor asked, getting comfortable. His voice was gruff, but not unkind. He stirred the contents of a pot hanging over the flames. "I will take that ravenous gaze of yours as enough of an answer. Here." He served some of the steaming bean and meat stew into a wooden bowl. "Have as much as you like."

She ate gratefully, unable to recall eating something more savory—as if senses long dormant were being reawakened. Theanor watched her with mild amusement before serving his young companion, who had joined them. A few others approached, three men and two women, all of them Illiri, to share in the meal. One of the women brought a large loaf of bread and passed it around.

After the meal, the others dispersed, including the younger man with the large scar. As the sky darkened, Namél remained with Theanor in quiet contentment.

He stared solemnly at the fire, occasionally stabbing its dying embers with a stick. "So, where are you from?"

"I was born in Hamath," she said quietly.

"Were you there during the war?"

She said nothing.

He did not seem to mind.

"The war took a lot from us." Firelight reflected on Theanor's eyes as he spoke. "I was born in Zirgalath myself, but I have not been there for—practically a lifetime. I no longer know the place, or its people. . . . Have you been to the south?"

"Once."

Theanor nodded. "So much destruction," he said, more to himself than to her, "and so much treachery. . . . I do not know how any of us survived. And for what, I wonder." He assessed their surroundings, raising his eyes to the treetops. "This is now our cause. We ally with the land against a new age and its players." He glanced at her. "How long were you in Tïrmen Prison?"

"Long enough."

He nodded gravely. "I admire your resilience. What did you say your name is?"

She did not answer.

He looked away, unfazed. "If you should decide to join us, you would be welcome." He stared at the flames. "Everyone has a role here. All belong." He wiped his face. "But you need not decide now. Your leg has to heal. You should go rest." He pointed. "There is a tent over there prepared for you. If anyone tries to bother you, they will have me to contend with."

Noting the place, she said, "Thank you," rose and walked toward the edge of the clearing where a small tent had been set up beside one of the white rock walls.

She passed a few shadowed figures and ducked down under the tent. It was little more than a thick canopy hanging from a single line. In the fading dusk, the firelight danced softly on the white stone beside the tent and on the surrounding trees above. A mat had been set with a blanket folded on top of it. She lay down and placed the blanket over her. It was not yet cold enough for the blanket, but it gave her a sense of protection from the night. She lay there for a while until raindrops began to patter delicately on the canopy.

Glancing out from the tent, she saw Theanor still sitting beside the fire. He pulled the hood of his cloak up over his head before poking the embers some more, apparently undisturbed by the weather.

Turning away, she closed her eyes and found peace in the melody of the rain.

She woke at dawn.

The crisp blue sky above suggested a bright summer day ahead. She removed the blanket, folded it, and placed it on the mat before leaving the tent. Many others were already moving about the camp. A few looked at her, but none said anything or stopped her as she approached one of the gaps in the stone labyrinth.

"Friend," someone exclaimed behind her.

Namél turned and felt her heart leap at the sight of Opal walking hastily in her direction, a wide smile on her milky white face. The woman's hair was a brighter red than Namél remembered—the tresses wavier, and her eyes bluer. The number *86-1-12* still marked the skin of her right jaw.

"I'm so glad to see you," Opal said, still grinning broadly. She pulled Namél into a tight hug. "Oh, how I've missed you."

"I have missed you too," Namél said, nearly overwhelmed with a surge of joy.

"How are you?"

"Well enough. Surviving." Namél noticed Opal's bulging belly; looked at her in alarm, but tried to retain her previous enthusiasm. "You are expecting?"

"Yes, within the month." Opal's smile faltered somewhat. She pursed her lips and shook her head, as if to shake a thought away, and then forced back a smile.

Namél wondered if the child had been conceived while Opal was still in prison, a result of one of the guards. She wondered if anyone could leave Tirmen Prison without both leaving a piece behind and carrying another on. The shade of emotion that had passed over Opal's face led Namél to not press the matter. It would serve no purpose anyway.

"You remember that fella I once mentioned?" Opal asked. "The one who told me about the rebels? Well, he's going to help me raise the child—like one of our own. We got married a few months back." Her eyes suddenly widened. "I got your message—from the healer. She's a crafty old fox, she is."

"I am glad," Namél said, thankful for Ida.

Opal drew Namél close once more, and held her for a while. "The note gave me such hope, Friend. Thank you. Truly." She released her. "Shall we walk for a while? It does me good."

Assuming a leisurely pace, they followed a gently rising path through the rock labyrinth.

"The days were colder after you left," Opal commented. "Some said you'd been executed, so I feared the worst. It wasn't until I got your message that I knew you were alive."

"How did you get out?"

Opal shrugged. "Just released one day, told my sentence was up. It may've had something to do with my being with child. I'm not sure. I was supposed to go to some place in Girion for women like me, to be cared for until the child is born, but I gave them the slip as soon as I had the chance. It was Rölf—that's my husband—who managed to find and help me. He's a clever one, strong and good." She paused, lifted her shoulders, all the while smiling. "Anyway, here we are. I'm going to have this child, regardless of who her real father is. She isn't the one to blame."

"You know it is a girl?"

Opal looked away, her eyes narrowing shrewdly. "I've got a premonition." They proceeded in silence.

"So what will you do?" Opal asked after a while. "Will you stay with us?"

"I have not decided," Namél replied.

"You should stay. Please, I want you to stay. You can be here when the baby arrives."

"Perhaps." Namél felt herself withdrawing. She cared deeply for Opal, but Opal also reminded her of the prison. She did not really know who she was anymore. She needed space away from the past. She needed time. She recalled her aunt, Corine, and wondered if she was still alive.

"What is it?" Opal asked.

"I am sorry," Namél said. "I cannot stay. Not now, anyway."

"Where will you go then?"

"I think I should go east, to Rodaním."

A veil of sadness lowered over Opal's face. "I understand. I do. I remember what you said about your mother. It's important you go."

They reached the top of the rise. A limp body hung from a nearby tree. The person's face was covered by a black hood.

"Pay that one no mind," Opal said.

"Who was he?"

"A Siligen spy," Opal replied. "Rölf says there're spreading through Illirium like vermin. The Reminax, I've heard them called—special agents of the king, I suppose." Frowning at the body, she added, "This one nearly caused our ruin. We've got to be careful."

Glancing away, Namél looked at the camp below. The stone labyrinth was at the center of a dell the shape of a wide-rimmed bowl. Though well concealed by the surrounding landscape, it did not appear able to provide any sturdy defense against attack. She wondered why the rebels used it.

"It was once the foundation of a small fortress," a man's voice said from behind them.

Namél turned to see the young, brown-eyed man with the large scar from the day before. He stood a few steps away, unsure whether to come any closer. He nodded at Opal, as if they knew each other, but avoided letting his eye linger on Namél. Instead he focused, or pretended to focus, on the dell. "Some say the Elphadém built it."

"The Elphadém?" Namél looked back at the labyrinth quizzically.

"An ancient race thought to have come here before all others," he commented.

"Does this place have a name?" Namél asked.

"None remember," he replied. "Captain Hectiliath was the one who knew of it. Yet he thought it better not to give it a name. Giving something a name risks it being more easily found."

Indeed.

The young man watched her with the same piercing expression as the day before. It made her feel uneasy. She turned to leave.

"May I walk with you?" he said abruptly.

She hesitated, looking over at Opal.

"I think I hear Rölf calling," the other woman said, a mischievous glint in her eye. "You have much to talk about, I'm sure, and I need to rest anyway." She squeezed Namél's shoulder. "I'll see you later."

What did Opal mean: *Much to talk about?*

As Opal left, the man came next to Namél. He indicated that they walk further into the woods away from the dell. She said nothing nor looked at him as they went. Though a little uneasy, she did not feel particularly threatened by the man. More so, she wanted to learn why he had singled her out.

For a while, she let the soft crunch of their footsteps on the pine needle-strewn ground fill the silence, and soon heard the steady applause of rushing water. She left the man to follow its call, but first came upon a narrow creek, which she followed downstream to where it poured into a large river over fifty feet below. To the right, mist rose from the base of a wide waterfall.

"Does this river have a name?" she asked.

"It does, but I cannot tell you," the man replied. She frowned at him. "I am not supposed to, at least."

"Do you not trust me?" The edge of mockery in her voice made him tense somewhat. He avoided her glance.

"We have to be cautious," he said.

She regretted her tone, so said more softly, "I would not trust me either."

He looked back at her. "I trust you."

"Why?"

"You do not recognize me, do you?"

She looked at him, met the steadiness of his one brown eye. There was indeed something familiar about his face, but she could not identify what it was. The sound of flowing water entered her searching memory. She recalled another stream on another bright sunny day—a day long ago. She took a step back.

"Rhoda." He reached out to her arm.

She took another step back, not wanting him to touch her. "Do not call me that."

"What is it? What is wrong?"

"I thought you were dead," she said more firmly, but then checked herself.

"Jed, where have you been?"

"After the war, I returned to Hamath looking for you." Jed extended his hand once again, but she took another step. "I saw your parents' graves, and learned that you had been sent to Tirmen Prison, but I could not get a clear answer as to when. I did not think you would survive there." He hesitated. "Rhoda, I am so sorry . . . I should not have given up."

"Do not apologize." She withdrew from his hand once again, but this time her foot slipped on a wet stone. Before Jed could do anything she fell back into the shallow water of the creek. He rushed forward to help her up, but she resisted. She did not want to be touched by him. "No," she said, but he managed to crouch down in the water and place his hands under her arms. "No," she repeated, louder, but still could not press him away. His hands held her firmly despite her efforts to break free.

"Let me go," she shouted, pressing harder. "Let me go."

He released her with a look of bewilderment. She stumbled out of the water and stopped at a tree, leaning against it for stability, trying to regain her breath. Meanwhile, Jed stood there watching, his arms and hands still slightly open and extended.

"Forgive me," he said.

She calmed after a few deliberate, slow breaths. "You owe me nothing, Jed." She straightened herself. "What we shared . . . that was long ago. I am not the girl you once knew. I am not her. There is nothing of that person—nothing left. It has all been taken away."

"That cannot be true." Jed sounded like he was about to reason with her.

"There is nothing you can say to me, Jed. There is nothing you can do. I need neither your help nor pity."

As he took a step toward her, she turned away and began to run. Her wounded leg felt as though it was being stabbed every step, but she did not care. She welcomed the pain. It was what she knew. It helped her channel the confused emotions coursing through her heart and mind. Without looking back, she ran until she could run no more.

The sun shone well below its zenith when three Illiri rebels found her sitting on the edge of a cliff, which overlooked the river far below.

"You have to return with us," the leader said.

She rose to her feet.

"We need you to put this on." He indicated a blindfold. She nodded acquiescently, and he secured it gently around her head.

They walked for a few hours, which confused her. Surely, she had not ventured that far. At last, she heard the stirrings of the camp ahead. When the blindfold was removed, she discovered a different camp than the one she knew. The woods had changed, the denser volume of pine creating a darker atmosphere. To the right was a large plain. Beyond the plain, a jagged line of snow-capped mountains glowed amber from the sunset.

Her escort led her to a stone outcrop that sheltered a small fire. There, Theanor sat the same way she had last seen him the night before. As she joined him, he offered her a flask, which she received gratefully, but was surprised to discover that it only contained cool water.

Theanor smiled gruffly to himself. "It is unwise to rely on spirits to improve one's condition. They only betray in the end. Besides," he chuckled again, more to himself than to her, "We have not been able to find any for quite some time."

He offered her his plate, which contained some bread, cheese, and dried meat. She received it and ate gingerly.

Noticing Theanor staring, she paused to meet his gaze. "What?"

"Forgive me," he said, turning his eyes away. "Most of my life has been spent in the company of men, in Zirgalath and then Pernor. I am still getting used to being around women."

She stopped eating again. "What happened to Pernor?"

"Fire and ash." He studied the flames. "That is most of what I remember. And death. . . . I understand that you know Jed." He looked at her for affirmation, and she nodded. "He was under my command—still is, actually. But Pernor feels like a long time ago, though it has not been that long. . . . What is the year?"

She did not know.

"633 EP, I think," he said, quietly, more to himself. "It has been about seven years—seven years since the war ended. Some call it 'The Illirium War.'" He shook his head. "Remarkable. The war only lasted months. Anyway, that is all gone now, and time means little here. Our lives are measured by deeds." His voice quieted. "I used to know why we fight, why we struggle on and on. The enemy once seemed so clear, but not anymore. No . . . now we fight our own, fellow Illiri. These Alöweans still live in another time. Though their empire is no more, we continue to follow them. Strange."

He shook his head and chuckled to himself. "I sound like an old man, and am not even that old. I imagine that I look it, though."

"The years have been difficult for many of us," Namél offered, staring at the fire.

"Indeed." Theanor stood and stretched. "I need to sleep."

He took a few steps, but then turned back. "By the way, if you would like to bathe, there is a nice spring nearby, about a half mile into the plain. I can have one of the women show you. We even have a few bars of soap. You will have full privacy. You have my word on that."

"Thank you."

"Please," he said, staring down at her arm. "It is the least I can do."

She looked down and realized that the skin of her forearm was exposed, revealing many scars. She pulled the sleeve down.

"Pardon me." Theanor's eyes wandered away uncertainly. "Goodnight."

The soft cold touch of the stream eased her leg, though she shuddered at first entry. Standing knee deep, she observed the mountains to the north, their snow-covered peaks like spikes of pearl in the moonlight, and wondered how far the water had traveled to get to her. Did the stream continue south to join the Menelmachar River? She thought of Mirror Lake, how its southeastern shores touched the border of Rodaním; how the Elentarí River ran south from the lake into the sea, toward unknown lands. What waited beyond the sea? Was there a place for the undesired, or a place of cleansing?

A pool had formed at the western bank of the stream. Retrieving the bar of soap and large sponge that had been given to her, she knelt in the pool's calm water. Looking down at the scars crisscrossing her arms, legs, and back, she hesitated. The front of her body had not received as many marks, but she knew it had been abused in other ways. She suddenly felt agitated, and began to scrub her body roughly with the sponge. Using the soap as well, she scrubbed her scars, as if doing so would make them disappear. She scrubbed everything within reach until her skin felt raw, wishing she could clean her insides as well. Yet none of it felt like enough.

She sank into the pool, allowing its cold depths to envelop her entire body and head. Under the surface, she listened to the dull chorus of water flowing across the rounded stones of the river floor. She imagined the invisible grime of the previous years carried from her body by the current.

If only it was that easy.

The pressure in her lungs increased, yet still she remained submerged, resisting the warnings of her body. Her heart began to pound until it was all she could hear. With what little breath she had, she screamed within the depths, though little sound came forth. She did not have enough air for it.

Slowly, she rose from the water and inhaled, all the while her heart continued to pound. She felt lightheaded, but welcomed the warm night air against her skin.

The night.

I am a creature of the night.

Leaving the pool, she made her way to the center of the stream, which rose up to her chest, and then lay back with her arms extended to let the current carry her. She breathed in deeply. The stars twinkled far above. The longer she stared, the closer they felt, until she thought she could reach out and touch them.

She closed her eyes, not caring where the stream would bring her. Her limbs were going numb from its chilling touch. Perhaps the water would thrust her over a precipice onto rocks. Or perhaps she would sink slowly into its oblivion. Neither outcome would be so bad. Keeping her eyes closed, she drifted into half-consciousness while perceiving the quiet murmur of the watery depths beneath and the dry sky above.

Rhoda.

Was someone calling her, or was it another dream?

"Rhoda?" The voice was closer, more urgent.

She sensed the noisy crashing of legs pushing through shallow water. A pair of hands came around her and pulled her away from the current. She was lifted up, but could not stand. Once out of the water, a cloak was hastily wrapped around her body. She was carried a bit further before being set down on soft grass. The night air still felt warm. Her blood began to flow more freely.

"Rhoda."

Opening her eyes, she saw Jed looking down at her with concern.

He exhaled sharply, straightened, and wiped his face. "Rhoda, what were you doing?"

"Why did you have to take me from the water?" she asked dreamily, stretching out her arms while continuing to lie on her back.

"Rhoda, you scared me. I thought you were dead."

"You need not worry about me," she said, almost amused. "I have survived a long time without your concern, and I will continue to do so."

Jed sat down beside her. "What is wrong with you?"

Bitterness overcame her joviality. "I told you. I am not that girl you knew." She stared at him. "You will never understand because you were not there."

"I want to understand."

"Forget it," she said. "It is too late for that. You are a part of a life that could have been, but not anymore. To go back would be folly, and I will not go. There is nothing for me there."

"I am here," Jed countered, "and I still love you."

She looked at him incredulously then rose to a sitting position. The cloak had absorbed most of the water clinging to her body, and was slowly drying in the evening warmth. She held the cloth closer about herself then stood. The action made her dizzy at first; but after a few concentrated breaths, she regained her composure, and walked along the spring in the direction she imagined the pool to be—to where she had left her clothes. Jed followed wordlessly behind.

"It is useless, Jed," she said after a while.

"What is?" He caught up to walk beside her.

"Your love. It is only the remnant of a past that would have been forgotten had we not met again." She stopped abruptly and looked at him. "You love the idea of me, of what I once was, but that is all."

After letting the comment settle, she continued on at the same eager pace as before.

"I never stopped thinking about you," Jed offered, pursuing her.

"I do not believe you," she retorted. "Anyway, who am I to distract you from the greater purposes happening around you?"

"Greater purposes?"

"This rebellion, for example. Is it not necessary? Is it not important? A power like Siligen should not be left unchecked. None should. You believed in that once, when you chose to serve at Pernor. Do not use me as an excuse to turn away from it."

"I do believe in what we are doing," he replied, "but . . ."

She stopped again to face him. "But what?"

He looked at her in confusion, but did not have an answer. She nodded knowingly and continued walking. "I have no space in my life for timidity, Jed. It is not the way to survive."

"I do not understand."

"I know."

They reached the pool. She retrieved her fresh clothes and began to dress without waiting for Jed to turn away.

"Where will you go?" he asked, turning his back to give her privacy.

She thought little about what she was doing; only that she was finally doing something. After a moment's consideration, she knew what to do. "I am going east."

"Where?"

"Rodaním."

"Let me go with you."

"No."

"I can protect you," Jed pressed.

"I can protect myself. I made it this far."

Part of her grieved to treat Jed this way, but she knew it would pass. She also wondered if she was fooling herself. After all that had happened, could she truly protect herself? Perhaps not, but she would not harbor fanciful ideals about her relationship with Jed. It had been good once, but she could not identify any goodness to be gained from it—for either of them. It was something youthful and detached from the real world. It made no sense in the present.

Dressed, she offered Jed his cloak. "Thank you."

He received it without looking at her.

"I am sorry it has to be this way," she offered, trying to soften her tone. "You will find someone worthy of your affection. It is just not me."

"I am not sure that 'worthy' is the right word," Jed said quietly. "When will you leave?"

"Immediately."

"You are not yet recovered," he objected. "You should rest more before going. There is no hurry. You are welcome to stay with us for as long as you need."

"To stay would only mean further delay," she replied. "My mind is set. I cannot stay here anymore. Will you help me? Will you speak to Hectiliath on my behalf?"

Jed looked at her with his one eye then nodded. "Yes." He then added more confidently. "Of course I will help you."

She felt her body ease. "Thank you." She almost wanted to touch his shoulder tenderly, but resisted. It now seemed a foreign gesture to her.

"Come," Jed said, noticing her hesitation. "Let me also gather you some provisions."

They walked back to the camp.

Hectiliath assented to Namél's request.

There were no long goodbyes. Except for Opal, there were no tears or signs of affection offered before departure. It was the way Namél wanted it to be.

"Come back as soon as you can," Opal said, holding her tight. She offered Namél a green scarf with patterns of light gray thread. "I made it for you.

It'll serve well in all weather, cool or warm, maybe even help keep your scar discrete." She indicated Namél's jawline.

"Maybe," Namél replied. "Thank you."

Placing the scarf around Namél's neck, Opal kissed the side of her face, close to her eye. "I love you, friend."

The kind words and embrace pierced Namél's heart, yet for a moment she could find no words to say back, nothing born of herself. She had no tears. Though the initial feeling vanished, she willed herself to murmur, "I love you too." Opal deserved that much. Though Namél could not grasp the weight of such words, she did not consider her reply dishonest. It was an echo of goodness, all that she could give at that moment.

Nor could she quickly forget the look in Jed's eye as she left him at the edge of the wood. There was confusion, but also grief. Was there really love there as well? Perhaps, but it did not really matter to her. She felt nothing for him that suggested love, only detachment. To consider what might have been would be futile, she reminded herself. Her chance with Jed had been lost long ago.

She glanced back at him as she reached the west bank of the stream. The moon, halfway down its western descent, hung over the forest where Jed stood. He appeared to be little more than a dark shape in a darker wilderness. Standing in the field, she imagined the moonlight casting a ghost-like aura on her form. It was fitting, she thought. The ghosts of another life may haunt a person for a time, but they too inevitably pass.

Or so she hoped.

Not looking back, she turned and made her way awkwardly across the stream: using her good leg to leap from the bank, she landed on an exposed rock, and then another, and finally to a third until she reached the other side without getting wet. Already, her good leg felt strained. She would have to be careful about overusing it.

She gripped the straps of her pack tighter, and with an enthusiastic breath started off across the plain. Recalling the map Jed had secretly shown her, she now knew it to be the Ilinoth Plain. The swiftest and safest route would be to proceed in a straight southeasterly line across it toward the western border of Norwood.

Norwood was the largest wilderness in Illirium: thousands of miles of uninhabited forest and hills, and home to the Alöwean's faded empire, Nemenelor.

"Most Alöweans have withdrawn far to the east, to Hamrothél," Jed had explained. "So you will not likely meet any along the way." By candlelight, he studied the map closely. "Where do you intend to go in Rodaním?"

"Yanweri," she said.

"That is well over six-hundred miles from here," Jed commented. "Your provisions will only last you five days, maybe six. I wish we could give you a horse, but we do not even have enough for ourselves. Anyway, be mindful of your surroundings. The safest settlement nearby is at least two weeks away by foot. It is known as Fumond's Hut, which is small, but well stocked. Fumond is a curious man, but generous and impartial to political affairs. We have done some business with him."

"I will be fine," she said. "I know how to survive in the wild."

"I remember." Jed studied the map further. "The lower Ilinoth Plain has a lot of wild berries, which are safe to eat; and none that are poisonous. Western Nórwood is the same. I will give you a knife, and even a bow with a quiver full of arrows, if you like. There should be plentiful game along the way."

"That would be helpful," she replied. "Thank you."

"You may also be able to arrange passage with a fishing boat or trading vessel near Mirror Lake's northern shore. They should be well supplied and might even bring you all the way across to Fumond's Hut. That would eliminate a few days on foot, anyway. But be careful; some vessels travel armed with Siligen soldiers or agents. Dwairian has also set up a small military outpost on the island at the center of the lake, the abandoned Tower of the Sky. They closely guard the western waters, and sometimes even move into the eastern half, despite it being under Rodaním's authority. It is a tense arrangement, so be careful who you trust. Dwairian has many spies in the east."

"I understand. It may be better to avoid any boats then."

"It might," Jed agreed.

As she now walked briskly across the plain an hour later, she slowed and ran her finger along her scarred right jaw. Even though the number was gone, it still felt like a part of her. Would people notice? What would they think? Though the tattoo was gone, Prisoner 43-1-12 was part of who she was, as was Namél. Would others discern such a confused identity by looking at her, noticing her scars?

She pressed onward, resuming as aggressive a pace as her injured leg would allow.

Part of her doubted that venturing into the east would bring any healing. While there would be less external reminders of her abuse, the memories would remain inside her all the same. Could she hope for rest when the images continued to visit her in the night? Could she really start a new life free from the past?

Her food lasted seven days, but her pace did not. Both calves ached relentlessly. She had formed a habit of compensating with her good leg, which made it painfully stiff. There was some hope in knowing that she was drawing close to Mirror Lake, that she at least was making progress.

The weather remained pleasant, but did little to improve her mood. Once she had reached the edge of Norwood, she proceeded under the shade of the trees to make her passing less noticeable. Besides, the direct sunlight would only hasten the loss of her already waning energy. She was glad she did not have to ration her water supply like her food. There were many streams along the way, most still swelling with water from the snow that had melted off the northern mountains—the Gírgash Range, she recalled from Jed's map.

When she was forced to hunt, on the eighth day of her journey, she managed to shoot a rabbit. It had taken a few tries, for she was out of practice; yet as she saw the creature writhing in the tightening hold of death, screaming, she could not help but feel remorse. She was tired of death.

Staring down at the rabbit, she knew she should end its suffering, but could not will herself to do it, which made her feel worse. Slowly, the rabbit died as she watched it passively, unable to divert her eyes. When it had finally become still, she removed the arrow and brought the rabbit to a cluster of large rocks in the trees where she had decided to make camp. She remembered how to prepare the rabbit; though it had been so long, her parents had taught her well. She had been fascinated by the process then, but now she felt sick.

The meat filled her stomach, but did not satisfy her hunger. She questioned whether she could kill again. If necessity drove her to it, perhaps, but then she shook her head. No, she did not want to kill another living thing again. She had defied her enemies with an enduring will, found purpose in the thought of retribution; yet all of that was melting away like the snow in the mountains. Ketash's death left her feeling empty. The thought of killing Nabilak offered little more. There had to be another way to find peace.

Wrapped in her cloak, she lay down.

It became difficult to breath. Memories of countless nights suffocated her like a chain around her neck. Curling up on her side, her hands over her face, she tried to shield herself from the memories, to ward them off, but they remained strong and relentless, winding about her thoughts like a fever dream.

After a restless hour, she gathered her gear and continued on through the night. Walking eased her body and mind somewhat, but weariness quickly crept in. There was also something intimidating about being in the dark woodlands. She felt watched or even hunted. Trying to ignore the fog of her thoughts, the fear, she pressed on, the pain in her legs keeping her in touch with the present. She began to perspire with the exertion. It felt good, she told herself, imagining that it released some of the poison within.

Many hours later, just as the moon reached its zenith, she came upon a creek. Having removed her pack, she collapsed at the bank, and buried her head in the water's cool depths. Not wanting the sweat to dry on her skin and clothes, she crawled into the shallow water until she was completely submerged. The soaked clothes pressed against her, so she removed them and tossed them onto the bank beside her pack. She picked up a smooth stone from the bottom of the creek, and began to scrub herself with it until her skin hurt. She tossed the stone aside in frustration.

If only it were that easy.

She rose and sat on a flat-topped rock, which jutted out near the bank, holding her knees to her chest and trembling in the cool night air. The feeling brought her back to the central prison when only the surface of her body was being destroyed—before the nights with Nabilak.

If only I had not been so weak, she berated herself, still shivering.

What else could she have done? His dominion of her would have come eventually, so she had seized the only trace of choice in the matter, ended the pain before worse could be done. She did it to survive, and had succeeded. Did that not make her the victor after all?

Or had he also succeeded in some way? She felt the scars across her shoulders, felt her arms and legs, and thought of the number once on her face. Nabilak and Ketash had done all they could to mark her forever. There was some relief in the realization that Nabilak had been unable to impregnate her. Further consolation came from the notion that she was leaving them all behind, for there was a certain freedom in that.

She left the rock and returned to her gear. Laying her wet, green attire out to dry, she thought about who had given her the clothes, how she too was a rebel.

Exhausted, she wrapped herself in her dry cloak, and lied down on a patch of grass near the shore. Resting her head upon her pack, she gathered a clump of earth with her hands and slowly let the dirt fall from between her fingers.

So much time had passed. So much time was passing. Where was she now in time; was it still the present, or had at long last the future been found?

Throughout the next day, the weight of sorrow lingered in her heart. Her legs buckled under its weight. She began to feel as though she wandered aimlessly. The wilderness grew vast and indomitable. Perhaps Nabilak had indeed impregnated her, only not with something tangible. Even the thought of finding her aunt in Rodaním did not motivate her. She did not have the strength to keep going.

Hunger returned, but she did not bother searching for food. She removed the quiver and bow and cast them aside, and then did the same with the knife. She did not want them.

Her steps faltered. Her legs throbbed. A few times she tripped and fell roughly to the ground. The sky was clear of clouds. She felt its heat pounding onto her, and wondered what it would be like to die of thirst.

Maybe she should go back to find the knife. Perhaps it would empty her of contamination. She turned around, took a step, but then wavered again. No. She did not feel like going back, so continued her original course.

Soon she reached Mirror Lake. It was larger than she had imagined, like the bay of a vast sea. She considered drowning herself in it. Walking shakily forward, she stopped as the ground fell away to at least thirty feet below. She stood at the edge of the cliff and gazed down at the rocky shore. Could those rocks empty her head of the past?

She could not bring herself to jump, and laughed derisively at herself. "Still so weak," she said, nearly shouting the words. "Why do you resist? Why are you here?"

Turning to the right, she followed a vague trail, which connected the cliff top to a long expanse of dry shore. She wandered along the shore for a while, noting the dancing blue shapes of the water's surface—shapes adorned with glittering stars of light. Looking through the surface, she found the ochre radiance of the underwater stones to be beautiful.

Up ahead, miles away in the distance, she spotted the Menelmachar River flowing from the west into the lake. Memories of the west filled her with disdain.

Her head ached, and she could not remember when she had last drunk some water. The waterskin at her side was empty. She considered the lake water, but did nothing. Returning her attention to where the river fed into the lake, she noticed that beyond it was a wide stretch of land with different vegetation: Marshwood. What secrets did it contain? Were they the same, she and it? Or was she so unclean as to pollute even a swamp?

Wandering forward, she suddenly smelled smoke, but saw no sign of its source. Following the coastline, her mind began to clear. The smell grew stronger, savory even, and revived her appetite. She soon heard the distant crackle of a fire.

The shore curved right into a small cove. She stopped at its corner, and peered cautiously around a boulder. Ahead, less than a hundred strides away, on the shore at the center of the cove, a figure sat on a large bough of driftwood before a small fire. His back was to her, bent over slightly as he focused on something she could not see.

She became conscious of sounds: trees conversing with the wind, water lapping near her feet, the snapping fire, and then something else.

Was that music?

Notes danced like sprites across the water of the cove to fill her ears. She felt her body and mind calming. Even her heart eased as a calcified layer around it began to crack. Unfamiliar sensations surged into her heart. She felt a pang of emotion, but did not comprehend what it was. Her mind was blank. She could not speak, and could not move. The last note of the song echoed playfully then vanished.

At that moment, the figure turned his head and looked directly at her.

Part 3: Medium

He stood.

Instincts sought to turn her away, but another part resisted: a fearless curiosity urging her to wait.

The stranger continued to watch her.

She observed him, all the while conscious of her pounding heart. It felt alive with anticipation—but of what? Was it the hope of a new beginning, or simply the anticipation of knowing she was free to choose whether to go or stay?

She wanted a fresh start. Its potential pulsated through her body. For so long she had known only imprisonment and wandering, fighting to survive and navigate an oppressive oblivion. This choice seemed different, however. It was not about rationalizing how to survive, but becoming open to the prospect of living again. She had felt it before, most recently with Opal, but never this clearly. Whatever it was, it had touched something deep within her: mind and heart, spirit, or soul—whatever composed the essence of a person. More than sound, the stranger's music had felt like an extension of goodness. She wanted to know that goodness, to understand and claim it. She wanted to discover if it could provide a lasting peace.

The stranger motioned for her to join him.

Defensive instincts once again sought mastery, and she tried to discern the stranger's intent while at a safe distance. With his hand, he gripped the neck of a lute while its round body rested gently upon his foot. She could see no evidence of a weapon. Smiling, he extended his free hand toward her again, beckoning her to come. She noted a canoe lying bottom-up on the shore not far from the man's fire. Perhaps she could steal it later, and use it to get across the lake.

Her stomach suddenly rumbled at the smell of cooked food. The stranger motioned to her a third time. Perceiving no immediate danger, she adjusted the green scarf around her neck, gripped the straps of her pack, and walked forward one measured step after another.

Seeing her approach, the man carefully placed his instrument to the side and turned to the fire. Adding some wood and poking the embers, his back was to her as she covered the final approach to his camp. Along the way, she seized a stick of driftwood and kept it close as if to use as a walking staff. She would be ready to defend herself.

The fire danced brightly. Staying a few strides away from the man, she made her way to the other side of the fire. The man raised an inquisitive eyebrow as she passed.

"Welcome," he said in a calm tone. "Please . . ." he gestured toward a smooth, pale log on the ground next to her, "have a seat."

She sat down slowly, keeping her eyes on him. Sitting felt like a relief, especially for her calf, yet it also reminded her how tired she felt. In an attempt to remain alert, she squeezed her new staff tighter as it rested across her lap.

"Are you hungry?" The man did not appear to notice her timid behavior. Instead, he lifted a thin stick from where it had been secured between the sandy beach and two stones, the contents at its end thus angled toward the flames. He stepped forward and offered it to her.

Gripping her staff, she tensed at his approach.

This he noticed, and stopped. "It is fish." His eyes indicated the small form at the end of the stick. "From the lake."

Without stepping closer, he extended his arm out to give the food to her. She stood and received it, watching suspiciously as he sat back down and retrieved another for himself. He brought the fish close and let it linger under his nose, inhaling with satisfied expectancy. He took a small bite and chewed, all the while gazing at the lake.

After swallowing, he said, "The fish here have more flavor than most. Yet they lack enough to really enliven the palette." He glanced at her with eyes that smiled. "What do you think?"

She looked at him for a while longer, and then down at the fish. Steam rose from its silver flesh, its cooked scent filling her nostrils. She bit into it. The meat tasted warm and succulent. After finishing the first bite, her stomach began to ease. "It is delicious," she said before taking another mouthful. After days alone, it felt strange to speak.

Looking pleased, the man nodded and returned to his meal.

They dined in silence.

Eventually, he offered her another small fish, which she accepted gladly. She ate four before raising her hand to acknowledge that she was full. He urged her to have another, but she declined. "Thank you." She felt some of her strength returning.

Placing the stick, which had contained his third serving to the side, the man slid forward to sit on the ground and rest against his own log. He stretched his arms out in contentment and looked back at the lake. Above, the sky was a gradient of soft blue with scattered clouds illuminated by golden twilight.

"Beautiful, is it not?" he commented, without averting his gaze.

She glanced up, but said nothing.

"Most do not appreciate it, I think," he added, "the wonders around us."

She had grown to cherish sunlight, but still said nothing. Instead, she simply inhaled the fresh, cooling air.

"It often speaks to us," the man continued, "but how good are we at listening?"

Listening to what, she wondered.

He leaned forward. "Some hear a voice, like a whisper, while others only discern its presence. To me, it is like music."

She considered the sounds around them: water lapping against the shore, a hush of wind through nearby trees, the fizzling collapse of wood in the fire. "I hear no music."

The man studied her, a hint of sadness in his eyes. "You are not the only one." He watched the flames, their red light dancing on his face. "There is much that smothers it."

She did not know what the man was getting at, but discerned grief behind his words. Studying his features—thick, short brown hair; smooth, tanned skin and a beardless face—she had first guessed him to be around her age, but now she was not sure. There was no youthfulness in his attentive, dark blue eyes. Those eyes had seen things. Furthermore, when he spoke, his voice was steadied by wisdom that could only be gained from many years. Something about him reminded her of the man with the bronze-colored eyes.

"Who are you?" she asked.

He looked over at her as if waking from a reverie.

"I mean . . ." Suddenly feeling self-conscious under his gaze, she rephrased the question, trying to make it sound more casual: "Where are you from?"

He smiled slightly, his eyes wandering to the shallow water lapping against the nearby shore. "Not from this place."

She continued to watch him, transfixed by his presence. It caressed her thoughts, made her feel at ease. She told herself not to trust it.

"What about you?" he asked. "Where do you come from, and what brings you to this part of Illirium?"

She reached for her chin to make sure the scarf still covered her scar. She looked down at the blue heart of the flame and at the glowing red embers. "Where do I come from?" she echoed. What had brought her to such a place? Like him, she would speak in ambiguities. "I come from fire."

"A curious response," he said, tilting his head inquisitively. "What does it mean?"

What could she say to him, and what did he really want to know? Recalling the man with the bronze-colored eyes made her think of the Hamath of her youth, which could not be dissociated from the war and what followed. "I rose from ashes," she replied, "but the wind scattered what remained—piece by piece."

"What remained?"

A hope in goodness, perhaps—in other people, in herself. "I am not sure."

The man listened intently, his brow lined with compassion. "Your words carry a great weight; however, there is also something beautiful in them. Despite the pain clinging to the spaces between your words, I discern strength within you—of having overcome much."

She felt a prick at her heart, though not entirely unpleasant. Unable to meet the man's gaze, she pretended to study her hands. Her left hand wandered over to her right wrist and brought her sleeve up until her first forearm scar was visible.

"What is your name?" the man asked, still with a gentle tone.

Another haunting question. "I have been called many names," she said, still staring at the scars on her arm.

For a moment, she imagined the tattoo once on her jaw, as if it was still there. *43-1-12.* She kept her chin down, but wondered why she bothered to conceal it from the man. It was just a scar. He would not know what it had replaced. Anyway, she had deeper markings within her, ones that could not be so easily seen or removed. She could keep those hidden.

She wondered what Nabilak was doing at that moment. Was he tormenting another, or had he used her alone to purge himself? *Namél.* Was he now with Vera? Did he treat her better?

The specters of abuse lingered within her thoughts and body. She wanted to be rid of the memories, but when she looked at the man, she thought of all the men she had known. Whether good or bad, were they not more alike than she had first surmised—weak, insecure, proud, distant? Was she any better? She felt tired of being guarded and afraid, but neither could she let herself be taken advantage of again. She would defy everyone, if need be, even herself, though the resolution felt hollow.

She was tired of her thoughts.

Straightening her posture, she let the scarf drop from her jaw line. The man's eyes shifted down her face, but his gaze did not linger.

"Not all names must be accepted," he said, meeting her eyes, "or carried with us."

He stood up and stepped toward her.

"Stop," she said firmly, seizing her makeshift staff. "Do not come near me."

The man stopped, and raised his hands in appeasement.

She stood, keeping the log between them, and held the staff ready, trying to look threatening. If only she had not so hastily discarded her knife.

Unmoving, his hands still raised, the man said, "Forgive me. I just meant to introduce myself properly." His hands rested on his chest. "My name is Bard ap Fili."

He extended his right hand. Calming herself, but still holding the staff in her left hand, she stepped over the log and placed her right hand in his. She tensed as his fingers closed gently around hers. There was kindness in his touch, but also power. He squeezed her hand affably before releasing it.

"I am glad to meet you," he said. Returning to his place at the other side of the fire, he added, "May I play you a song?"

Stunned by the simple cordiality of his gestures, she did not reply. Uncertain, she sat back down and placed the staff next to her, and considered whether she had overreacted. *No*, she told herself. She had to be smart.

Bard reached over and brought the lute to rest on his lap, looking down at it meditatively. He plucked the first note and let it disperse into the night; then plucked a second note, letting its resonance do the same. Slowly the notes came together, crossing the chasm of time and space. A melody formed.

Trancelike, she watched his fingers dance to the right and left, up and down the instrument's long flat neck. Its hollow wooden shell was filled with his life. It breathed his breath. It thought his thoughts. It said what could not be said: a language extending beyond reason and objectivity. It became a tender, compelling voice.

Bard leaned intently over the instrument, pouring his will into its frame, until his form blurred in her vision. Soon, she no longer saw, but only heard; for the melody became a presence that could not be seen. Her spirit was cradled by it. Her hearing was the door through which it entered and soothed her consciousness. All other sensations were diminished as the song held her. At first it had seemed so foreign, almost discordant—as if denying the treacherous world she knew—but then it overwhelmed her with a touch of peace.

The sporadic snapping of the fire suddenly reclaimed her attention. She looked up and realized the song had ended. Warm silence lingered in its place. Cradling the instrument in his arms, Bard studied her. His eyes shone less brightly than before, his demeanor tired but content.

Her eyes felt the pull of sleep. Without further consideration, she leaned over to lie down on the soft sand of the beach. Resting the side of her head on her bent arm, her thoughts drifted, disregarding all previous concerns. Once more, images faded to sounds. Sounds faded to quiet. Before sleep enshrouded her entirely, she felt warmth settle upon her body. Her eyes flickered open to see Bard crouched down beside her, adjusting a blanket. Slightly alarmed, but strangely not afraid, she let him raise her head and place his rolled-up cloak underneath it as a pillow.

"Do not be afraid," he said softly, moving away.

"Wait," she heard a voice say. It was her voice, but she felt detached from it. Was something else within her speaking? It sounded too tender, too trusting. "I was once called Rhoda," it said. Why did she tell him?

"Rhoda," Bard echoed thoughtfully. "That is a beautiful name."

She felt so tired.

Water splashed playfully against a sandy shore. Trees murmured. Birds whistled.

All sounded content.

She opened her eyes.

Above, a falcon soared across the blue sky to where clouds hung over a rising sun.

She sat up and recognized the cove from the previous evening. Though her physical weariness had lost some of its power, her spirit still felt vacant. She removed the blanket and stood, squinting to take in the details of the lake: light glittering brightly across its surface.

Aside from a heap of burnt logs and ash, as well as the blanket beside her, there was no trace of the stranger. The canoe was gone. She sat back down and tried to collect her memory of the previous night. Her head ached slightly. Her throat felt dry and sore. Reaching out to retrieve her waterskin, she realized it was gone.

The sound of gentle splashing caught her attention. She looked over and could not help but feel some relief at seeing the stranger steering his canoe toward the shore where she waited. With a firm, final stroke of his paddle, he drove the nose of the craft onto the bank, stood, and leapt out. His movements exuded a cheerful vigor.

"Good morning, Rhoda," he said, offering her a smile before he pulled the canoe completely out of the water. "I hope you slept well."

The name was jarring to her ears. She watched him uncertainly.

"Here." He offered her the waterskin she had missed; only now it was full.

She received it and drank gladly, letting the cool fluid cleanse her mouth and throat.

He brought a bundle out from his pack, opened a cloth and offered her a small loaf of bread. "It is still soft."

She took it.

He retrieved something else from the canoe then returned to sit next to her on the log. Tensing, she shifted to the left so as to allow more space between them.

"I found some berries and honeycomb to go with it," he said, offering her some before nibbling on what he had reserved for himself.

After watching him eat for a few moments, she took a bite. The thick texture of the bread with the sweetness of the berries and honeycomb revived her senses. She could not remember the last time she had eaten something so delicious.

"You like it?" he asked, noting her expression.

She nodded, wondering how he had kept the bread so fresh. Perhaps he had not been on the road for long.

"Sometimes it is the simplest gifts that keep us going," he said.

"Pardon me, but . . . what did you say your name is?"

"Call me Bard," he replied, still chewing the remains of a mouthful.

"Thank you for your kindness, Bard," she said, more shyly than she intended. She looked away. Noticing her staff still leaning against the log, she decided to abandon it.

"Please," Bard replied softly, focused on taking another bite, "it is the least I can do."

Once again they finished the meal in silence.

Afterward, while packing away a wrapped bundle into his canoe, he said, "You are far from civilization, but do not appear equipped for a long journey. Do you need help?"

Not exactly. Weariness washed over her anew. "I am going east."

"Do you have people in Rodaním?"

"I have no people."

He appeared to consider her reply.

The quiet unnerved her. She felt the urge to stand and walk away, yet something kept her seated. It was not antagonistic, but an inclination beckoning her to wait once more. It shook the foundations of her resolve, made her doubt herself. Yet she also remembered Jed's warning about Siligen patrols and spies. Distrust vied once more for her attention. *You should not linger*, it reasoned. *It is not safe.*

"Would you like to accompany me?"

Bard's question took her by surprise, temporarily silencing her thoughts. "What?"

"For a while," he added, "or as long as you wish."

"Why?"

"Would you rather travel on your own?" He hesitated. "I understand if you do. It is just that I have traveled enough miles alone with my thoughts. I am tired of their company." He offered a wry smile.

"Where are you going?" she asked.

"I also look to the east."

"To Rodaním?"

"No." Bard gazed solemnly at the eastern horizon. "To the Upper Mountains."

"I have not heard of them."

"The Upper Mountains belong to no one," he said, "at least to no one living." His tone grew somber. "They border Rökad and what remains of Nemenelor, though none in those lands dare enter."

"Why not?"

"They fear a world beyond what is seen," he replied.

"What do you mean?"

"Some call it death."

"Death?"

"It is as I said," he replied, "The Upper Mountains are no place for the living."

"Then why go there?" Surely, he did not really mean death.

He smiled faintly to himself, but did not look at her. "Because that is my path. Death is the door to something more: another land and meaning . . . an imperfect conception of a perfect truth."

"I do not understand."

"I have said more than I should. Anyway, I cannot explain it with words." He studied the ground, as if searching its sandy surface for an answer.

She could not help but stare at him as he did so. There was something different about him, but what was it?

Bard's eyes wandered over to his lute, the head of which jutted out from inside the canoe. He went over and retrieved it, sat on the log beside the fire pit, and held the wood body. Leaning over the instrument, he looked pensively at its neck, which was partitioned by strings and perpendicular metal lines.

"When I look around me, I see a myriad of possibilities," he said. "And when I listen, I discover their voices. Moreover, when my fingers take their first step on this instrument, a journey begins: often into memory, but sometimes into a world beyond what is known in the present. The Upper Mountains are another gate into that world."

She still did not understand.

Bard continued to study the lute. "I will try to explain, but not with words." His left hand came up to more resolutely grip the instrument's neck. For a moment his right hand stroked the strings where they ran over the shape of a small tree carved at the center of the main wooden body, the empty spaces between the tree's branches serving as the passageway for sound.

He began to play.

There was no single melody. The notes were soft and delicate, like the first drops of rain on a lake surface, or like scattered birdsong in a waking forest. The song carried with it peacefulness, anticipation, longing, but it also resonated with somberness. A presence moved within the waves of each note—mysterious, like hope. As she heard its call, her heart yearned to reach out and touch it—to know it was real.

She realized the song had ended. Bard sat staring blankly at the ground.

"I like that song," she offered.

He smiled faintly. "I am glad."

"It feels like it should be longer."

"Indeed," he replied. "That is the manner of a beginning. Like a door, it is neither complex nor extensive, but simply shows one to a new place, revealing what was previously foreign. Each step along the way builds upon the last. There are no futile steps in such a life."

"But surely, some things should be avoided," she countered, "or at least forgotten."

"Possibly."

She held his gaze for a while, but could not do so for long. Sometimes it felt like he could see into her own memory, and she did not like it. It reminded her that she was contaminated. Bard would likely be disgusted to learn what she had gone through, what she had allowed, and what she had done. How violence had begotten more violence. It would mute the pure timbre of his music. As he carefully placed the instrument back into its cloth case, she resolved not to let him know.

"So have you decided?" he asked, focusing back on her. "Shall we journey together for a time, discover the revelations each step will bring?"

He stood up, securing the strap of his instrument bag over his shoulder. She hesitated, remaining seated, confused about what to do or where to go. She looked eastward across the lake. The unfamiliar landscape suggested something more; not only Rodaním and her mother's family, or a widening distance from Siligen and her past, but something more certain. What was it? She had felt its presence before—in the kindness of another person, in light—and now in Bard's music. Were they connected? Could Bard help her learn the answer?

What was the risk; that Bard would betray her? No, she did not think he would. She discerned goodness within him, but was hesitant to trust it. Anyway, she had defied others before. Could she not do so again?

Bard extended his hand to her. She looked at it for a moment then up at his face. He was watching her expectantly.

Tired of fighting, she wanted to trust him. Yet she also reminded herself to remain cautious. She could not sink into complacency, no matter how charming the way might seem.

She grasped his hand, and felt her thoughts clear somewhat as Bard helped her stand. Once again, she felt his immense but controlled strength. His handhold lingered while his eyes studied her. Her heart beat louder, but she could not determine whether it was out of fear or anticipation.

"Come," he said softly, smiling. "Follow me."

More abruptly than she intended, she withdrew her hand from his, but Bard did not seem to mind. As they approached the canoe, he said, "It is a four-day journey east to the mouth of the Illüväter River. From there we will continue on foot."

"What about supplies?"

"I have enough."

She scrutinized his gear while he finished adjusting it in the canoe, but saw no indication of sufficient provision.

"Trust me," he said, noticing her gaze.

Though she did not entirely trust him, she decided to allow a few days to see what would happen. In a way, it would be safer, or at least less suspicious, for her to travel with someone else. Siligen soldiers could be looking for a lone woman.

She helped Bard push the canoe back into the water. He held the craft steady as she climbed inside near the prow, and then followed after her to sit at the stern.

"Ready?" he asked.

"Yes."

They paddled out from the cove onto the main body of the lake. There, they were met by a warm breeze. With his paddle, Bard steered them left toward the still rising sun.

The slight headwind made it difficult at first, but she was glad for the work. It sharpened her senses and made her limbs feel strong. She reveled in how the simple movement quieted her mind, but most of all she welcomed its sense of freedom.

Each evening, as the sky darkened crimson and violet, Bard steered the canoe to the lakeshore to make camp. Each night, he provided fish and bread for supper.

The simple meals never tasted bland to her. The fish and bread varied in kind. Sometimes the meat was white, other times gray. Occasionally, the bread was textured with oats and grains; other times it was smooth. She could not guess how Bard managed to preserve so much bread. An assortment of berries was often added to their meal, sometimes with honeycomb. At midday, they always ate a sliver of a fruit she did not recognize. The fruit's pale gold skin felt smooth to touch, and its white flesh tasted crisp and juicy. She thought it strange how such a small morsel could fulfill her appetite and waning energy. Every time she asked about it, Bard merely said the fruit was rare and came from far away.

At night, after they had eaten their fill—there was always enough—Bard would lean back, bring out his lute, and play. At first she thought it was only for her, but she came to realize it was as much for him. He appeared to pour himself into it, becoming one with the instrument. The music enlivened him, echoed his thoughts, told of his past. Yet none of it was offered in terms she could fully comprehend.

Bard more eagerly asked her questions than talked about himself. She responded to his inquiries with vague brevity, but sometimes elaborated. There was something cleansing about talking. Still, so many memories had fragmented, their details forgotten. Mainly, she focused on her childhood, only sharing a few details about her life after the war. She did not want to speak about Tïrmen Prison.

Sitting next to a small fire, or lying back while gazing at the starry night sky, she preferred to listen to Bard's music. It calmed her. Increasingly, she wondered about the other world Bard had suggested. Did it have something

195

to do with the Fields of Gedáron, which her mother had spoken about—or Gedáronith as Ida had called it? The desire to understand became a guiding star, a faint reason to press on. She wanted to know where it would lead. Regardless of what it was, it gave her a trace of hope.

"Where does it come from?" she asked the night they camped at the mouth of the Illüväter River.

Bard glanced at her. "Where does what come from?"

"Your music . . . what inspires it?"

Above them, the moon was full, illuminating the surrounding forest with soft blue light. Nearby, the river murmured happily. Bard considered her question while staring into the small glow of the fire's cooling embers. Though his face was partially shadowed, his eyes remained clearly visible.

"It is hard to make tangible that which is intangible," he said. "Do you really want to know?"

"I do."

He focused back on the embers. "To me, inspiration comes from everywhere—from all life. Look closely and listen. Everything offers its own kind of music, most of it good, and that music yields more. That is the truth I grasp. Sometimes it is like a chorus of voices, while other times it is only one."

"What do you mean by truth?" she asked.

"Truth is an unwieldy word," he said, sighing. "In a basic way, it is the power holding everything together, giving it meaning and purpose. If there is no fundamental truth for all of us—some reality transcending the self, enabling us to connect with other living things—then what is the point of existence?" He shook his head. "Without some truth, life seems lonely and hopeless."

"I suppose you are right."

"But that is still the start of an answer," Bard said. "What is this underlying truth? That is the real question, which further unveils the mystery of inspiration. The power does not originate from this world, but neither can it be dissociated from it. I believe everything was formed from its nature, by its voice—its breath. This power is the first creative spark, the prime mover;

not just an idea, but a perceptible presence: Elíbom Prímom."

Had the light she had experienced in glimpses, the moments of warmth and goodness, been a testament of such a presence? The term, *Elíbom Prímom*, was familiar to her, but only in association with how time was measured. The current year was 633 EP, *Elíbom Prímom*, or 7 AEP, *After Elíbom Prímom*. Furthermore—assuming for the moment that Bard was right, that there was some fundamental spark of life—in changing the naming of time, had Dwairian been consciously trying to change the truth?

"Regardless of what it is called," Bard continued, "this view of power is a way of comprehending the unity possible in the world. By unity, I mean a deep and lasting peace. Elíbom Prímom is boundless, yet somehow also personal. How are we to think of, let alone describe, such a person? It, he, she—all these pronouns are too limiting. I like to think of music as the voice of Elíbom Prímom, though that too is a frail metaphor. My point is that music reminds me that there is something more to this world than what is readily perceived with our senses."

"But how do you know for certain?"

"How can we know anything for certain?" he countered. "Each of us must choose to believe in something. Eventually, that trust becomes a kind of knowing. It begins with knowing that I am real, and that this instrument is real. It continues with knowing how music is created, such as by the cause and effect of plucking a string over a hollow wooden body. There is a definitive craft to composing a song, yet there is also an art—subjective, inexplicable. There is still a cause and effect—sounds gathered in a pleasing harmony—but the question of why they are harmonious and pleasing delves closer to the mystery of inspiration. I may not fully understand it, but I have come to know it—at least in part. Its boundlessness compels me, challenges my perception of the world, and calls me to explore further. Thus my belief is gradually guided into a sense of purpose, which provides me with meaning. Music has the power to influence people, Rhoda. Sometimes I think of myself as its herald, even its guardian."

"A guardian of what, though?" she asked, still not understanding.

"The power of music," he replied, "Its voice whispers about a way to peace,

197

even love."

She did not know what to say to that. If the notion of peace felt distant to her, love felt far more remote. "How is love connected to all of this?"

"Love is at the heart of peace," he replied. "I have traveled throughout most of Illirium; however, from what I have seen, that truth is fading." He took a deep breath. "I realize that truth, peace, and love are abstract concepts. While I am trying to speak of them with clarity, I ultimately find it more productive to show them rather than speak of them. In other words, they find their greatest meaning as part of a movement of choices, actions, and reactions, which are the essence of music. Though it is not fully tangible, it is one of the most tangible means I have for comprehending and sharing these ideas.

"Music is not merely a vessel through which the power of truth speaks, it is a means by which barriers can be conquered and wounds healed. Somehow, music heightens my awareness of that which is true—to being aware, for example, of the unspoken pain revealed through your tone of speech, the glint of weariness in your eyes, and the tension of your posture."

She glanced down, self-conscious under his gaze.

"They do not tell the whole story, of course," he continued, "but they echo the truth. Music is not a passive force, Rhoda, but can help each of us navigate confusion without losing sight of good."

He tossed a twig into the fire, tensing his jaw. He looked older again, the lines around his eyes more numerous. "I have not talked about this with many people." He rubbed his eyes. "Has what I said made any sense?"

"A little," she said. At least, she resonated with the fundamental desires he had addressed. She too wanted something to guide her beyond herself. She wanted to trust that life could hold meaning, peace, and even love.

"As the power of music is as abstract as truth," Bard said, straightening, "there are no adequate words, or I am ill-equipped to speak them. I have been given this tool." He rested his hand upon the lute. "Music, like truth, is not a commodity, nor should it be considered one—something to merely duplicate, repackage, and sell—but instead it is a gift to be shared. Sharing a song, in other words, helps it grow and develop greater meaning. For example, your receptiveness is a reason I like to play for you."

"Will you teach me?" She indicated the instrument.

"You want to learn?" He looked down at the lute then back at her.

She had not really considered what she was asking. The idea asserted itself, pressing her forward before she had time to overthink it and retreat.

"Yes." A smile formed at the corner of Bard's lip. "There is no better way to try to understand the mystery. I must warn you, however, that it will be frustrating at first, the rewards few. It has taken me many years—most of my life—to gain this skill. There are no shortcuts."

"I am willing," she replied, trying to sound confident, though she felt misgivings. The rhythm of her heart increased. She trembled slightly, but could not tell whether it was from nervousness or excitement. "I want to defy the confusion like you do." For so long, her efforts to overcome it had felt futile.

"You can," Bard said, a youthful vigor returning to his gaze, "and you will. But it will not be easy."

"Nothing ever is," she replied.

Learning how to play the lute proved harder than she had anticipated. Her untrained fingers felt awkward and disobedient; it took a lot of conscious effort to form the right fingerings. There was so much to think about. Her initial optimism about replicating the beauty of Bard's melodies sank into a bog of frustration.

"This is how it always starts," Bard tried to console her. "There is no rhythm, but merely scattered pieces we must work to bring together. Be patient with yourself, Rhoda. A new beginning is rarely natural, and never without mistakes."

There was no music. There were only shuddering noises, half-expressed sounds, and hesitancy. Anger welled anew within her. Sometimes it took all her will to resist taking the lute by the neck and smashing its body to pieces on the ground.

"I cannot," she mourned on the fifth day. "I do not have the talent necessary." She hated herself for wanting to give up so soon. She hated the whining

199

tone she had adopted.

Quietly, Bard received the lute back from her and put it away.

They had been paralleling the northern bank of the Illüväter River for five days on foot. The canoe had been left behind, hidden away in a gathering of trees not far from where the river flowed into Mirror Lake. The path they had been following was narrow, but in good condition—apparently maintained and used regularly, though they had seen no one else on it. Only deer and small rodents crossed their path. Bard explained that most Alöweans had withdrawn to Hamrothél further east, and that only a few from Rodaním ventured this far north.

Gazing up at the tree branches sheltering their campsite, Bard commented, "This land is scarred with memories wishing to be forgotten."

Like me, she mused. "I am sorry I am not a more patient student."

"There is no need to apologize," he replied, still staring up at the branches. "I told you it would be difficult."

"I wonder if I am focusing too much on the end result," she said. "Have you ever felt that way?"

"Absolutely." Bard leaned forward. They had made no fire that night, but still she could see his eyes. "The beginning is the hardest, but if you press through it . . ." He offered a smile. "You become boundless. There will still be challenges, of course, and limitations, but I have come to think of them as opportunities." He leaned back, slowly inhaling. "They give each work of art its own character. Such art can even heal us, as I have suggested before."

What kind of healing had he needed, she wondered. "Do you mean to say you have found healing through music?"

"Music is part of it." His eyes caught her gaze. "It offers me a medium by which to release some of the pain. But that only happens when it is partnered with honesty, however ugly it may feel. Dishonesty reinforces the defensive barriers we create to protect ourselves."

His words remained both compelling and strange. She suddenly felt tired.

Without saying more, Bard took the lute out of its case and stood. "Excuse me, I need some time alone." He walked away toward the river.

Quiet lingered.

She reflected on how Bard respected her space, rarely coming close. While she would not have let him touch her, a part of her wished he would. She discerned no malice in him; his friendliness was no charade, yet something within her resisted letting him get closer—old defenses, but also a desire to choose when to reach out to him, if at all. She chided herself at the thought. What was human contact, but a false sense of security? Thinking of Nabilak, she was not sure if she wanted to be touched by a man ever again.

Her mother had disappeared into the night, and her father had slowly wasted away—both buried in earth. The bodies of Sindor and Ürstus were lost somewhere in the Kurshemnt Mountains. She thought of the cruelty of Malech, Nabilak, and Ketash, but also remembered the warmth of Opal and the kindness of Ida. She missed that kind of intimacy. She thought of Jed, how he had been before vanishing into memory. There were others, their motivations ambivalent, antagonistic, or supportive. Where did Bard fit, and was he another temporary presence? Did she have the strength to endure another departure?

What do I want?

She closed her eyes and lay down on her side. The night sky looked too bright. A pressure in her chest robbed her of breath. She rolled over onto her stomach, with her hands pressed against her chest as if willing the pain to submit or shift to the immeasurable mass of earth beneath her.

Clenching her teeth, a sob escaped her throat. At first she tried to contain it, embarrassed that Bard might hear, but she quickly discarded such self-consciousness. She was tired of pretending to be stronger than she felt, tired of pretending there was much left of her. Agitated by grief, she rose to a tight kneeling position and cried against the earth and darkness. She could no longer bear the pain of loss, guilt, anger. She wanted it to be taken away.

Please take it away.

Her vision blurred with tears, hands still clutched at her chest. She shuddered.

Please.

"Please," she cried.

There were no more words. The pressure within her rose up from her heart and burst out her mouth. Still bent over, with her head against the ground, she sobbed. Sounds poured out from her throat: broken sounds, pained, enraged, searching, begging.

She no longer thought, no longer resisted. Sounds flowed from her—at first haltingly, as if navigating sharp, broken stones with bare feet. But then the sounds pressed through all hindrances, like a dam of debris washed away by the flood of her grief. Her voice grew stronger. Pleas gave way to mourning. Mourning gave way to emptiness. Emptiness . . .

There was something else . . . The tension within her dissipated. She relaxed and listened. There was music. She could almost touch it, the notes like small lights floating through the darkness. The music warmed her, filled her emptiness. Her spirit overflowed—not with pain, but longing. Other sounds rose to meet it. She found herself lying on her back. Countless stars smiled down at her from above. She felt her heart ease.

The music continued.

But something had changed.

She listened, and then realized the music was coming from within her. Softly, she hummed the song's melody. At the sound, the shadows gradually receded until she found herself in a simple forest, a harmless gathering of trees. The space no longer felt like a wilderness. There were no watchers in the shadows. It was just a forest, an unfettered place brimming with life.

The song quieted.

She stared up at the indigo sky for a while. Hearing a footstep, she rose to a sitting position and looked over. Bard stood nearby, holding his lute at his side, while his eyes glistened. There appeared to be joy in those eyes, but the word seemed insufficient. There was more: peace, though it too transcended the notion of the word. Assurance? Still more. She became attentive of the steady rhythm of her heart, of a hope being renewed within her. Goodness no longer felt so impossibly distant. It was within reach, within her. She looked into Bard's eyes, somehow so clear in the night.

"Your voice," he began, his tone hushed. "That is a gift."

"A gift?"

He came closer. "There are some things that cannot be taught."

She recalled singing as a child. "What am I to do with it?"

"Help it grow." He came and sat next to her. "And share it."

"How do I share something I do not understand?"

"I will offer what I can," he said, "but you are the one to ultimately answer that question."

They walked in silence the next morning. Bard led the way at a relaxed but steady pace. Meanwhile, the happy, content sounds of nature resonated all around. The air smelled fresh with the fragrance of damp earth and pine. Embracing such sensations further calmed her mind.

Around midday, the path left the river to ascend a lush valley. There, rivulets trickled down from the adjoining hills, gathering as a chorus into a brook at the valley floor. Where the path climbed the right side of the valley, the density of coniferous trees increased. They provided welcome shade against the bright sun. Few other plants grew on the steep, rocky hillside.

A breeze rushed through the treetops.

She decided to ask the question that had been forming all morning. "Bard?" she began, wishing her voice did not sound so hoarse.

Without changing his pace, he glanced back at her. "Yes?"

She paused to drink from the waterskin strapped across her chest. Quietly clearing her throat, she continued. "Do you share your music with others as you have with me?"

He did not look back. "Not often anymore. Not in these lands, anyway."

"Why not?"

"No one listens."

She found that hard to believe. "I listen."

He said nothing, but focused on the path as it zigzagged up the valley hillside. She wondered at Bard's silence. The soft, crunching cadence of their footsteps accompanied by their labored breathing took precedence. She was grateful that the arrow wound in her calf had become no more than a dull ache.

An hour later, they reached the summit of the hill. To the left of the crest was the narrow valley from which they had come, while the Illüväter River could be glimpsed down at the right. Bard motioned for them to sit and rest, so she placed her gear on the ground and rubbed her sore shoulders and calf. The breeze quickly dried the sweat that had soaked through her shirt under the straps of her pack. Looking north through a gap in the trees, she studied a large expanse of rolling forestland. Beyond it, farther north, loomed the sharp pinnacles of a mountain range.

"Are those the Upper Mountains?" she asked.

Sitting on a small rock and removing his boots to air out his feet, Bard glanced up to see where she was pointing. "No, that is the eastern fist of the Gírgash Range. The Upper Mountains are further east. We should be able to see them in a few days—after we reach Lake Cüivenen."

She wanted to return to their previous conversation—or her attempt at it anyway—for she felt unsatisfied with Bard's answers. Why had he been so evasive? "Last night, you said I should share my voice," she began. "You called it a gift."

He drank a mouthful of water and nodded.

"So how can you neglect to share your own?"

"It is not a matter of neglect," he replied.

"Then what is it?" she pressed. "As you have said, your music wields the power to influence people. Surely, you can see it affecting me."

"I am glad if it is," he replied, avoiding her gaze, "though I wonder at it."

"What do you mean?"

He looked tired, focusing downward as if deliberating with himself. She wondered what he was thinking.

"For seven years," he said, "I have explored Illirium. Yet in all that time, no one has responded to my music like you. Some are mildly amused, but nothing more. I suspect they do not know what to do with it. In this battered, war-tainted world, music no longer seems to have a place. People are more interested in what is practical. It is the show of authority by force or the threat of force that captures their attention the most. They want progress, with less concern about how it is offered."

"But your music communicates a kind of authority," she countered. "And besides, change is an aspect of progress."

204

He said nothing.

"Look at me," she said. His dark blue eyes rose up to meet hers. Was he trying to hide something? "Why do you wonder at your music changing me?"

"I wonder at your courage." His voice was gentle.

"I am not that courageous."

"I disagree," Bard replied. "For one, you are here. Against your instincts, you chose to come with me, a stranger. That demonstrates a courageous trust."

"Some might call it foolishness," she said.

"One person's fool is another's hero. I will come to my own conclusions." He leaned forward, resting his elbows on his thighs. "It is about more than your courage, however. In you I discern a unique ability to overcome."

"Overcome what?"

"Anything."

She felt strange talking so openly with him, but also empowered. Reminding herself that she was his equal caused her hesitations to fade. She went over and sat beside him. "For a while now," she said, "I have tried to dissociate from my past, hiding in some dark corner to be forgotten." Her heart beat faster. "Yet no matter what I do, the splinters of memory remain: moments, faces, words, pain. Whether I want them to or not, they influence how I approach the future."

"Are you saying you feel helpless?"

Perhaps. Well, sometimes. No, not always. "I do not know," she said.

"What will you do?"

"I wish I knew." She was tired of suppressing the fact that she felt weak and lonely, and that her wounds were real. "Do you really believe it is possible to find healing?"

Bard nodded. "I do. But it is a journey. To begin, you have to identify the pain and share its history. Eventually that can lead to forgiveness, and sometimes reconciliation."

She could not imagine forgiving Nabilak, let alone coming to some kind of understanding with him. "What about justice?"

"What does justice mean to you?"

"I am not sure."

She remembered the three men who had tried to rape her outside Hamath. She remembered Malech, Ketash, and the Tirmen guards. Many were dead, some by her hand. Yet most of all, she hated Nabilak. Perhaps she should have killed him, regardless of the consequences. Would that have satisfied her? Had the deaths of any of her assailants given her peace? Though her rage had been placated by reciprocating their violence, the outcome had left her confused and horrified at what she was capable of doing. Had it gone beyond self-defense? Was she violent by nature, or was all humanity cursed with it?

Justice was about Nabilak both realizing and confessing the evil he had inflicted on her, how manipulative and abusive it had been. Acknowledgement was not enough, however—it was not enough to know it in his mind, or to admit it with his mouth—he needed to know her pain by sharing it. There needed to be punishment. How else would he know the impact of his actions?

Yet to punish Nabilak required authority, a dynamic of power she did not really have. She was a convict, a rebel. The law was not her ally. So did that make justice about a struggle for domination? She had asserted a form of power in taking the lives of a few assailants, but that brought her back to questions about the cyclical nature of violence. It made retribution and justice appear the same, dancing together in some masquerade of oblivion. If power defined justice, and those in power were corrupt, then justice was corrupted. It could not be relied upon. She had defied the authority of her oppressors by turning their weapons against them. There was a shade of justice in that—fairness. Yet it pulled her into the mire of fighting for control. It made her barely distinguishable from those she detested. Was that how she wanted to use her energy? Was it how she really wanted to live?

Perhaps that was the real question.

She had once known goodness, even love. Her parents had introduced her to it when she was young. Love was about willingly sacrificing aspects of one's power to gain not only peace, but intimacy. Like purpose, intimacy provided meaning to life. Having witnessed it in glimpses since then, could she reclaim the power of such goodness, or was it an idea swaddled in something too fragile to survive? Was the hope of healing some faulty notion about reclaiming innocence, or was it about something else?

Patiently, Bard watched her. Did he know the answer? He had said that the first step toward healing was to identify the pain. The pain was not simply some element to extract like poison from a wound, it was part of her, and had shaped her identity. But did she have to define herself by it permanently?

Perhaps by telling Bard the truth, by bringing him into the wilderness of her identity, he could help her discover a way through. She was tired of trying to navigate it alone. She wanted to tell him what had happened: about her life in Hamath after her father had died, about Tïrmen Prison, about Nabilak. Everything. She wanted to try. After all, what was the risk? That Bard would not understand or would withdraw from her in disgust? Did that matter to her? Why not tell him? There could be power in speaking. Did it not at least release some of the pain imprisoned within?

She decided to tell him.

For the remainder of the day, as they continued to follow the path, and on to the night after they had set up camp, she spoke. There were words and tears. There were moments of quiet. Sometimes there was even music.

Bard listened attentively as she exposed the charred framework and darkened corners of her story. It was in no particular order. Her story felt like shards of who she was, both attached and detached from her present self—like sparks floating up to a vast expanse. Something was releasing them: some unseen, burning hand of flame that simultaneously seared her gaping wounds. Scars would remain, but their hurt would not last.

The scars of the past only told part of the story, however. Which was more powerful: past or present; and what of the future? Or were they somehow all equal, complementary, forming a whole? Could she be whole again?

Singing wordless melodies gave her a taste of peace, and helped focus her mind. The future was not about following a predetermined road, but about choice. It was her choice to press on. The music helped her identify the sources of her pain and acknowledge their role in her suffering. It whispered to her consciousness, "It is not your fault." Thus speaking, whether through words or song, her oppressors' hold on her will loosened. Her spirit felt liberated.

But that was just the beginning.

Once free, what was she to do? Where was she to go?

She was surprised to find her tears coming easily. *What are you doing?* she scolded herself. Old instincts tried to spin webs to ensnare and immobilize her sense of vulnerability. Memories of torment refused to be so easily released. They beckoned her to withdraw because abandoning her rage would be to surrender her power.

That night at their camp, as she finished telling her story, she felt dazed and exhausted. Sitting next to her, Bard placed his hand on her shoulder, but she slid beyond its reach and stood up. She did not look at him as she walked away into the darkness beyond their camp.

"Rhoda," he called.

She stopped, but did not look back.

"What happened to you was evil," he said, "and I am so sorry."

She took another step.

"Wait."

"What is it?" she said, more tersely than she intended.

"I want to show you something."

She turned around. "What do you mean?"

He hesitated. "You are right to be angry, and suspicious . . . of anyone. You should go to Rodaním and find your aunt. . . . But if you can trust me, and are willing to delay your journey a while longer, will you come with me to the Upper Mountains? There is something there I want you to see."

Despite her uncertainty and lingering defenses, part of her had hoped he would ask. She was not ready to say goodbye. "And after that?"

A glimmer of firelight shone in Bard's eyes. He smiled knowingly. "That will be for you to decide."

Three days later, they reached the shore of Lake Cüivenen.

Along the way, each evening after making camp, she would go off on her own to think and practice singing. At first, she felt self-conscious about her voice, constrained by timidity, but she willed herself to persevere. The desire to discover where the music could lead became stronger than her reservations.

Bard offered to listen and instruct her, but she declined.

"This is something I must do on my own," she said.

"Well, I am here if you need me," he would say. Every night he would say it.

She did sometimes ask him to play while she was away. Not venturing far, she could still hear his music. It provided a melody to follow or interact with. Thus she conditioned herself, noting the tonal changes vibrating from her vocal cords. She suspected it was an insufficient process, however. To grow further, she would have to be heard more directly by others.

But not yet, she would tell herself. *I am not ready.*

On the evening of the third day, after they had eaten their supper, she and Bard left their camp to watch the sunset from the Cüivenen lakeshore. To the right, southwest across the water, stood a grim silhouette.

"Anaríl," Bard explained, "the once proud capital of the Alöwean Empire, Nemenelor."

"It reminds me of Tïrmen," she said, sitting next to him. The sandy shore was soft and cool, a welcome respite from a warm day.

Bard nodded. "An age has passed that cannot be reclaimed."

"I want to know more about where you come from."

Bard watched the rippling, silver surface of the lake.

"Please," she added.

"I am not sure you will believe me."

"Let me decide that."

He looked at her. "I am not supposed to speak of it . . . but you deserve to know. You entrusted me with your story, so I will entrust you with mine. What do you know of your people's history—that of the Illiri, Mankind?"

She shrugged. "Why is that important?"

"It is a framework for understanding who I am and where I come from."

209

"Well," she said, searching her memory, "There were originally twelve Illiri clans. Now there are eleven, or ten. It depends who you ask. They settled here before the Alöweans; and now that the Alöwean Empire has diminished, the Illiri are regaining control. The clans remain divided between Siligen in the west and Rodaním in the east. My mother said it has always been so."

She stared at the ground, recalling her family. "That is the way of the world, is it not—families and society at war with each other? I suppose it does not matter, really. Death is impartial. Anyway, I grew up learning more about nature. I was never a good scholar."

"You know enough." Bard shifted his sitting position. "Were the Elphadém ever mentioned?"

"Yes." Jed had mentioned the name recently. "Once, at least."

"Well, I am one of them."

She was not sure how to process such a statement. "An Elphadém?"

"Yes," he replied. "Obviously, we no longer dwell here in Illirium, not in your sphere of existence anyway."

She found herself growing skeptical.

"There is another world, Rhoda," he explained, "unseen by mortal eyes. In places, our two worlds overlap; I do not merely refer to Illirium, but also Alöwe across the sea—and everything in between. Our two worlds are similar, but not the same. There are different barriers, and different manifestations of power. For example, what you refer to as death is simply the place where our two worlds most clearly intersect."

She thought of her mother. "Are you talking about the Fields of Gedáron?"

"What do you know of those fields?"

"Only a little," she replied. "My mother spoke of it as a place for those who overcome the spirit of death. She thought the Fields could be found by strength and cunning." She remembered Ida's words. "I know some call it Gedáronith, and believe it can be reached with the help of a guide called the Canta."

"Those are portions of the truth," Bard commented. "The Fields of Gedáron are real, but not exactly in the way you have been told. The Fields comprise a vast valley between two clusters of tall mountains; and along the base of the northern range is Rühílis, the city of the Séorans. Outside the city is a large, walled garden called Elím, 'Place of Rest,' or the Garden of the Upper Kingdom. Some refer to the Fields and Elím together as Gedáronith. Either way, it is where the spirits of the dead may go to dwell until the Restoration."

Could it actually be true? "Who are the Séorans?"

"Theirs is another story," Bard replied. "They are the servants of Elíbom Prímom, and existed before the beginning of the world—before the Elphadém, before everything—but their city is now hidden from mortal eyes. I mention them for some context; for it is by their labor, under the direction of Elíbom Prímom, that Elím was created and is maintained."

"But who are the Elphadém, exactly?"

"We are your forebears," Bard said, "the first of Mankind. Our history begins at the creation of the world, and it is intertwined with yours more than you or the Alöweans seem to remember. Even the origin of the Alöweans is connected to us. The rift between our races began long ago—with the Corruption, and then the First Unrest. But most finalizing of all was the Elphadém Civil War four hundred years ago, in which we nearly destroyed each other here in Illirium. You see, I fought in that war . . . and died in it."

She looked at him in surprise.

"That is not to say I am over four hundred years old, not in the physical sense anyway. I do not entirely understand it myself. My point is to tell you that Elím is where I dwell, or where I came from, and it is to Elím that I return."

Doubt pressed against her mind.

"Try to understand," Bard continued. "As your mother taught you, or as Ida suggested, death is not the end of life, not in the full sense." Leaning closer to her, he spoke in a hushed, imploring tone. "There is a door, Rhoda. For those who know how to find it, it leads to Elím, which is a resting place, a safe haven. Many of my people dwell there, preparing for the Restoration. But we are not alone. There are Alöweans, Illiri, and others from every race of the world with us."

If the Fields of Gedáron existed, had her mother found a way to it? Would Bard know if she had, or could he find out? She was trying to process what he was saying, but the ideas kept compounding on each other. "Do you mean to say you are some kind of ghost?"

"In a way," he replied, smiling to himself. "But that oversimplifies the truth. I am not a lost apparition, if that is what you mean. I am real. Here. Now."

He held out his hand. Hesitantly, she touched it. It felt as tangible as any other person's hand. Confusion and disappointment filled her heart. What Bard was saying sounded too foreign, grand, mythological. But then again, she had discerned something unusual about him from the beginning, and there was much about the world she did not know.

She recalled how the presence of the Dryden had felt. She had not touched it, but it too had been real. Surely, she had not imagined it. She thought of how Ida grappled with the strange elements that had influenced the war—like a dragon. The Ülak attack of her family's ranch had certainly happened. They had burned her home, killed their horses, ranch hands, and presumably her mother. She had killed at least one by her own hand. With all she had experienced, was it so hard to believe there were forces beyond what she comprehended?

"I am sorry if this is overwhelming," Bard said. Their eyes met. "I do not have all the answers, for there are many forces at work. What is most important is to trust that my purpose is guided by peace, a peace that will one day govern everything again. That is the promise of the Restoration. Imagine, Rhoda, a world with no more evil or pain."

"I cannot imagine such a world," she replied. The notion was appealing, yet sounded too good. "What has led you to trust in such an ideal?"

Bard exhaled slowly. "As I have said, the power of music gives me hope; not only in the sense of peace, but a tangible power: Elíbom Prímom, the Creator of Worlds."

"How do you know such a being exists?"

"I know Alíndor," Bard replied, "the living spirit of Elíbom Prímom. She looks human, but it is impossible to truly identify her with any gender or race. She manifests for our benefit, and not always in human form, for the Creator of Worlds is not limited by matter and comprehension, masculine and feminine. Elíbom Prímom is presence, wonder, and unity, the source of all power and goodness. You and I are part of a larger story, Rhoda."

"But if such a power is all encompassing, how do you reconcile it with the corruption of the world? What about the Dryden?"

"Corruption occurs because we have the power to choose."

"Choose what, exactly?"

"Everything." Bard leaned back, his face sober. "To pursue peace or turn away. It will not remain that way indefinitely, however. In the Restoration, all powers resisting the dominion of Elíbom Prímom will be overthrown."

"That does not sound like peace."

"Peace is costly."

"I have heard that before," she said, "from men like Dwairian, Malech, and Nabilak."

"I do not purport to understand all of Elíbom Prímom's ways," Bard replied. "I just know that each of us has the capacity for goodness and peace, and that those who scorn it, who inflict evil, will be held accountable. That includes the Dryden, though its history is complicated."

She wanted to return to the heart of her questions. "But why are you here?"

"I am here under the authority of Fréalwë, who is the first Elphadém and Steward of Elím. In the Restoration, the gates of Rühílis, the city of Alíndor, will reopen, and the invisible will be reunited with the visible. Fréalwë sent me to scout Illirium for signs of readiness . . . for someone."

"Did you find what you were looking for?"

"No. I fear the hope that Fréalwë seeks has retreated into the shadows and cannot be called back. Not by me, anyway. I tried to reach—." Bard caught himself and shook his head. "It does not matter now."

As the layers of mystery increased, she felt small and unaware. Once again, the world was proving larger than she had thought.

Bard continued, "Honestly, I have found little encouragement in these lands. Hope has fallen like petals from a wilting flower. That is the message I was prepared to bring back to Fréalwë . . . until something changed." He matched her gaze. "I met you. You are different, Rhoda. I discerned it from the start. Not only did you dare come with me, but your voice . . . it is music, unfettered, blossoming anew. It comes from deep within you, preserved despite all you have been through. You have already begun to recognize this, I think. Here, in the last days of my journey, your voice has given me hope, altering the message I will bring back."

"How has it given you hope?" she asked. "I do not understand."

Bard took her hand with both of his. She tensed. The impulse to withdraw shouted at her, but she forced herself to remain still and focus on the warmth of his touch. Still, her heart raced.

"The truth will become clear in time," he said. "Can you trust that?"

She did not know what to say.

"I wish I could give you more," he added, "but I do not think I am meant to. I am only part of the beginning for you."

The beginning of what? Her head ached, but she tried to center her thoughts. "You said these are your final days. What does that mean?"

He continued to hold her hand. "Fréalwë gave me seven years, which are nearly spent. In two weeks, the Door will be closed to me. If that happens, I will fade away, trapped in the unseen dimension of Illirium until the Restoration. I would become more vulnerable to the invisible powers governing here—powers that resist the rule of Elíbom Prímom. Not all Séorans follow Alíndor. Their power is increasing. I suspect they have already sensed my presence, maybe also marked my progress. If I am trapped here, they could capture, bind, and torture me for what I know." The strain on his face softened. "Even if I could or wanted to stay, it would not be the best for you."

Her heart sank as he released her hand. She warmed her other hand with the one Bard had held. As she did so, she observed the scars on her arms, imagined the many branches leading to her back and down her body. "Maybe I do understand," she said softly. "Everyone must leave."

"It will not always be so."

"I do not want you to go," she confessed.

His expression bore sadness and weariness. "I am not what you seek, Rhoda. Not really. If I do anything, it is merely to help you find the way."

She did not know what she ultimately wanted, but the thought of being alone again drained her vigor. "Find the way to what?"

"To hope," Bard replied, "peace, immortality. But our time together is not yet over." He stood and offered her his hand. She received it, to which he helped her stand. "Trust in your voice, for it is one of the most tangible hopes you have. Let it continue to heal and strengthen you, and give you a means to examine what cannot be easily understood. Purpose can grow from that."

They walked back to their camp. "I am sorry," he added. "I wish there was an easier way."

"There is no easy way," she replied.

They followed the main road east from Lake Cüivenan. She could hardly believe how far east she had made it. At last, old hopes for the future were taking form.

"We are entering Nemenelor," Bard commented.

As they ventured deeper into the High Hills, a hush like an invisible mist lingered upon the landscape. It did not feel hostile, but rather mournful. It also suggested that though the war had devastated the Alöwean Empire, power remained concealed within its old boundaries. She felt like they were being watched.

"The last seven years have been difficult for the Alöweans here," Bard said. "Lord Däne of Hamrothél struggles to meet his peoples' needs. Outside Hamrothél's walls, thousands of Alöwean refugees have extended the city limits with a makeshift camp. Most of them are veterans from the war, idle and bitter from defeat, and estranged from their families. Most of the women, children, and elderly were evacuated through the Door of Anaríl to Alöwe before the capital fell. That Door is now closed, as are all the main Doors."

"What are the Doors, exactly?" she asked. "Is the Door of Anaríl like the Door you are going to in the Upper Mountains, the one leading to the Fields of Gedáron?"

"Yes . . . and no," Bard replied. "I am somewhat surprised you do not know more about the Doors of Nemenelor. As far as I am aware, they were no secret. But then, you did live most of your life in Hamath removed from the Alöweans. And, of course, though you visited Nemenelor's western capital as a youth, you would not have been allowed near the Door of Tïrmen. Still, you never heard them mentioned?"

"No," she replied, but suddenly recalled the cave in Tïrmen Prison, how she had discerned something unusual about it. "When I was a prisoner, something did make me wonder. It looked like a dark passageway."

"Ah yes, I remember that part of your story: the cave in Tïrmen's highest tower, its entrance lined with runes?"

She remembered it clearly. "Yes."

"That must have been the Door of Tïrmen," Bard replied. "I should have thought of it sooner. If you had ventured into the cave, you would have found nothing more than a wall of stone. The Door of Tïrmen was shut like the others. When open, each Door provides direct access from one place to another—like any door or passageway—except the two places it connects are separated by a vast distance, usually hundreds of miles. The Door of Tïrmen was designed to link with Anaríl, a bridge between Nemenelor's two capitals.

"The knowledge of how to build a Door is well guarded and known by few. The first was built centuries ago when Alíndor taught Fréalwë, who then wrote down the lessons in *The Book of Doors* to preserve such knowledge. The book was eventually stolen, and a great conflict resulted, the murmurs of which still persist and will not be resolved until the Restoration. In the meantime, the book was reclaimed, and Lord Theaníl, Steward of Alöwe, mastered some of its secrets. He constructed the Doors of Tïrmen and Anaríl to unite his people, here in Illirium and to their homeland of Alöwe. Those Doors are weaker than the ones created by Fréalwë, more easily manipulated. Alíndor created her own Doors as well. The Door of Rühílawë, for example, to which I now go, cannot be found or used by the living. Anyway, the history of the Doors is long and complex, entwined with all the events of creation."

"I am beginning to understand," she said. The world was not only larger, but more wondrous than she had ever imagined. "Can a Door be reopened, such as in Anaríl to reunite the Alöwean families?"

"It could," Bard replied, "but only by one who knows how, such as Lord Theaníl. After the war, he shut all doors for the security of Alöwe. There are—." His expression suddenly became alert.

She followed his gaze to the right. "What is it?"

"Nothing," he said after a moment of uncertainty, all the while scanning the terrain.

"Are you sure?"

"Come."

They proceeded in silence.

Thin clouds veiled the sky. Occasionally, the sun shone through, though its warmth could be felt all the while. All her extra layers were rolled up and strapped to her pack. As mid-afternoon approached, she felt the sweat on her back soaking through her tunic. The shade of the trees did little to improve her condition.

They reached a rivulet, which trickled across the road and down a narrow gulley, so decided to stop there to refill their waterskins and wash some of the heat from their faces and limbs. Once done, she adjusted her pack and stepped over the rivulet. Bard lingered on the other side, crouching down with his hand in the current. He studied the water flowing around his fingers, but then glanced up and caught her staring at him. Grinning self-consciously, he withdrew his hand.

Watching the water roll down his hand and fall in beads from his fingertips made her shudder. She did not know why until she remembered the room in Tirmen and the cold water flowing into puddles around her bare feet. To repel the memory, she turned away and focused on the stretch of visible road ahead.

"Come," Bard said, appearing beside her.

She followed a few steps behind.

The next day, they encountered people on the road.

Seeing them reminded her that agents from Siligen might be searching for her. Or was that paranoia? Surely, her escape was no great loss to them.

Would they care to the point of venturing this far east? Regardless, she told herself not to take any chances. Most of the travelers were Alöwean, yet there were groups of Illiri as well.

"Rodaním continues to trade with what is left of Nemenelor," Bard explained. "I doubt the Alöweans would have survived without them. Their economic alliance is a source of great tension between Rodaním and Siligen."

"If it disturbs Dwairian," she said, "then I am glad."

"The alliance is fragile," Bard continued, "for the Alöweans are not ready to forget how Rodaním did not come to their aid during the war."

"I thought Rodaním helped defeat the Küllka invaders." She recalled how Ida's husband had been killed in the last battle.

"They did," Bard replied, "but not until after Anaríl fell—after Nemenelor was crippled beyond mending. Such is the way of kingdoms and alliances. Opportunism dictates the affairs of this world."

By nightfall, they reached a crossroads. One road ran north and south. The second road, on which they had been traveling since Lake Cüivenen, continued east. In that direction, not far past the crossroads, a sizeable gate blocked the road. Stone walls, about twenty feet tall, extended north and south from either side of it.

"The Norwood Wall," Bard explained. "The Alöweans began building it after the war. When I was last here, seven years ago, only the gatehouse had been finished. The wall will one day encircle all the land around Hamrothél. Non-Alöweans are not permitted through without a permit signed by Lord Däne."

She studied the defenses. Blue light from small stones set along the arch of the gate illuminated the final approach. The gate opened for a double-line of Alöwean soldiers wearing green tunics lined with black. Once they had marched through, the gate was closed and locked from the inside. Meanwhile, archers patrolled the wall walks, their darkening silhouettes visible as they passed the gaps between the merlons. She felt their eyes upon her.

"So where do we go from here?" she asked.

"North," Bard replied, studying the wall as well. He continued in a hushed tone, keeping close to her. "The road to the left leads to the Kingdom of Rökad, but we will turn northeast well before we near its border."

"How long will it take to reach the Upper Mountains?"

Bard's voice remained quiet. "It will take seven days to reach the Rökad border. From there, it will take at least seven more days to get to the Door. The mountain terrain is difficult to navigate, despite the remnants of ancient paths."

Only days left together. She felt her heart sink at the thought. "Could I go with you through the Door to see what lies beyond?"

"The Door is not for the living, remember."

"I am not afraid of death."

"I am sorry, Rhoda." Bard rested his hand upon her shoulder and squeezed it tenderly. "It is not your time." She did not recoil from the gesture. "One day you will see what lies beyond. I will show you everything, just not yet. You still belong here." He removed his hand. "But let us not dwell on that."

She looked around, noting the merchants and travelers settling into their camps on either side of the road.

Bard stepped off to the left. "Let us make camp here for the night."

She followed him to a group of Illiri merchants sitting around a fire.

"May we join you?" Bard asked.

"Surely," said a bald, burly man with a white beard. He motioned for them to sit.

"Thank you."

As she sat, she noticed other fires being lit. A man wrapped in a faded black cloak sat at an adjacent camp watching her. Or she felt him watching her. She could not see his face, for it was shadowed by his hood. A long gray beard rested upon his chest. His attention made her uncomfortable. She checked that her scarf covered her jaw line, only feeling herself ease once the man's attention shifted to address someone next to him.

The burly man in front of her attended a large pot of thick, steaming stew. Its smell elicited a rumble from her stomach.

"Are you hungry?" another man asked.

"Yes, thank you," Bard replied.

"Then you're just in time," the burly cook commented. He proceeded to fill small wooden bowls, and passed them out to everyone around the fire.

They ate in silence.

Afterward, Bard rested his empty bowl on a knee in satisfaction. "Delicious."

"Yes, thank you," Namél added, addressing the cook.

"You're more than welcome," the latter replied.

A gray-haired woman, the only other woman beside Namél around their fire, placed her bowl on the ground then brought out a pipe. She had red designs painted on her pale face. Her hair was gathered back in tiny braids clasped by a variety of beads. After lighting her pipe, she assumed a more relaxed sitting position. Her eyes settled on Namél. "So where do you come from?"

Namél glanced at Bard. He offered a faint smile to the woman. "From the west."

"From Siligen?"

Bard said nothing, though his smile did not fade.

"Not an easy venture in these times," one of the men grumbled. "The west has changed so much, I hardly recognize it."

"Indeed," the woman with the pipe said.

"I come from Zirgalath myself," the first man commented. "Where are you going?"

"North," was all Bard would say.

"Not a lot of business in the north," the woman said. "Not worth the venture as the Rök keep to themselves these days. They want little to do with what we've to offer."

"What's that you're carrying?" the cook asked.

"A lute," Bard replied.

"Well then, how's about a song?" the woman suggested, turning to her companions for support. "In exchange for the meal, shall we say?"

"Yes, play us a song," others murmured.

"It's been quite some time since I heard any music," the cook said, addressing Bard. "That's part of the trouble with living on the road, though cities aren't much better. Music's been replaced with the chorus of drunkenness, orgies, and the clanging of coins."

"And the songs of the dying," the man from Zirgalath added, staring blankly into the fire.

Bard looked at Namél, but hesitated.

"Please," she whispered.

"As you wish," he replied, his expression exposing some uncertainty. The others around the fire voiced their approval as Bard removed the instrument.

"What songs do you know?" one of the men inquired.

"The songs I play are my own," Bard replied, "I know few others."

"Well that's all right," the woman offered optimistically. "Most of us can't remember the names of songs anyway. Play us something you've written. I'm always one to welcome new things."

"Very well," Bard conceded.

The man from Zirgalath addressed Namél with a timid tone. "Do you sing, miss?"

Her heart froze.

"It's been so long since I heard a woman sing," the man added. "And Yolanda here is no songbird."

The others around the fire chuckled.

"That's the truth," the gray-haired woman replied, grinning with the pipe between her teeth.

Namél looked at Bard, who offered a smile of encouragement.

She brought his ear closer to speak quietly. "I am not ready."

"Oh, come now," Yolanda said with some vigor. "We're but humble merchants. This be no throne room or court. Let's hear you sing. I'm sure you have a charming voice."

Namél saw from their faces that she could not escape. "All right." She looked at Bard. "But only if you play the song."

"The song?"

"The one you played the first time I met you, that you have not yet found a name for."

Bard smiled and nodded. He looked down at the instrument, closed his eyes, and breathed slowly. The others around the fire grew quiet in anticipation. Namél also closed her eyes, focusing on the silence surrounding them: the crackle of the fire, the creak of swaying trees, the murmur of voices in other camps.

The music began slowly, like the stirring of a warm breeze. She welcomed it, breathed it in, felt her lungs expand. As the song swelled with fervor, she imagined it filling her with strength. Calmly, she exhaled. As she inhaled once more, out from the depths of her being came her voice. It started with smooth humming, but as she opened her mouth it became resonant. She felt power in it, focus and resolve. There were no words. Not yet. The music was enough. It flowed from her freely.

She felt peace.

It stayed with her, held her. As the last note faded softly into the night air, she opened her eyes and looked around. Everyone present stared dreamily at the white glow of the flames, their faces tranquil as if transported somewhere else. Others nearby had also noticed, for the neighboring camps had quieted. The silence lingered in a way Namél had never experienced—not intimidating, but assuring.

"Remarkable," the man from Zirgalath whispered, as if hesitant to disrupt the reverie.

"I've never heard anything like it," another added.

Yolanda looked over at her. "What's your name, child?"

"My name . . ." She hesitated, glancing at Bard. He smiled, but said nothing. She returned her attention to the woman. "My name . . ." She was tired of being a prison number, a slave, nameless. She no longer needed to carry them. Their meaning dissolved. At last, the truth freed itself from deep within her. "My name is Rhoda."

"Well, thank you, Rhoda.," Yolanda shifted her attention to Bard. "And thank you, young man."

The others voiced their agreement.

"I wish there was more beauty in the world like that," the cook commented.

It was getting late. Many around the fire wished each other a good night.

A few lingered.

"Thank you again," the man from Zirgalath said, offering his hand to Bard and Rhoda. "Goodnight." With a smile, he withdrew to his covered wagon.

"Rest well," Rhoda said.

After watching the man go, she noticed that Bard had not shifted his position. Still cradling his instrument, he watched the fire as if deep in thought. Rhoda looked him for a while before his head turned to acknowledge her.

"I too want to thank you," he said.

"For what?"

"For helping me see." He looked around at the wagons and tents. "And for your courageous spirit. . . . I wish I could give you something in return."

She looked away, feeling self-conscious. "You have given me so much already."

With a hand, Bard gently turned her face back to meet his. His eyes lowered to her lips, and as he leaned toward her, she felt her heartbeat increase. But he hesitated, and a shadow passed over his expression. Was it doubt? His eyes had not shifted, but he would not move closer. She studied his face, searching for an answer, but there was none she could discern. He looked away and withdrew.

"What is wrong?" she asked.

He stared into the fire. "Rhoda." He said the name as if measuring its sound. "You have given my song meaning, including a name."

"A name?"

"Your name," he replied. "May I call the song 'Rhoda'?"

"If you wish," she said. The request seemed strange to her, while also heartening.

"Thank you."

He returned the instrument to its case while Rhoda looked at him. A forgotten feeling stirred within her, overwhelmed with memory and longing. She resisted the doubts pressing her to withdraw. *No,* she thought. *I know what I want now.*

"Will you hold me?" she asked.

Bard looked at her in surprise.

She shifted closer beside him, and slowly leaned against his shoulder. He remained tense at first, but then let his arms come around her. As he did so, she closed her eyes to all else. Tears flowed as his embrace tightened and he rested his head on hers. She let herself be held—held in a way she had forgotten. The tangible goodness filled the empty depths of her heart, washing over so many memories. Though she knew that resting in his embrace could not last forever, she was thankful for it and let it nourish her present.

She woke with such a sense of comfort, its serenity so real and pure, that she wondered if she had passed into the other world. She basked in its glory: carefree, restful, safe—like a sanctuary. Yet gradually, she remembered where she was. Across the forested landscape, birds sang about the dawn. Embers smoldered from the previous night's fire, their scent tickling her nostrils. Shifting from lying on her side to her back, she realized that Bard was still holding her, shielding her from the cold.

She studied his face. There was no trace of the agedness she had sometimes witnessed. Peace emanated from his sleeping form. As his eyes calmly opened, he stared back at her with an expression of mild curiosity until recognition slowly washed over him.

He carefully withdrew his arm from around her body and sat up. Drawing his cloak tighter about himself, he gazed blankly west toward the still darkened horizon. Rhoda looked east as the sun crested the hill, its rays reaching through the trees like fingers caressing locks of hair.

A few others in the camp were also waking. Returning her attention to Bard, she watched him rub his face and stand. After looking around a while, his expression hardened. She followed his gaze and saw the cloaked figure from the night before watching them. Still hooded and expressionless, the man leaned against a nearby tree. As they noticed him, he shifted his weight and casually walked away.

"We should go," Bard whispered, his tone lined with urgency.

"Is something wrong?"

"Come." He helped her up, all the while mindful of the departing figure.

After two hours of walking at an aggressive pace along the northbound road, Bard finally relaxed. "Excuse my haste," he explained. "I have seen that man before—twice, which cannot be a coincidence."

"He made me uncomfortable," she said. "Do you know who he is?"

"I think he is an agent of Siligen," Bard replied. "I have heard rumors about a new order called the Reminax. Its agents are said to be tasked with learning Alöwean secrets, for example about the Doors. They move about more openly in the west."

Reminax sounded familiar. Rhoda suddenly remembered Opal mentioning it in association with the spy hanging outside the rebel camp. "Do you think he recognized you?"

"I am not sure. I first encountered him in the Hoch Hills, and he was not alone. I evaded them without being identified, but stumbled into them again in Tïrmen—before it was made a prison. They tried to corner me, but I managed to slip away once again."

"Do you think he will follow us?"

"He was probably not at the crossroads for me," Bard replied, "but was investigating a way into Nemenelor. Whatever his intent, we should be more careful."

As the journey north passed without incident, Rhoda put the cloaked man out of her mind. She did not want to waste time on him. Nor did she want to keep track of the days, for doing so would hasten them to their end. Yet every step reminded her that it was inevitably coming; that soon she would be alone again. Grief besieged her heart. Bard tried to console her, but he too seemed to be fighting an inner conflict. There was little more to say. Silence filled most of their hours. Even the music was quiet.

How would they say goodbye?

After days, the road was traded with a narrow path, which wound northeast through a muted forest with numerous steep valleys. Reaching the foothills, they entered the Upper Mountains. Since arriving to Zirgalath a year earlier, she had thought about mountains as another means for escape. Now, as she finally reached them, she longed to turn back.

Along the way, Bard identified various landmarks that would guide her back out of the mountains. "I will not have you getting lost once I am gone," he said, trying to sound lighthearted.

She forced a smile in return, but could not give it true life.

Nine days after leaving the crossroads, the small path vanished, forcing them to venture cross country over sharp woodland ridges and around outcrops of increasingly exposed rock. Rhoda could see no trail, yet Bard navigated the terrain as if there was a path. Snow lingered on the mountain peaks beyond. While the landscape felt uninterested in Bard and her passing, she became conscious of an invisible presence. Each day they climbed deeper into the mountains, the power of the presence increased.

Four days later, the density of trees thinned to become a barren and rocky landscape. Following Bard through a small ravine, Rhoda glanced up and suddenly noticed a woman dressed in gray. Crouched at the edge of a stone outcrop above, she watched them with bright green eyes. The head of her staff bore the curved horns of a ram. Her thick black hair was gathered behind her head in a vertical set of three dense knots. She looked like an Illiri, but her brown complexion was unlike any Rhoda had ever seen.

"You return so soon, Bard ap Fili," the woman called in a deep resonating voice.

Bard did not appear surprised to see the woman. "Hello Äelmich."

The woman smiled faintly. "Have seven years already passed?"

"They have," he replied. "But you knew that."

"Yes." Äelmich's tone remained calm, while echoing authority. She indicated Rhoda. "Why have you brought this Illiri girl?"

"Her name is Rhoda," Bard replied. "She has eaten fruit from the Balmwéa Elíf."

"From the what?" Rhoda looked at Bard intently.

"So that is it." Äelmich studied Rhoda a while longer. "I perceived something different about her." Her attention returned to Bard. "Why did you give her the fruit? What did you think to achieve?"

"Hope," he replied.

"You know that is not enough here," Äelmich said, though appeared to consider his statement.

Rhoda did not know what they were talking about.

"I want Rhoda to see and learn," Bard pressed, "not only for her, but the good of all. She will not pass through the Door."

"She could not, even if you wanted it." Äelmich shifted her weight. It was then that Rhoda noticed a small sword strapped behind her back, partially concealed by her gray cloak. "The Warden of Rühílawe is attentive, and questions your mission here—even if Fréalwë himself commanded it. It was dangerous and foolhardy, Bard ap Fili."

"Nevertheless," Bard replied, "something had to be done."

A moment of silence passed.

Äelmich studied the sky. The sun had begun its afternoon descent. "Time is burning away. You must reach the Door before it is too late." She extended her arm toward the rising mountainside. "Go."

With a hand on his heart, Bard bowed his head. "Thank you. I wish you well."

Hesitantly, Rhoda followed Bard out of the ravine.

"We are watching," Äelmich called after them. "Do not stray from the path."

When Rhoda glanced back, the other woman had vanished. She turned to Bard and spoke in a hushed tone. "Who was she?"

"Äelmich is a Séoran. She guides the spirits of those who seek Elím. You know her as the Canta."

"She was the Canta?" Rhoda could not contain her surprise.

"Yes."

So the Canta was real, and in a way more tangible than the Dryden. Rhoda could not decide what that meant to her. "Every day, I understand this world less and less," she commented, more to herself.

"Do not be hard on yourself, for most do not understand." Bard stopped and looked at her, placing an assuring hand on her shoulder. "But you are different, Rhoda. Already, you are developing eyes that see and ears that

227

hear. Give yourself time."

He continued walking.

"If I had asked," she began, catching up to him, "would she have told me about my family?"

"What do you mean?"

"Whether they reached the Fields of Gedáron or not."

"She might have."

"Do you know if they did?"

"No," Bard replied, focusing ahead. "I left Elím before their passing. But if you wish, I will search for them when I return."

The idea seemed so extraordinary, unfathomable. "Thank you."

"If I find them," Bard added, "what shall I say?"

"Tell them . . ." She hesitated. Could it be possible? The thought stirred hope in her heart, as did the prospect of one day being reunited with them. Yet there were also so many lingering doubts. Would they be proud of her? "Tell them everything . . . how I have survived, and how far I have come."

"Anything else?"

"That I love them."

"Of course."

"You discussed fruit," Rhoda said, wondering if she should be concerned and defensive. "What were you talking about?"

"The Balmwéa Elíf is a tree that grows in Rühílis," Bard replied. "A fruit plucked from its branches will not spoil for many years. It is powerful, sustaining the spirit's vigor—for both the living and the dead. Though the city of Rühílis is currently closed to all but the Séorans, they still share the fruit of the Balmwéa Elíf with those of us who dwell in Elím. I was given some for my journey here, and I decided to share it with you."

"But what has it done to me?"

"Do not be afraid, Rhoda. What I said was true. The fruit of the Balmwéa Elíf helps restore life in the fullest sense. Its influence is like any good food, yet stronger and longer lasting. I am sorry. I should have told you sooner."

"If it is so normal," she pressed, "why mention it to the Canta?"

After some thought, Bard replied, "She needed to know—not only to let you pass, but . . . so that she knows to watch over you when I am gone. That is my hope, at least."

"Watch over me in what way?" She did not like the idea of being guarded again.

"In her own way, unseen."

"I can watch over myself."

"I know." Bard's voice grew quiet, his eyes downcast. "But as you have attested, the world is large and layered with mysteries. Honestly, none of us can navigate it, not in the end. I do not doubt your strength, Rhoda. I care for you."

She felt her defenses lower somewhat. While the thought of being watched by the Canta remained both unclear and unsettling, she trusted that Bard meant what he said. She cared for him too.

A few hours later, after scaling a steep rise, they faced a large granite cliff. Its flat stone surface extended far above them and out to their left where it dropped thousands of feet below. The rise they had climbed continued a short way up until meeting the rightmost edge of the cliff, the final ascent littered with loose rock.

Bard allowed Rhoda to catch her breath before climbing the remainder of the rise. Once they reached the point she had seen, he led her left to where a narrow ledge cut across the stone wall. Trying to ignore the long fall to her left, she concentrated on the placement of each step. At the center of the cliff, the ledge ended at an overlook, which jutted out like a small platform over the abyss. There Bard stopped.

Studying the smooth rock, Rhoda noted an arched indent, the base of which was as wide as the platform. If the cliff was a face, the shallow indent was its open mouth while the platform was its lowered jaw.

Here, the power that Rhoda had been conscious of was at its strongest. It felt familiar, reminding her of the cave in Tirmen Prison. "Is this the Door?"

"Yes."

She walked forward and touched the cold stone. "How . . ." She turned to face him.

"It is time," he said softly.

Her heart became heavy. She nodded, lowering her eyes.

"I want you to have this." He held out the lute in its cloth case.

"But it is yours," she protested. "How will you play?"

"I will make another one."

"But I do not play it well."

"You will learn," he said. "May your voice find strength with it." He held the instrument out to her. "Please."

She received it reluctantly.

Bard smiled, though the expression looked pained.

"I do not want you to go," she said.

His eyes were sad. He reached out to caress her face, his fingers brushing across the scar on her jaw. "Remember who you really are, Rhoda, and who you are becoming. Identity is a living, growing thing."

Her tears wet his hand. It seemed strange to her how easily they came. "What happens next?"

"We continue," he replied, "each on our own journey. I return to Elím to serve Lord Fréalwë, and you go to Rodaním to find your aunt."

"Yes," she said. The thought of finding her aunt, Corine, gave her a sense of purpose. "But after that?" The future seemed like an empty land.

"Tell your story, about what you have seen and heard." Keeping the palm of his hand against her face, he gently stroked her tears with his thumb. "I cannot see what lies ahead, but I believe it will be good." His other hand came up to help cradle her face. "That all can be well . . . and all will be well."

Closing her eyes, she wrapped her arms around his torso, resting her face against his chest. He held her tightly, his hand cradling the back of her head. She did not know how long they stood like that. She did not want it to end.

Bard stepped back, his hands lingering on her shoulders until he turned to the Door. The stone between the shallow indent had vanished. Through it, foothills meandered down to a valley of forests and fields dappled with flowers of many colors. At the far end of the valley waited a walled garden with numerous plants and trees. To the left, beyond the valley, glistened a blue sea. An eagle called, and was answered by a thrush. The sway of trees and the chorus of waves on sandy shores mixed with the giggling laughter of children at play.

Closest to Rhoda, just through the Door, stood Bard. He looked at her with eyes full of grief, compassion, and affection. "Farewell, Rhoda," he said. "We will see each other again."

The image faded to gray stone.

Prelude & Fugue

There was music.

Yet to simply call it music, a mere word, seems so vacant and intangible. There was a song, a depth of longing, a spirit within the spaces of those melodic pinnacles and valleys—a duet of questions and answers. There was a man, a patient presence with searching eyes and a heart that saw beyond the world I knew. For this world is not all there is. He came from more. His music heralded it.

I listened and came to play that song on my own, a song both strange and familiar—like a memory that is not mine alone, but part of a community. It is a living thing, a voice; sharing it strengthens its power. In that way, it defines all other songs, as they too define it: those that were, those that are, and those that have yet to be. Like names past, present, and future, they are part of a whole: distinct notes formed in the depths like roots of a tree—a tree of meaning.

From it grows my own song. It radiates, enlivens, guides.

"Where, and for whom?" one might ask. I often do.

Well that is part of the mystery, and part of the hope. Questions and answers. I trust it will one day produce fruit.

Meanwhile, the seasons turn. Leaves grow and fall. The cold is not the same as it once was, the darkness no longer night. Questions and answers. All the while the branches remain—the notes remain.

Listen. The music is written in the silence as well as the sounds.

Look. Wonder is all around. Its lines are even on my skin: to wonder at survival—its power and limits. Though it is not easy, I read the scars and remember that I choose to journey forward, and that healing is possible.

That I know who I am now.

That I can feel again.

And that I am coming, for a new movement has begun.

About the Author

Passionate about art, outdoor adventure, and world travel, J.D. Grubb has lived chapters in the United States and Europe, and wants to explore every corner of the world. He currently lives in northern California. *There was Music* is his debut novel, the introduction to a series.

You can connect with him at:
- jdgrubb.com
- twitter.com/ jd_grubb
- facebook.com/ jdgrubb
- instagram.com/ jd_grubb

Subscribe to his newsletter:
- https://mailchi.mp/1d560a0a2083/jdgrubb_newsletter

www.ingramcontent.com/pod-product-compliance
Lightning Source LLC
Chambersburg PA
CBHW050350190726
48284CB00007BB/2223